MW01616612

No
Matter
What

a novel by

Mary Saracino

spinsters ink
minneapolis

First edition.
10-9-8-7-6-5-4-3-2-1

Spinsters Ink
P.O. Box 300170
Minneapolis, MN 55403

Cover art and design by Teri Talley
Production by: Sacha Bush   Lou Ann Matossian
                Melanie Cockrell   Mev Miller
                Joan Drury   Stefanie Shiffler
                Kelly Kager   Liz Tufte
                Lori Loughney

This is a work of fiction. Any similarity to persons living or dead is a coincidence.

Library of Congress Cataloging-in-Publication Data

Saracino, Mary 1954–
    No matter what / Mary Saracino. — 1st ed.
        p.   cm.
    ISBN 0-933216-98-X (cloth)
    ISBN 0-933216-91-2 (pbk)
    I. Title.
PS3569.A65N6   1993   93-26212
                                                    CIP

Acknowledgments

I was blessed to have many loving arms around me as I wrote this book. These friends and family, colleagues and "guardian angels" helped lessen the solitude that's required of such a long process. Each, in their own way, made it possible for me to write this novel, and I am deeply grateful.

Special thanks to Rosemary Martin, whose gift of healing helped carry me to the place where the writing could begin; to Judith Katz, whose first words of encouragement set me on this journey; and to my writing group—Pam Colby, Nancy Kelly, Blake Lynden, Ilza Mueller, Ann Monson, and Elissa Raffa—whose exceptional feedback and invaluable moral support helped sustain me through many revisions. These fine women are a gift no writer should be without. I send extra thank-yous to Elissa for her detailed critique of my final draft. I felt so cared for and listened to.

For reading first drafts and offering insights, suggestions, encouragement and lots of love, I thank Jane Hoback, Colleen Convey, and Kate Houston. Many thanks to my Loft Mentor Series mentors—especially Jessica Hagedorn and Sandra Cisneros. Their constructive criticism and critical feedback helped me turn an essential corner and write my story with passion and conviction. I am grateful to my editor, Joan Drury, for the magic of her red pen and the gift of her insights. Her respect for me as a writer is truly a blessing. To all the other women of Spinsters—especially Kelly, Liz, Mev and my copy editor, Lou Ann—thanks for making the publication journey one of joy and celebration.

I thank Marie Traver whose gentle, strong hands soothed my knotted shoulder muscles. Her constant support of my writing means the world to me. Deepest thanks to my partner, Jane Butz, who loves me, no matter what. Her gift of laughter and her generous heart mean more to me than words could ever say. I am grateful to my mother, father, sisters and brothers—who understand that wounds need love to heal. And finally, loving gratitude to my maternal grandmother, Fiora Vergamini, for showing the way. Mille grazie di tutti.

For Jane

And for my sisters and brothers

No
Matter
What

PART ONE

September 1966

ONE

Long ago, I made a promise to myself to love my mother with my whole heart and soul. No matter what. Sometimes it's really hard to keep that promise. But I do. Because she has a sad face and she needs me to. Fridays are the worst. Mama's always in a hurry to go see Patrick. If we're not out the door by three her temper bumps against the ceiling. She gets all grouchy, like now, and stands at the front door tapping her fingers on her dress-up handbag. She squints and yells, "Come on, Peanut! Grab your coat. Get in the car." Her voice stretches. She raises her hand to swat me and yells some more. I get mad right back at her, but I don't show it. I tuck it away in the pocket of my heart for later, when I'm all alone. Then I take it out and bounce it around the room.

"Regina Giovanni, are you listening to me?"

I only pretend to listen. I glance at her once in a while, so she thinks I'm paying attention. But I'm busy. I'm thinking about my best friend, Amelia, and how I wish I was over at her house right now, playing June Taylor dancers on her back patio—twirling on my tiptoes, kicking my heels in the air, my long braid swinging around and around and around. Instead I'm rushing around, changing my clothes, trying to hurry, hurry, hurry because Mama hates to be late on Fridays.

"Regina! You know how important this is. Now, get in the car. Your sisters are waiting."

"Yes, Mother," I say.

Mama's all jumpy now. She's on the edge of her skin. She's gonna slip off unless I come take her hand right away. I poke myself and remember my promise. Before we go, I give my dog Zoomer a quick hug.

Under my breath, I whisper into Zoomer's soft neck, "You'd think we were gonna visit the Pope." Then I run outside and slam the screen door behind me. All the way to the car I stew about how when I'm a famous Broadway dancer she won't be able to make me go with her on Fridays anymore.

My sisters wait in Daddy's blue Rambler. Little Winnie's only two. She's in the front seat, playing with the radio knobs. She likes to turn them this way and that, messing up the stations. Rosa's five, so she has to sit in back with me. Today she's plopped next to the window on my side of the car. I open the door, yank her ponytail and push her over the seat.

"Move, Rosa. That's my place."

She's got brown hair like Mama's, and I'm jealous.

"Ma!" Rosa screams.

I slap her arm. "Shut up, brat."

Winnie sticks her tongue out at me. I poke at the slimy thing with my finger.

"Make her stop, Ma!" Rosa yells. She grabs for my hair, but I duck fast and escape.

"I didn't do anything!" I shout. "You two always gang up on me. I hate you both!"

"Peanut, why can't you act your age? You are ten, for Christ's sake." Mama screeches as she opens the front car door, barking out orders.

"Rosa, come up here, next to Winnie. Let Peanut ride alone in back for a while. Give her some breathin' room to cool off that hot head of hers. Sometimes redheads take longer."

Her face is all twisted from shouting. It makes my stomach ache just to look at her. That's how it is when we have to go see Patrick. No matter how hard I try, I can't seem to be the good girl Mama wants me to be.

The car is hot. My eyes burn from trying to keep my grouchiness inside. I lean my head against the window and close my eyes. I stretch my legs over the seat and cross my ankles like I'm in charm school. The back of my thighs stick to the vinyl, so I uncross my legs and pull my knees up near my chest and get comfortable. I roll down the window and breathe. The air feels good, like a cool hand touching me.

When I open my eyes, Mama's settling herself into the driver's seat. She looks calmer now that we're all in the car. She tosses her head from side to side, shaking the hair out of her eyes. Her perfume crawls up my nostrils. The whole car smells of it, now. It's sweet, but not like flowers. More like cinnamon or nutmeg or both mixed together. She tucks her fancy pocketbook next to her leg and adjusts the mirror. She stares at herself a second, pats her curly hair and checks her cherry-red lipstick one more time before we take off.

Mama glances over her shoulder as she backs the car out of the driveway, catches my eye and smiles. Then how I love her pushes up and the warm isn't just inside the car anymore. It's inside me, too.

My mama. She looks so pretty on Fridays. Prettier than an angel on a holy card. No more frumpy ole grouch. No more tired, I-can't-take-it-any-more, long-face complaining. No more wrinkled eyes. No more stiff corners for a mouth.

On Mondays and Tuesdays and Wednesdays and Thursdays, Mama wears the same clothes—faded blue jeans and my daddy's old tan work shirts hanging down to her thighs. Most of the time she doesn't even brush her hair, just hides the messy curls under the blue-and-red kerchief she wears when she cleans and cooks. And her eyes are puffy brown spots in the middle of her skinny face, just staring out. Mama lost a baby once, right when it was being born. And sometimes, when her face gets all thin and stretched and worn out, she looks like she's staring out the window, just waiting for that dead baby to come over the hill and home to supper.

I was born a year after that baby died. My brothers, Danny and Joey, were already here, so I was Mama's first daughter. She named me Regina Maria, like the Blessed Virgin Mother. She nicknamed me "Peanut" because I was tiny. Daddy used to hold me in the palm of his hand, like a five-pound sack of pasta flour.

Mama laughed more when I was younger. She'd hold me close and tell me I was her special present. God had given her back the baby girl He'd taken away—all fresh and new and alive. Sitting close in her lap, Mama rocked me and hummed. Her warm skin smelled like tiny lily-of-the-valley bells. And I felt perfect and good. Until she got sad, remembering the other baby, the one that died. She'd set me on the couch and run away, sobbing and sobbing. The empty rocking chair creaked in the corner, and I felt scared and all alone.

With each new baby Mama went further away. After Rosa was born, Mama got more grouchy, more tired. "I haven't got time," she complained, when I asked her to sing me a song or let me show her how I could stand on my tiptoes like a ballerina. After she had Winnie, it got even worse. Mama snapped at me more, and her face complained all the time. "Heat up Winnie's bottle. Hand me a diaper. Watch the baby while I fix dinner."

Having babies just makes Mama sadder and sadder. I feel sad a lot, too. Especially when we have to go to see Patrick on Fridays. But I try not to show it too much. I don't want to upset Mama. I don't tell anybody, but I have a twin soul. Half of it's mine and the other half belongs to the lost baby. When I make Mama happy that's the lost baby part, the good me shining through. When I don't do my homework or sass back or get in trouble at school or make Mama late on Friday, that's the bad side poking its stubborn face out.

I try to show the good-girl side most of the time. When Mama gets her faraway, sad look I try extra hard. I pick her favorite flowers—black-eyed Susans. I sing show tunes—the ones she loves as much as I do. We play the records and sing along sometimes when we wash dishes after supper, if Mama's in a good mood. I belt out songs in my best Ethel Merman voice—"Everything's coming up roses"—until Mama's eyes clear and her mouth un-wrinkles. Then I feel special again. I celebrate each time Mama's face comes back home and her brown eyes smile at me.

But no matter how hard I try, nothing makes Mama happier than visiting Patrick. Something happens then that's like a kiss good-night and a blanket tucked in tight when you're sick. Just that little bit of something that makes you feel a whole lot better.

Fridays are different from every other day of the week. In the morning before I go to school, Mama puts *My Fair Lady* on the record player while she washes her hair in the kitchen sink. I eat Cap'n Crunch at the table and watch. She splashes the water all around, soaps up her hair, then swims her hands around in her tangles so slow and gentle it makes me want to cry.

When she's done, she wraps her hair in a towel and sits at the kitchen table. She combs out her tangles, then twirls the wet ends into small Q shapes and presses each one in place with black wire bobby pins. All the time she hums soft and sweet to the music—"Wouldn't it be lov-er-ly." After that she goes upstairs and takes a long, hot bubble bath. The lily-of-the-valley smell sneaks into my nose and stays there all the way to school. The lost baby must have smelled that way: good and clean.

When I come home from school, Mama's in the bath-room again, this time in front of the mirror, brushing out the tight Q shapes. I hold my breath for just a second and pretend I'm diving into the deep, brown curls. I imagine that the lost baby had brown hair like Mama's, not red like my own and Daddy's, rough and loud. But soft instead, as soft as chocolate pudding in a cool, glass cup.

When Mama's done fixing her hair she brings out the small glass bottle she hides in her dresser drawer. She splashes on fancy perfume—the kind with the funny name, half American, half French. "Chanel No. 5," she calls it, in a make-believe accent. It's her favorite. Patrick gave it to her last Christmas. The way she touches herself reminds me of Mrs. Rossi and Mrs. Del Vecchio, two old women I stare at in church. They squeeze their eyes shut and pray after they brush their foreheads with holy water.

Finally Mama pulls off her blue jeans and tosses her shirt in the dirty-clothes pile. She stands there in her underwear for a second, looking at herself in the mirror, then she reaches for the hanger and puts on her Friday clothes—ironed black cotton slacks and her white sweater with the small blue flowers and pearl-colored buttons.

"I want to look just right," she says.

Mama pulls the car out of the driveway, careful not to run over Winnie's green tricycle or my brother Joey's baseball cleats. "Goddamn kids," she mutters. She sounds like my brother Danny. He thinks he's a big shot, just 'cuz he's sixteen. He swears a lot—when he gets mad. He calls Patrick a no-good son of a bitch, but not so that Mama can hear. Only me and Joey. But I don't tell on him. Sometimes I agree.

Mama squeezes the steering wheel. I check her eyes in the rear-view mirror. The wrinkles are caving in, and I know she's mad at me for dragging a leg and making us late. "What time is it, Peanut?" she snaps.

I check my Snow White watch. "It's ten after three."

"We're gonna be late," she says. She frowns, and I stare at Snow White's clock arms, wishing they could move backwards and give us more time.

"Don't worry, Mama, we'll get there soon." I wish I could take away her frown, erase the frumpy lines around her eyes. But she's got Patrick on her mind. Only Patrick.

Patrick is sort of like a second daddy. At least that's how Mama wants me to feel. Mostly I think of him as a pretend daddy. On Friday, we meet him at the coffee shop in Cayuga. That's a city with wide sidewalks and buildings taller than trees. Nobody we know lives there. We just go to visit Patrick. Mama says it's because it's halfway between where he lives and Pisa. That's where we live. Pisa, New York. Sometimes I call it Pizza, New York, to make Mama laugh. Our town is named after some place in Italy. That's where my grandmas and grandpas are from. Mama says they moved here because they needed jobs, and there were lots of other Italians here, so they wouldn't feel homesick. Pisa is littler than Cayuga, but it's prettier. The street lights remind me of sleepy eyes, and there's lots of chestnut trees and maple trees and houses that sit back from the road with gravel driveways and crooked front steps. We live across the canal from the light bulb factory where my daddy works. At quitting time the whistle blows so loud it fills me up.

When Patrick first moved to Pisa my daddy invited him over for supper. I was only seven then. I had just made my First Holy Communion. And Winnie wasn't even born yet. There was only Danny and Joey and Rosa and me. Daddy took him in, made him part of our family, and every Friday we said the rosary together, before dinner.

"The family that prays together, stays together," my daddy says before he bows his head. He holds the first bead between his fingers like a pea.

That first night Patrick walked into our kitchen, he reminded me of the cowboys at the Saturday afternoon movies: tall and thin with handsome black, wavy hair. But he was softer than a real cowboy. His blue eyes looked like shiny marbles in his smooth face, and his hands were pretty, like a lady's. He laughed like a garden hose, gushing out water. Mama told me later he was Irish, and that's why he laughed like that. "Hearty and full of life," she said. He likes to tell stories like my Uncle Tony. But Uncle Tony talks about bocce ball and dunks cookies that taste like licorice into his wine. And he laughs, too, but his laugh is wild like a bunch of birds taking off, loud and excited.

Patrick wasn't much like my uncle. He smoked Lucky Strikes and smelled spicy, and he chewed his zitis with his mouth closed. He didn't talk until after he finished eating, except a few times to my daddy. Mostly he just sat and listened to all of us going on and on about this and that, like we always do at supper. Joey yakking about baseball, Danny talking about the drug store where he works after school, Rosa giggling about something, and me trying to get Mama's attention in between her going up and down to scoop more sauce or slice more bread.

After supper Patrick thanked Mama. He said he never had homemade Italian food before. I thought that was kind of funny, him calling it Italian food. It's just macaroni.

Mama poured him a cup of coffee, and he drank it without any milk or sugar. That's when he started telling stories about the time he went to Rome and saw some statues and old paintings and how he even got to meet the Pope. Daddy liked that part the best. His lips curled at the corners, and his eyes opened wide.

Even though it was May, it was hot and sticky that night, and Patrick sweated a lot. He wiped his face with a fancy white handkerchief with letters stitched into the corner. When he finished, he folded it and put it back in his pants pocket. He stayed a long time, talking with my mama and daddy. When I saw him after Mass that Sunday, he touched my head. The lace from his priest clothes brushed against my eyelashes and tickled my face.

In the beginning we had to call him Father Patrick. His whole name is Father Patrick Michael Shaughnessy, and he's from Buffalo. That's a big city, far from here. He came for supper every Friday for that whole summer, then all winter and into part of the next summer, too. He brought us small presents every week, dimes and nickels for candy, baseball cards for the boys, sometimes paper dolls for me and Rosa. After Winnie was born, he brought a big teddy bear and boxes and boxes of baby clothes— pink pajamas, frilly white-and-yellow dresses, and fuzzy little toy animals that squeaked when you pushed in their bellies. What I liked most about Patrick's visits was how his laugh filled up the kitchen, and how his just being around made Mama's sad face open up.

After a while we got to call him just Patrick. No more "Father," no more "Sir." That was before Daddy got mad and talked to Father DiSante about sending Patrick away. Right after summer vacation started, Daddy went to the rectory and I followed him, even though he told me three times to go home. He made me sit in the big, round chair in the rectory parlor and wait for him. When he went into Father DiSante's office I got up and leaned against the wall outside the door. "Get him out of here. He's destroying my family," I heard Daddy say, in a whisper so thick it stuck to my ears.

Later at home, Daddy yelled, "You should be ashamed of yourself, Marie. Think of your children, your family." Mama screamed back, "Go to hell, Paulie. You can't stop me." Her face slammed shut.

By the Fourth of July, Patrick had moved away. Things got really bad after that. He didn't come for supper any more, and Mama cried all Friday afternoon.

"What's wrong?" I asked.

"I miss him so much, Peanut."

Like you miss the lost baby? I wondered to myself, then asked out loud, "Where did he go?"

"Far away. They transferred him, honey."

"Can't he ever visit us again?"

"You don't understand," was all Mama said.

Other things happened, too. Mama wouldn't let Daddy sleep in their bedroom any more. Every night, he stayed on the couch in the living room. And Mama stopped eating for a week. Just black coffee and cigarettes. The broken ends of her Chesterfields looked like dirty fingertips sticking out of her ashtray. She didn't take a bath, and she didn't wash her hair. She just wandered around the house with her pajama bottoms stuck into the top of her slippers and her bathrobe belt dragging behind her. She wouldn't let me play the records or even hum. She cried and cried, holding her long fingers over her face.

I picked black-eyed Susans for Mama that whole week. Every day I put a handful of fresh ones in her favorite clear-glass vase and set them on the table near her bed. The doctor said she had to rest, and he gave her some small white pills. "Don't worry, Mama," I said, handing her two pills and a glass of water. "It'll be OK." Then I tried hard to smile my good-girl smile.

Mama cried a lot the rest of the summer. And she stared out the kitchen window, looking. She was gone to some faraway place, never to come back. The house was quiet and empty, like church after Mass.

By the time school started up again, she was better. She remembered to fix us breakfast in the morning, and she had lunch ready for us most days, too. But things weren't all the way back to normal. Whispers and gossip poked at us everywhere we went. In the grocery store, Mrs. Tanturri's eyebrows stretched up and Mrs. Scalamassi's mouth turned upside down. At the beauty parlor, Mrs. Salvatori, Mrs. Parma, and Mrs. Manelli clammed up as soon as the little bell on the door jingled and me and Mama appeared on the other side of the see-through glass. Mama's face got hard, and the bone in her jaw popped out like a sourball in her cheek. I pretended I was a big, shiny shield of metal, with swords and crosses and barbed wire. I would protect her from their evil eyes.

"Pisa's a little town," Mama says, "with its own little ways."

I agree. It's like when I play hopscotch with my best friend Amelia and her older sisters. If you play fair and throw your stone inside the right boxes, you get your chance to jump. You get ahead, maybe even win. But if you cheat, you're out. Mama doesn't follow the rules. She's an outlaw. Patrick is an outlaw, too. Since I go with

Mama to visit him every Friday, I'm one, too. That's what I told the principal when she asked me why I hit Timmy Carelli in the playground during recess after he called my mama all those dirty names. "I'm an outlaw." I said it proudly.

One day, after Patrick left, Mama sat me down and stared at me with her sad eyes. If I looked too close, I'd fall in and never be able to crawl back out again, so I stared at the floor as she talked.

"Peanut, next week we're gonna go on a little trip. Just you and me and the girls. We're gonna go visit Patrick and have some dinner with him. But this has got to be our little secret. Just between you and me. Can I count on you to be Mama's good girl?"

I glanced up, and Mama looked like Rosa does when she wants me to share my Halloween candy with her. I nodded and said, "OK, Mama."

That's when our secret visits started. Mama and Rosa and Winnie and me. Never the boys, never Daddy. Mama said it was because there wasn't enough room in the car. It would be our special time, just us girls and her and Patrick. And I couldn't tell anyone. Not my friend Amelia. Not the teachers at school. Daddy knows and the boys, too. But I'm not supposed to talk about it with them, either.

"Why get them all upset over nothing?" Mama asks.

***

Fridays make Mama happy and everybody else sad. Daddy prays his rosary and goes to church. Even more than before. And he's real quiet on Saturday mornings. His eyes pretend to be reading the newspaper, but they wander away sometimes to stare at Mama. And he looks lonely. Danny and Joey get mad because they can't come. They think they're missing out on something fun. But

24

they're not. We don't do much. Mostly I watch Rosa and Winnie, so Mama and Patrick can talk and hold hands. If I had it my way, we wouldn't even go. I think it's kind of dumb, driving so long just to eat dinner. If we met Patrick in town, Danny and Joey could come, too. But Mama says we can't do it that way.

I go with her every week because I'm afraid someday she won't come back. I'd rather have Mama and Patrick than no Mama at all. But I have double feelings about it. Patrick makes Mama's eyes get all soft like baby roses. That's the good part. But deeper inside, behind my heart where it's cold like winter, I get scared. I cover my eyes and pray, and a voice whispers and tells me Mama's lost baby is coming back someday. And when it does, there won't be any more room in Mama's heart for me. Patrick and the lost baby will fill it up, and I'll have to knock and knock at the door and hope someone opens up before I freeze to death.

I'm not making this up. I'm not lying. I know because I hear Mama and Patrick talk about it sometimes on Fridays. Patrick says he wants them to have kids of their own—be a real family. I get nervous. I know how sad Mama gets when she has babies. I lose little pieces of her every time she brings a new one home from the hospital. I don't want that to happen again. Ever.

Mama pats Patrick's hand and says,"Someday honey, someday."

Then she looks away. I feel funny, like I'm watching something private that I'm not supposed to see. Then Mama looks back at Patrick as if he's a fancy Christmas present she can't wait to open. That's how I know the lost baby will come back someday. Patrick will tug and tug at Mama's feelings until she says yes to another baby. He'll make promises like he does now, and he'll get her to think it's the best idea ever. And it will be harder and harder for Mama to say no.

He makes promises all the time. At Smiley's coffee shop he talks about going to Happy Town. He says it's a special place where, someday, we'll all live together. "Danny and Joey and Daddy, too?" Rosa asked once. But Mama blushed and looked down at her fingernails. Patrick said, "No, honey, just the five of us." Mama interrupted, "The boys can come later."

In Happy Town, we can have potato chips and chocolate cake for breakfast if we want. Patrick promised. And Mama says we get to sleep in white lace canopy beds, like the ones in the Sears catalog. Amelia says all famous Broadway stars sleep in them. Every year at Christmastime, I cut that picture out of the catalog, tuck it in my Sunday purse and take it to Mass, hoping Christmas morning I'll wake up with my head plopped on a white lacy pillow, staring up at a ruffled canopy sky. It's my favorite wish. At home I have to sleep with my sisters. Rosa drools, and Winnie wets the bed sometimes. I want a room all to myself, with a big fancy bed like a grownup. I want it so much, I can't hardly let myself think about it.

Mama says there won't be any more fights in Happy Town. I like that idea. She and Daddy yell all the time. About grocery money. About phone bills and heating bills and the time Mama had to take Danny to the dentist when he cracked off the edge of his front tooth horsing around on the cement floor in the cellar. They holler about Daddy spending all his time in church or reading his *Lives of the Saints* book instead of helping Mama.

She yells, "Are your hands broken, Paulie? You son of a bitch. You never lift a finger to help out around here. I'm not your slave."

Daddy shouts back, "My hands are fine, Marie!" He shakes them at Mama's face. "See? Look at this thick

skin! I know what hard work is! Who are you to
bellyache?"

I can't remember ever seeing their hands quiet down
and touch each other in soft ways. And they never give
each other little kisses with their eyes, like Amelia's mom
and daddy do or like my mama and Patrick do.

✳✳✳

Mama speeds now, trying to make sure we won't be
late. I watch the country whoosh past the car window.
Lots of hills and white farm houses with tall round silos
next to them. Cows and chickens and fences everywhere.
And in between, wide pieces of land with nothing on it.
How can people live out here? Especially at night, it gets
so dark. I hate the night. It makes me feel so little. I stare
at the trees. The wind waves the branches, collecting up
everybody's loneliness. Then it tucks all the sadness
under the leaves, in the space between the air and the
light, and kisses it with a tender kiss, like my mama
kisses me sometimes. I put my sadness there now, so I
can forget about it.

"You roll it, you pat it, you mark it with a 'B'."

Rosa and Winnie's voices push everything out of my
mind. They're not outlaws. They're just silly little girls. All
they ever want to do is sing stupid songs and play dumb
games.

"Can you turn on the radio, Mama?" I ask. I move forward and rest my elbows on the back of the front seat. I
want to get as close to her as I can.

Mama clicks the knob and pushes the black buttons.
"What station do you want?"

"I don't care, Mama. Aren't we almost there?" I whine,
even though she doesn't like it when I whine. "I'm
hungry," I add. I move my nose closer to the back of her

head, tickling my nostrils with the tips of her brown curls. I want to eat them like a piece of chocolate candy.

"Just about. Ten miles or so."

"Are we going to Smiley's again?" I close my eyes and move my face closer still, brushing my eyelashes against her soft sweater. I breathe, sucking up her perfume smell.

"Yes..."

"Yippie!" My sisters stop singing and clap their hands.

"Can I have a milk shake tonight, Mommy?" Rosa pleads. Her eyes are big, round, hopeful.

"Yes, Rosa," Mama says. "You can always get what you want. What are you hungry for, Peanut?"

I don't answer. I lean back into the seat, close my eyes and listen to the song on the radio. My chest could burst if I tried to talk.

> Somewhere my love
> There will be songs to sing
> Although the snow
> Covers the hope of spring ©

It's Mama's favorite. The love song from *Dr. Zhivago,* the movie she took me to. I felt so grown up. I was on a date with my mama. Just me and her. Not Danny, not Joey, not Daddy, not even Patrick. She bought me popcorn and Reese's peanut-butter cups, and when she cried and cried through the whole movie, I gave her one of my napkins, even though it had butter grease on it.

For her birthday last year, Patrick gave Mama a tiny box with that song inside it. She keeps it in her dresser drawer. Sometimes I sneak in there when she's busy and can't see me. I open the box and listen until my insides get all sad and lonely. I close my eyes now, listening to the radio. I think about being on the run, in the middle of cold, lonely Siberia, calling for Lara, feeling all broken up. My heart is cold, like chips of ice. I squash my face against the car window to keep the sadness inside my eyes.

"We're here, girls."

I swerve away from the window as Mama turns the car into the lot. Smiley's Coffee Shop sign blinks on and off, an icy blue smile.

Then I see Patrick's big, shiny, red car parked two down from us.

"He's here already, Mama."

I open the car door, but don't feel like getting out yet. I take my time and try to push the snowy Siberia feelings away.

Patrick doesn't like me, I can tell. Every Friday he hugs us in this order: Winnie first, then Mama, then Rosa, then me. If I push ahead and grab for his hand, he pats my fingers, then wraps his arms all the way around Winnie. Later, when we're done eating, I try another way. I tell a story or a joke, and he listens for a tiny bit, then hurries me through so he can set Winnie on his lap. She combs his hair, and they play beauty parlor. I sit and wait and wait and wait, but he still doesn't play with me. I'm too ugly. My hair's too red and too thick. And I'm too old to sit on his lap.

"Are you feeling better now, honey?"

Mama's question splashes my face. Her front teeth creep out from behind her stiff, red lips. The worries smooth out of her face.

"Yeah," I lie. I get out of the car, look the other way. I push my sneaker into the pavement. "How about you?"

"Yeah, much better." Her smile is huge. "Let's go give him a hug, OK?"

Mama hums as she leads the way to the cafe. She swings her fancy pocketbook. Winnie and Rosa walk right behind her, and I'm behind them. Patrick's waiting at the door, jingling his car keys. I imagine Mama's face, bright as a neon sign, greeting him.

Smiley's wouldn't be so bad if we could come here without Patrick. I like the red booths and the black-and-white checkerboard floor. I like how the long ceiling lights shine on the silvery soda machine. I like how the whole place smells of coffee and cigarettes and french fries. And how the waitresses pin black-and-white lacy hankies to their chests with funny names on them, like "Betty" and "Pearl" and "Muffin." They always have a treat for us kids, suckers or Tootsie Rolls, or a shiny, polished stone to take home.

Mama pushes the cafe door open and light from inside spills its thick, oily glow all around the edges of her hair and her shoulders. Then Patrick's eyes hold Mama's. "Hello, Marie," he says, with a smile that stretches across his face. And I know, right then and there, why I keep Mama's secret. More than anything else in the whole world, I want my mama to always be smiling, full of light. On Friday night, happiness spills out of her and the cold sadness slips away. I take a deep breath, wait my turn to hug Patrick, and try to grin my best smile.

Two

Friday afternoon study hall drags on. Joey plays with his history book, bending the cover back and shuffling through the pages fast and steady. His legs fidget, and his eyes wander to the clock on the wall near the door. It's still only a quarter to three. It seems to him that it had been that the last time he looked. Goddamn, why can't it be three o'clock? Fifteen more minutes. Fifteen more minutes.

The last period of the day, last day of the week, and he's itching to get out. He slumps forward, rests his head on the edge of his book. He imagines getting up, bolting across the classroom, out the door, down the hall and into the September afternoon. He can't be late, not today. He sits back, slaps his textbook shut, picks up his pencil and drums it on the edge of his desk.

"Mr. Giovanni," Mr. Flynn, the study hall monitor, calls from the front of the room. "You are disturbing the other students."

Joey looks around at the roomful of ninth graders. Only Tony Malone and Teresa Rossi are actually doing homework. Johnny Scarpelli, the class creep, is busy wadding spitballs and piling them in long rows in the pencil well on his desk. In grade school, Scarpelli and Joey used to be best friends, but now Johnny's mom won't let him hang out with Joey any more. Scarpelli calls him "bastard boy" and "priest kisser." Sometimes in the locker room after gym class he yells, "Your mother's got bigger balls than you do, Joey boy." But he's a reject anyway. Joey's good buddy, Stevie Androzzi, is sprawled over his math book, sleeping. Maria Ponti files her nails and blows on the tips of her fingers. And John Barnett is picking his nose and sticking boogers under his chair.

Looks to me like I'm really disturbing the peace here, Joey says to himself. He shoots a glance back at Mr. Flynn. His eyes say, "Who the hell you kidding?"

"Don't give me any of your looks, Joseph, or you'll find yourself in detention all next week," Flynn says, matching Joey's stare. "That should give you plenty of opportunity to find ways to productively use your time."

Joey lays his pencil down and shoves both hands out in front of his chest. His cheeks feel sunburned. "No problem, Mr. Flynn." The last thing he needs is to cause trouble and wind up in the principal's office. It's already two fifty-five.

Mr. Flynn looks away, and Joey stares out the window. The sun touches the edges of the leaves, just beginning to turn gold and red, and out beyond the school playground, the grass is still green and inviting. Joey thinks about baseball and dirt, and ice-cold lemonade to wash away his thirst, but it's September now, and he can't quite get used to being back at school, smelling antiseptic hallways and breathing stale air in crowded classrooms. His legs twitch and his fingers curl, holding an imaginary bat. Being fourteen isn't all it's cracked up to be. Ninth grade is cool, but all the homework drives him crazy. It ties him down. It's not like grade school when he could rush home, everyday, to his baseball mitt and cleats.

Being on the move is all he ever thinks about—running, dribbling a basketball, throwing a baseball, swinging a bat—outside, inside, even in the living room—it doesn't matter to him. Only to his mother who gets pissed off every time he bounces a ball against her clean walls. She doesn't understand that he can't help himself. He likes the power of his body in motion. It makes him feel as if he has control over something in his life.

It's two fifty-seven. Three more minutes. If I don't get out of here soon, Ma will be gone for sure. She said she'd wait.

That's how he remembers it, and he's counting on her to come through for him today. This morning he tried to convince her to take him with her, this afternoon, to see Patrick. They argued in the kitchen while she packed his peanut-butter-and-jelly sandwich into a brown paper lunch bag. Even then, he darted around the kitchen, his arms and legs full of restlessness.

"Can I go? Can I go?" he pleaded.

He hounded her as she moved across the kitchen putting away the Wonder bread, the Peter Pan peanut butter, the jar of A&P grape jelly. She tried to sidetrack him by saying, "Joey, can't you sit still for one second? You're worse than a goddamn gnat."

He wouldn't give up. He grabbed the back of a kitchen chair to steady his urge to follow her everywhere. He trailed her with his eyes, hoping to change her mind, make her see it his way. "Just wait 'til I get home from school this afternoon. Three-fifteen. I'll hurry. I promise."

"Why do you want to go?" she asked. "Wouldn't it be more fun to stay here with your brother?" She bent the ends of the paper lunch bag into a tight crease. "We don't do anything special, you know. It's not like you're missing out on anything."

"No. Honest," he said. "I don't have fun here with Danny. I miss you guys when you go."

"But you see me every day. How can you miss me for the few short hours I go see Patrick?"

"But I do. I really do." He was starting to sound like his little sister Rosa, so he took a deep breath to coax his voice back to being fourteen again. "And so does Danny."

"Daniel's nearly a man," Ma said, shaking her head. "I'm sure he has more important things on his mind than missing his mother on Friday nights."

Her hesitation had nothing to do with Danny, and Joey knew it. She was still sore about the time she took Joey to Finger Lakes State Park for a picnic with Patrick and the girls. Danny was there, too. Joey let loose, got rowdy on the jungle gym in the playground near the picnic tables, and started pushing kids off the bars.

Some lady yelled "Stop it right now, young man, or I'll have to speak with your father." She pointed at Patrick, sitting nearby, holding Ma's hand.

"Go ahead. He ain't my father," Joey sassed. He felt so smart, thinking he found a way to get the pesky woman off his back. "He's just some old priest who thinks he's my father."

The woman's eyebrows jumped into her forehead, and her mouth swung open. She huffed off the playground, folding her kids to her side, and headed straight towards Patrick. "You ought to be ashamed of yourself." Then she turned and marched back to her own picnic site and started gossiping with the other picnickers.

"Joseph, Danny, Peanut, Rosa, Winnie, come on kids," Ma fired off their names. She waved to them with a frantic sweep of her arm. When Joey got to the table she swung at his butt and yelled, "What did you do?" He swerved and missed the blow.

"I didn't do nothing, Ma," he insisted. He raced around the far side of the picnic bench to escape her.

"Well, we've got to go home now," she said as she packed the cold chicken and covered the potato salad. "You've spoiled it for all of us."

"Why'd you have to be so stupid, Joey?" Peanut snapped.

"Lay off him, Peanut," Danny defended.

"All of you shut up and get in the car," Ma ordered.

From the look on her face, Joey knew she'd taken a memory trip back to that park, that woman's screeching voice, the shocked stares of the other picnickers. "Ma, I'll behave. It won't be like that one time," Joey said. "I promise."

"You upset Patrick very much the last time we took you, Joey," she said. "You upset me, too. Can you learn to keep your mouth shut?"

She handed him his lunch bag. "I won't say a word, Ma. I promise. Please let me come with you tonight."

"Get going or you'll be late for school," was the last thing Ma said before she kissed him on the cheek and nudged him out the door.

***

The school bell rings inside Joey's chest. His heart races. "It's three o'clock," Mr. Flynn announces. "Class is dismissed. Have a good weekend, ladies and gentlemen."

All twenty ninth graders spring to their feet and swarm into the corridor. Joey pushes past the others, trying to get to the door. "Hey, Joey, wanna go hit some balls?" Stevie Androzzi calls as Joey heads down the steps. "Naw," Joey yells back, over his shoulder. "I've gotta go somewhere with my ma this afternoon. Maybe tomorrow."

A spitball stings the back of Joey's ear as he pushes

the school door open. "You're scum, Giovanni. A mama's boy," Johnny Scarpelli laughs as Joey disappears into the school yard. He brushes the wet wad away and takes off down the block.

If I run hard, I can still make it home in time. I can't be late.

He pumps his legs and swiftly covers the several blocks from the school to the bridge that spans the canal dividing the town in half. His lungs burn as he races to the other side, his side of town. Three more blocks. She just has to still be there.

He runs into the wind. It billows against his open jacket. He presses on, pounding his sneakers harder on the sidewalk. Two blocks and he'll be home.

I hope we go to that coffee shop that Peanut is always talking about. I'm gonna get a burger and fries and a strawberry shake.

One block from home. He can almost taste the sweet, soft ice cream, smell the hot, salty potatoes. He stretches his stride and clips past the houses at the end of his block. Halfway down the street, he sees the empty driveway.

"Damnit." He shortens his step. "Goddamnit." He slows to a walk, wadding his fists.

Maybe Dad took the car today. Maybe Patrick is gonna come by to get Ma this time. She's inside, I know she is, waiting for me at the kitchen table.

He opens the porch door. Zoomer yawns, shakes back his ears and stretches to a stand. Joey walks past him and goes inside the house. Everything is quiet. No radio blaring, no soap operas on the TV, like regular afternoons during the week. Only the soft hum of the refrigerator buzzing in the kitchen. He heads in that direction, hoping against the odds that Ma is sipping a cup of coffee, puffing on a cigarette at the end of the table, waiting for him. "Ma?" he says her name like a prayer. "Ma?" he calls, louder, to the walls this time. "Ma!" he screams as he walks into the empty kitchen.

Maybe Peanut was late coming home from school, and Ma had to go pick her up. She'll swing by the house and get me before she heads out.

He pulls out a chair and sits at the kitchen table, pretending he's waiting for a car horn. His eyes fall on a note propped against the red ceramic sugar bowl in the middle of the yellow Formica table. He picks it up and reads it out loud: "Joey. Couldn't wait any longer. See you tomorrow morning. Hope you understand. Love, Mom."

He checks the clock above the stove. Three-eighteen. "She couldn't have left more than a few minutes ago." He crushes the note and throws it against the cupboard.

"Jesus Christ. She never meant to wait for me. She could have given me a note to leave study hall early. No way did she want me to go."

He picks up the sugar bowl and throws it against the wall, then swings around and kicks a chair, sending it rattling across the linoleum floor. He pounds the table with his fists until his knuckles are numb.

She don't care about me. She goes off with that turd Patrick. She never gives a second thought about me. Or how it feels to come home every Friday to this creepy house.

"What the hell you doin', Joey?"

Danny's voice startles him and he jumps back, embarrassed. "What the hell you doin', sneaking up on a guy like that?" Joey yells. He wipes his face, trying to remove traces of the panic that snuck out from the corners of his eyes. "Aren't you supposed to be at work or something?" he asks. He looks away from his brother's stare.

"No, I switched with some kid who needed to take

tomorrow off," Danny says. "Why'd you throw the sugar all over the place?"

"She didn't wait for me, and I asked her to," he says, trying to swallow the tears caught in the back of his throat. Danny touches his shoulder. Joey wants to bury his hot face in his brother's chest and scream, but he stiffens his back, brushes Danny's hand away, and stares at the mess on the floor.

"Come on, Joey," Danny says. "You know she don't want us along. Just that sissy pants, Peanut, and the little ones. You're too old for that shit anyway. Hang out with me and Dad."

Joey shakes his head and stares at his sneakers. In the run home, the laces had loosened, and now they lie tangled around the toes of his sneakers. He stoops to tie them and thinks about his brother's suggestion. Be one of the guys, that's really all he needs. She's not worth it. But some small, swollen place in his heart screams for her. He wants to sit in the middle of the kitchen floor, surrounded by red shards of sugar bowl and granules of sugar, and never get up. He looks at Danny, leaning against the back door, waiting for him to do something. He swallows hard, ties his shoelaces, then stands up with tight, hard fists and grabs the broom and dust pan.

"Guess I better clean this up before Dad gets home."

"Guess so," Danny agrees. "Then let's go hit a few balls at the field."

"OK."

Danny gives him a small grin. "It'll be OK, Joe. You don't need her anymore. You got me. And Dad."

Joey sweeps the mess into the dustpan, opens the broom closet and dumps it into the garbage can. In the center of that small, swollen place in his heart, that place where his mother lives, is a hard knot where Danny and Dad live, where he can breathe, away from the pain, away from the waiting and the longing for comfort. It's as big and as dirty as a baseball diamond, and it smells like summer all year round. Even when the leaves fade, even when the snow falls, white and thick as sugar, he's safe at home plate.

He grabs his bat and ball and follows his brother out the door. He'll feel better when he gets to the field. He won't care anymore that Peanut and the girls get to be with Ma. He won't care that she forgot about him one more time. At the ballpark, it doesn't matter anymore. He slips on his glove. He rubs his fingers against the soft leather, feeling for comfort.

"Danny, do you think she'll ever leave?" Joey asks. He pulls his Yankees cap over his thick hair and walks down the driveway beside his brother.

"What ya thinkin' about shit like that for, Joey? It'll just get ya upset again." Danny stuffs an extra baseball into his pocket.

"I don't know," he says. "But do ya think she will?"

"Sometimes I wish she would and just get it over with." Danny kicks the gravel stones beneath his sneakers. "All this mickey-mouse Friday-night stuff drives me crazy."

Joey agrees, but he can't say it out loud, like Danny. Danny's tough. It all still bothers Joey. He wishes things were still the way they used to be when they were little— Danny and Joey and Peanut, too. Things were better then. Mom and Dad didn't fight as much. Patrick wasn't around. Ma stayed home every Friday with the rest of them. And everyone ate supper together. Sometimes Uncle Tony and Aunt Stella would come over to play gin rummy. But that was a long time ago.

"What ya got that long face for?" Danny says. He knocks Joey on the arm, takes off running for the field.

"Last one to the field's a bastard Irish priest," he yells into the wind.

Joey chases after Danny, pushing his lungs until they can't hold air fast enough. When he gets to the ballpark, Danny's waiting on the bleachers. He tosses a ball at Joey. "Knock their heads off, pal."

Joey steadies his breath as Danny heads for the outfield. He takes a few practice swings, then pops a high fly out to center field. Danny back-pedals to nab it.

"Just like the Yanks, hey, Danny?"

Danny throws the ball back to Joey at home plate. Joey tosses it into the air and swings his bat smoothly through the strike zone, connecting with the stitches, spinning the ball down first baseline.

"You're hot tonight, Joey, ole boy!" Danny yells to him.

Joey laughs. Nothing feels better than practicing ball with Danny. He tosses another ball into the air and slams it. Then another and another until his muscles burn from swinging and connecting. When he's had enough he calls to his brother, "Let's go now, Danny."

He picks up their gear and inhales slowly. He's calmer, now. His arms are tired, and his heart isn't screaming anymore. "Beats sitting in some dumb ole coffee shop listening to Peanut bellyaching, don't it, Joey?" Danny says.

"Yeah. Who needs 'em anyway." Joey punches Danny's arm and his brother jabs him back.

"All you need, you already got, Joey. Just remember that. Me and you. You don't need nothing else," Danny says. He grabs Joey across the shoulder. The weight of his arm feels good against Joey's neck.

"I'm hungry. Do you think Dad's home yet?" Joey asks.

"Yeah, probably," Danny says.

"What do ya think he's making for supper?"

"It's Friday. It's gotta be fish sticks," Danny grimaces.

Joey makes gagging sounds like he's going to throw up. "I hate fish sticks." Danny bats at his head.

"It's either that or burnt hot dogs," Danny says. "And you know we can't eat meat on Friday."

"Mortal sin," Joey cackles. He makes the sign of the cross with his right hand, and both boys laugh. "You're gonna rot in hell for sure now, Joey," Danny teases him.

Joey swings at his brother. Danny pulls the bat away and tears off down the street. Joey tucks his glove under his arm and races after him. A few blocks from home they slow to a walk. They aren't in any hurry to get there.

THREE

There's hardly anybody at Smiley's coffee shop tonight. Betty, my favorite waitress, waves from behind the cash register as we crowd in through the door. Winnie's already all wrapped up in Patrick's arms. She's kissing his cheek. Her lips look like the tiny candy hearts my best friend, Amelia, gives me on Valentine's day, no bigger than a dime, the kind with little promises on them, like "Be mine," or "I love you." Winnie hugs Patrick's head real tight. He kisses her face over and over again.

I hate this in-between time, after we get here and before we sit down. It feels like a million eyes are staring at us. I wish we were back in Pisa right now, eating fish sticks with Danny and Joey and Daddy.

But every Friday night Mama says, "No, we've got to go."

The only time we stayed home was last winter, when it snowed so hard she couldn't see to drive. Even then, she tried. I helped her bundle the girls up, and we sat in the car hardly able to move our arms and legs; we had so many clothes on we looked like human stuffed animals, furry and pink-faced. We only made it as far as the thruway, slipping and sliding. The state troopers closed the highway.

"Too icy, go home," they said. Mama turned the car around and cried all the way back to our house.

Patrick reaches into his pocket and pulls out some quarters. "Here, go pick out some songs for us," he says to me and Rosa. "The booth's over there."

He's generous that way. Always has some change if we want an ice cream or some little thing. That's one of the things Mama loves most about him. He tries to make us happy. Not like Daddy, who snaps, "Get out of here. You think money grows on trees?" whenever I ask him for a pack of gum or a candy bar at the grocery store. But Daddy doesn't mean to be grouchy. Danny says it's the fighting and the bills that make him that way. I wish I could plant a forest of dollar trees. Daddy could go out there and pick a bushel, and then he wouldn't have to worry so much.

Patrick pats Rosa's hand, then points to a booth with a tabletop jukebox, near the window. I follow his arm all the way out to the tip of his finger. His nails are clipped and rounded, and they shine like they're dipped in clear nail polish. They're so different from my daddy's dirty hands, with thick, greasy knuckles and hard, rough callouses.

While I'm thinking about hands, Mama presses hers against my back and nudges me. Her voice sneaks up, "Go on now, do as you're told."

I open my mouth, but nothing comes out. I want to say I don't have to obey him, he's not my daddy, but I can see Mama too busy eyeing Patrick to listen to me. He puts Winnie back down and reaches for Mama. His armpits smell like wet cardboard when he stretches over my head to hug her. Mama and him smack a kiss, and I make a face like I've just picked away a scab. Then I run to see what Rosa's up to.

I notice the cat family's here already. They're weirder

than we are. They eat at Smiley's every Friday night, too. I call them the cat family because the mama wears black, pointed glasses that tilt on her face like Siamese cat eyes. She has two daughters, and they have the same glasses, too. Those cat girls sit so quietly across the booth from their mama and daddy; I don't know how anybody could sit so still for so long. Their daddy doesn't wear glasses. Who knows, maybe he's not really their daddy? Maybe the cat woman and her daughters meet the man without glasses in secret, every Friday. I don't know for sure, but the cat girls have sad faces, and their eyes are droopy, so I guess maybe it's true.

"Hello, Red. What ya staring at?"

I jump back, scared I've been caught gawking, but it's only Betty. She smiles as she rushes past me, heading toward the cat family's booth, with an armful of plates that rattle like a bracelet when she walks. I smile back because I like her. She's got red hair, like me. And white teeth that shine like snowflakes in the sun.

"How's my favorite family tonight?" Betty asks, not waiting for me to answer.

"Fine," I start to say, but I stop myself when I remember Daddy's home, and we're here with Patrick. Nobody's ever told Betty that Mama and Patrick aren't married. Sometimes I pretend that we really are a family, just like Mama wants us to be, and we're here eating supper and laughing, and when we leave we all go home together. But then I think of Danny and Joey. And Daddy. Eating cold fish sticks in our quiet kitchen. The picture I have in my mind of my family is upside down or backward or something, and I get dizzy thinking about it all. So I don't.

I slide into the booth, next to Rosa. Winnie's there, too, hanging her head over the top, waving at a family with a small baby, sitting in the booth behind us.

"Sit down, Winnie."

I yank at her arm to pull her around, but she kicks my leg and ignores me. I kneel and look over the back of the booth, too. Drool runs down the sides of the baby's chubby chin. Its mama kisses its head and offers it a bottle. She looks up at me and Winnie and smiles.

"Hello, girls," she says, and I want to smile back but I can't. My lips are afraid to open up. My brain's thinking, I don't want Mama to see this baby. It will get her thinking too much about dead babies, then the evening will be ruined for sure. Winnie giggles at the lady and the baby, then she gets shy and turns back to bug Rosa. I nod my head "hello," polite, like my mama taught me to be with people who aren't family. But my stomach flips, and I turn away, too.

"Let me pick one," Rosa yells.

"No!" Winnie hollers. "Me. Me."

Sometimes my sisters are stupid twerps the way they fight about dumb things like a jukebox.

"You two can't even read, how do you even know what songs to pick?" I say in the sassy way I always do when I have to watch them and make sure they behave. I slide into the booth, opposite them.

"Peanut, tell her to let me do it," Rosa pleads.

"No!" Winnie yells back.

"Give me the quarters, and I'll do it," I say.

"Read 'em to us, Peanut," Rosa demands.

"You want the Beatles? Or the Beach Boys?"

"Beatles," Rosa says. Winnie nods her head, too.

I flip through the plastic song menu. "B10, 'She Loves You,' H5, 'I Wanna Hold Your Hand,' and C22, 'Roll Over Beethoven.' How's that sound?"

"What's all the commotion about over here?"

Patrick startles me. "Didn't mean to scare ya." He laughs and tickles Winnie. He slides into the booth beside her and Rosa. Mama settles in beside me and puts her arm around my shoulder. "Did you pick us some good songs, honey?"

"Yeah, Ma, your favorites," I start to say, but I'm interrupted by Betty.

"Howdy gang, what'll it be tonight? The usual? Three burger plates and two chicken dinners?"

We're not supposed to eat meat on Friday, but Patrick says it's OK. He's a priest, so he can give us a "dispensation." Mama says it's like permission. We get to eat whatever we want.

"Yep, Betty," Patrick says. "Burger plates and chicken dinners. Same as always."

Patrick smiles, but the rest of his face isn't happy. He looks more like Daddy tonight, except his hair's black instead of red, and his eyes don't look delicious like Daddy's. Daddy's eyes remind me of hot chestnuts on Christmas Eve.

"OK," Betty says. She digs into her apron pocket and leaves some crayons for Winnie and Rosa. They start to draw on the white paper placemats. After Betty goes, Patrick looks across the tabletop at Mama.

"Well, how was your week?" He touches Mama's hand, then pulls away and taps the top of the booth with his clean knuckles.

I think a minute about punching in the jukebox songs, but something about how Patrick is tonight makes me nervous. Usually his hair's all combed just right, and he smells handsome. And he laughs like a movie star and kids around and smiles at Mama all the time. But not tonight. He takes sips of water and swallows hard. Mama doesn't seem to notice, though. She tells him all the news. Danny got an A on his biology test. Joey got a new baseball mitt for his birthday. She even tells him I took first place in the song-and-dance competition at the Knights of Columbus. She doesn't see Patrick's eyes get all dark and worried or how his cigarette shakes when he holds it to his mouth and sucks the smoke in, real deep.

"Peanut, did you bring your blue ribbon to show Patrick?"

"I forgot, Mama," I say. I look quickly at her, then back at him. The corners of his mouth twist down a little, and his eyes slide back and forth from me to Mama. He takes a deep breath like he's storing up oxygen for a long speech, and I sit real still like the cat daughters, waiting.

"I've been thinking all day," Patrick says.

He stares right at Mama. I feel invisible. Me and Rosa and Winnie are ghosts at the table, listening.

"About how nice it would be to be with you all the time. You know. We've been wanting to go for a long time. Almost two years. I don't see any reason to wait any longer."

"What do you mean, Patrick?" Mama pretends she doesn't understand. She cocks her head in a carefree way.

Happy Town. He means Happy Town, I want to say. I take a deep breath and hold it until it burns, and I have to let it out or I'll explode. I slip my breath out slowly, so no one knows I've trapped it inside. Mama's expression changes. Her smile turns under. Her white teeth hide behind her red lips. Her eyelids narrow, so I can hardly see her eyes any more. Those are the danger signs. I know them by heart. I sit still beside her—listening, looking, waiting.

"I mean—Hell," Patrick says. The sweat drips down the side of his neck. "I mean, Happy Town is as close as a car ride away. If we left tonight, after dinner, we could be halfway there by morning."

I check Mama's face, scrounging around for some clue. Her mouth doesn't change, and her eyes stay the same. I can't move my legs or my arms. They're frozen to the booth. I keep track of everything with my eyes.

Mama looks at Patrick, then she stares at the table top, then at Winnie and Rosa. My sisters just keep drawing on the placemats. They sit quietly next to Patrick, across the booth from me and Mama.

Finally Mama says, "Patrick, I don't want to rush into this." Her voice is chilly and sweet like a popsicle.

"Rush into it?" Patrick says. He squints. His face gets all red and puffy. He squeezes a paper napkin between his fingers and tears it apart, little by little. "I feel as if we've waited for years. I'm tired of it."

The air is thick and smoky. I can hardly breathe. And my shoulders feel like someone's sticking a fork into them. I worry that everybody in the restaurant can hear us. I look around. The cat family is busy eating dinner. If they hear anything, they don't let on. I listen back behind me. The couple with the baby is singing along with a song on their jukebox. I don't think they're listening either. The waitresses are busy taking orders, delivering food to the other customers. Nobody seems to be paying any attention to our booth. My skin starts to tingle. Something inside is trying to crawl out, float away, out the door, down the road. The only thing I can think to do is pray: Dear Holy Mother of God, make Mama say no.

"Patrick," Mama interrupts him. "I've got five kids."

"I know that," Patrick says. "Five kids and a goddamn husband. We've been all through this. Many times. But what about us? When is there ever going to be time for us? We'll send for the boys later. It'll be all right."

His voice softens at the end. He's trying to convince Mama. I don't believe him.

"But the girls," Mama says. "We don't have any clothes or any money or any place to live when we get there."

Patrick smashes his cigarette into the ash tray. He pinches the bridge of his nose and looks straight at me. I try not to flinch. I hold my eyes against his until they burn. He looks at my sisters, then back at Mama. He slouches over the table and brings his face closer to Mama's. I chew my bottom lip and stare out the window at the parking lot.

"I've got money, Marie," I hear Patrick whisper. "I closed out my savings account today. I've got $2,000 in a safety deposit box in the trunk of my car. It's enough to hold us until I find a job. We can buy clothes when we get there. And we'll find a place to live. A nice place."

I close my eyes and try to imagine Happy Town and a special house all our own. I try to feel happy, try to picture myself in a canopy bed with lavender lace pillows. I try to picture Mama in a bright yellow kitchen with a window that looks out on a flower garden full of red and yellow tulips. I try to see Patrick coming through the front door after work, smiling. I hear a baby crying in a room, in the back of the house. I open my eyes quick and see Patrick wiping his face with a handkerchief. The baby in the booth nearby is crying. "Hush, hush, honey," its mama comforts. "Where's the bottle," its daddy says, trying to help.

Betty whooshes by to drop off chocolate malts. Patrick and Mama ignore her. Betty puts the tall glasses in front of us kids. "Thanks," Rosa says. Winnie reaches for hers and almost knocks the glass over, but I catch it before it topples. Betty whirls away and I wish I could jump in her apron pocket and go with her.

"I just don't know, Patrick," Mama speaks first. "I don't know if I'm ready." Her voice sounds far away. Her words are trapped deep inside her. I move closer to hear.

Patrick sits back, puts his hands flat on the table and sighs. "What's that mean, you're not ready?"

A deep line runs across his forehead. He looks worried now. "We love each other. We have a family here," Patrick says, nodding at Winnie, then at me and Rosa. My sisters sip their malts and smile. I wiggle a little and watch the thin line of chocolate ice cream slide down the outside of my malt can. I feel cold and hot at the same time.

"I'm sick of this, Marie," Patrick says, under his breath, then slightly louder, he whispers. "I want to marry you, you know that."

I blow air into my straw. The thick ice cream bubbles up like lava. The baby in the booth behind us cries again. I want to cry, too, but I squeeze back the hot feelings and suck cold ice cream up the straw filling my mouth. My teeth ache.

"Marie," Patrick's voice comes on strong now. "Let's ask the girls. Let's see if they want to go."

I stare at the napkin next to my malt glass, so I don't have to look at him looking at me. "Girls," he asks, "do you want to go to Happy Town tonight?"

Rosa answers first. "We haven't eaten yet."

"After dinner, honey," Patrick says. I picture him dressed like the wolf in Little Red Riding Hood, smiling that big smile of his, promising we never have to be afraid of anything.

"I tired," Winnie whines. She rubs her eyes and yawns.

"You can sleep in the car, sweetie," Patrick says, all lovey and gentle.

"Will I still be able to go to Lisa's birthday party tomorrow, Mama?" Rosa asks. Her voice squeaks, so I know she's nervous.

I wait for Mama to answer, but she doesn't. When I open my eyes, Patrick is staring right at me.

"How about you, Peanut?"

51

His mouth is wide, and his lips shake just a little. I stare at the cigarette stains on his teeth and say nothing. I look at Mama. Her face is as white as a fresh placemat.

"Peanut, do you want to go?" Mama finally says. She grips her coffee cup.

"Do you want to go, Mama?" I ask back. I don't want to say no if she wants to go, but I don't want to say yes if she doesn't.

"Well, it is what we've wanted for so very long," Mama says. Her voice trails off, then she glances out the window.

Mama looks like an empty house, all lonely and quiet. That's how she was when Patrick first went away. It scares me. All the doors are locked, and I'm pounding and pounding, but she won't let me in. Something inside me slams shut and I wonder, should I say yes or should I say no? What's the magic word that will make everything all better? "Yes" means I'll never see Zoomer or Amelia or Danny or Joey or Daddy. "No" means Patrick will be mad at me, and maybe Mama will be too. I search Mama's face one more time, hoping the words that come out of my mouth will be the ones she would have picked.

"Sure," I say. The words slip out of me in a funny way. I sound littler than Winnie. "Yes, I want to go to Happy Town. If you want to go, Mama."

Patrick's face relaxes. A small noise slips out of his throat. "Well, what do you say, Marie? The girls all seem to think it's a great idea."

My armpits itch. My chest feels as if Patrick's voice is pounding hard against it.

"Patrick, I..." Mama's words don't come out easy, either. "It's just not that simple. I can't just get a divorce."

The sweet smell of chocolate malt makes me want to throw up. I push the glass away and fall back into the booth. I said yes. I picked the wrong answer. If only I

52

could take it back, say no instead. Now, if we go, it's all my fault.

"What can Paulie do, Marie? If you leave him, he'll have to give you a divorce. It's the law."

Divorce. I'd heard that word before, at the beauty parlour when Mrs. Tanturri gossiped about her cousin Silvia Androzzi. She said that word, "divorce," like it was bitter, and she had to spit it off her tongue. I'd seen the word plenty of times before that, plastered all over the covers of the movie-star magazines the ladies read when they sit under the hair dryers.

"They drop each other right and left, carry on as if there's no tomorrow," Mrs. Salvatori complained.

"They think they're better than the rest of us," Mrs. Rossi snipped.

But divorce only happened to movie stars. Not to people in Pisa. Not to Catholics. Is that what Mama wants?

"Maybe it's the only way out," Mama says, softly. She wants to cry. She takes a deep breath, sips some coffee and lights a cigarette. "Maybe it's the only way out," she says again, as if we didn't hear her the first time. A few minutes later she adds, "OK. But I want to bring the boys, too."

"They aren't here right now," Patrick says. "We'll send for them later, just like we planned."

Here he goes again. Mama brings up the boys, and he squashes her talk. I want to put my fingers in my ears, shut their voices out of my mind. My head aches. I want them to stop talking about Happy Town and if the boys can come or not. I think about the fight I had with Joey yesterday morning after he ate the last of the Cap'n Crunch. Danny shouted, "Just pick another box of cereal, goddamnit, before you both drive me crazy." Maybe the boys would be happier if we didn't come home tonight.

"OK," Mama says. She sounds the way I do when I'm trying to convince Amelia to play Barbies instead of Chinese Checkers. "But we've got to send for them right away. As soon as we get there."

"We don't have that much money, Marie. As soon as I get a job, we'll send for Danny and Joey."

"I can't leave my sons," Mama says. "Not with Paulie."

"Marie, you're not making any sense. It's only for a little while. They'll understand."

The veins in Patrick's neck pop out like thick blue worms. Maybe he'll explode right here all over the restaurant. Wiggly blue worms will spill from his neck, and we'll have to call an ambulance and have someone take him away.

Mama starts to cry. "Do you think so?" she asks. "What if they don't?"

I slip my hand into hers and hold on tight. I want to bop him in the face. I want to be big and holler and carry on and say everything I'm thinking, but his blue eyes barrel down at me, and I feel little, sitting across the wide booth from him. He slaps the table, and my face gets hot. All I can think of is to think fast and blurt something out.

"Mama," I say. "I've gotta go to the dentist on Monday, and Joey's getting his baseball award the week after that. You said you'd be there, remember?"

They aren't very good excuses, but they're the only ones I can think of with his eyes fixed on me. Mama squeezes my hand.

"Yes, Peanut, I remember." She wipes her eyes with a napkin.

"For Christ's sake," Patrick says.

He looks like he's ready to give up. He grabs for Mama's free hand and holds it. My heart beats in my ears.

"Maybe it's not such a good idea," he says. "Let's just forget about it all for now."

I don't know why he gives in. When he lets go of her hand, he looks like he's gonna cry. He stares out the window.

Mama lets out a tiny sigh, and the tight wrinkles relax around her mouth. It's a good sign, even if Patrick is mad. Mama looks at me with grateful eyes, and I smile at her.

"Here ya go!" Betty announces as she appears at the end of our booth wearing a big, embarrassed smile. She's got platefuls of burgers and fries and chicken dinners lined up along her arms. "Enjoy your dinner." She leaves as fast as she appeared.

Rosa and Winnie drop their crayons and grab some french fries. I reach for the ketchup bottle for something to do, then I pass it to Mama, who's busy now, holding Patrick's hand.

"I'm alright," Patrick says. "We'll go some other time."

"We can go soon, I promise," Mama says. "Just not now, not tonight, not this way, so suddenly."

Nobody says anything all through dinner. Mama smiles a few times when she hears the baby behind us giggling. It makes me nervous, but Mama doesn't seem too preoccupied with it, so I try not to think about the lost baby. Patrick picks at his chicken dinner. I eat a few french fries and watch the cat family pay their bill and leave the restaurant. I stare out the window as they all get into the same car. My sisters finish their burgers and Rosa asks me how come I haven't picked any songs for them to listen to.

"I forgot," I say. I wipe my hands and punch the buttons on the tabletop juke box. When her favorite song comes on, Rosa sings along, "She loves you, yeah, yeah, yeah." Winnie joins in, "Yeah, yeah, yeah."

That makes Mama laugh. Patrick, too. He looks more relaxed now. He smiles and joins in the singing. He kisses the top of Winnie's head as she bobs to the music. When the last song is over, Patrick pays the bill, and we leave the restaurant. He kisses us all good-bye in the parking lot. He kisses Winnie soft on the lips. He kisses me and Rosa on the cheek. Then he kisses Mama hard on the lips, like how they kiss in the movies. He holds her tight, and they close their eyes. He pulls away and says, "It'll be OK. It'll all work out. I love you."

We pile into Daddy's car, and Patrick closes the door behind us. He leans through the driver's side window and looks at Mama. "See you next week," he says, as he touches her arm. That deep line in his forehead is back again.

"I'll call you soon," Mama promises. She waves good-bye one more time.

I watch Patrick walk to his car. His head is bent down. He stares at his shoes as he crosses the parking lot. He looks like Joey does when he drops an easy throw to second. I lock my car door and hold onto the arm rest.

Mama pulls the car onto the highway and we head back home to Pisa.

F OUR

It's quitting time in Pisa, and a line of cars as steady as a work whistle sweep pass Danny and Joey as they round the corner to their house. Fathers, all over town, pull into driveways, open front doors, come home to their families. Danny swings his baseball bat, pretending to hit passing cars.

"Out of the park," he says. He swings again. "Line drive past third base." And again. "A swing and a miss. Strike three, you're out," he says, pushing his bat at the air.

He rests the bat on his shoulder and slows down as he and Joey pass the Browns' house across the street from their own. Through the side kitchen window Danny watches his father's boss, Andrew Brown, sitting at his table eating dinner with his wife and kids. He wants to look away, but he can't stop himself. It's like watching a TV show with the volume turned off. The characters' mouths move. They laugh, but the sound stays trapped inside, behind the windowpane.

"Man, they got it made, huh Joey?" Danny pulls his jacket up around his neck. "See what ya get if you're a big-shot foreman, Joey. You got to make something of yourself in this world. Or else you wind up with nothing."

Something aches inside him, and he can't shake it. He stares at the Browns' house with its new pale-blue aluminum siding. He admires how it sits, neat and clean, in the middle of a manicured lawn. Mr. Brown's black Chevy is parked in the driveway, all shiny. He polishes it every Sunday, in summer, and covers it with a tarp in the winter when it snows. For once, Danny's glad Dad's rusted-out Rambler is nowhere in sight.

He glances back across Chestnut Street at their house. The front porch slants, and the cement sidewalk is cracked. The old two-story exterior needs painting, and the yard is thick with weeds and tall grass. His father will make him mow it this weekend; he'd bet on it. After Danny got old enough to do the job, his father never touched the mower. "That's what sons are for," he'd said.

That son of a bitch. Nothing changes. The whole place could go up in smoke, and he wouldn't give a damn. He stopped caring a long time ago. He'd rather pray for help than help himself. He'd never fix up the house unless Jesus sent down a work order with a big check stapled to the corner. Danny laughs, imagining Jesus wearing a pair of dirty overalls, handing a wad of money and a hammer to his father.

"What's so funny?" Joey asks.

"Nothing," Danny says. He shakes his head and crosses the street. "Come on, let's go see if the old man is home yet."

He hopes his dad is still at work. Once in awhile, he pulls a second shift on Friday nights. He doesn't like to be around, to be reminded of his wife and daughters being gone. Danny likes it that way. He prefers the house quiet. No one around to mess up the silence. Joey's allowed. He belongs there, just like Danny. They know the silence, know it like they know their own breathing. Their dad fights the silence. He makes a profession of running away to his recliner for a nap, or to a church pew, as if kneeling could push the emptiness away, fill up the ache that rattles like a box of bones.

Danny pulls the door open, and he and Joey go inside, into the darkness. He flips on a light, and Zoomer stretches to greet them. Danny brushes the top of the dog's head and hollers, "Dad? You home?"

The living room is quiet. His skin feels cold in the stillness. The brown, worn couch rests near his father's green recliner. Across the room the TV set sits on a short wooden table. A statue of the Sacred Heart of Jesus stands on top of the TV, resting on a crocheted doily, its pierced hands held out in a bloody welcome. On the wall behind its head, a spray of last year's Easter palm is wedged into a framed picture of the Little Infant Jesus of Prague. A frayed, braided rug lies on the scuffed wooden floor. To the right of the TV, beige cloth curtains are pulled open, revealing a small crack in the bottom left corner of the large picture window. Danny's eyes take it all in, catalogue each object, each piece of furniture, so he can be sure it's all there, the same as before, the same as always. The certainty of it calms him.

"Looks like we beat him home," Joey says, as he heads toward the kitchen.

"I thought he might be working late," Danny comments.

He follows Joey into the kitchen and flips on another light. He pulls himself onto the yellow linoleum counter-top. Everything in the kitchen is yellow. Not bright, sunshiny yellow, but faded, dingy yellow. His mother's Chanel No. 5 lingers in the air. The paint on the wall behind the stove is cracked and peeling from years of splattered olive oil and steam from stove-top pots and pans. He imagines her standing at the old GE stove, stir-ring a pot of spaghetti, laughing the way she used to when he was little. The stove, the refrigerator, the washer and dryer are hand-me-downs given to them by his Uncle Tony who long ago bought new ones for his wife Stella. He thinks of Andrew Brown's house—of the avocado stove, the matching refrigerator, the smooth white walls, the shiny surface of the new linoleum flooring. In his mother's kitchen, the window over the sink is the only clear, bright spot. Frilly white-and-yellow checkered curtains frame its panes, out of place in the otherwise gloomy room. He closes his eyes for just a second, to gather in the silence.

When he opens them, Joey's eyes meet his. "What you staring at?" Danny hollers.

"Nothing," Joey says. "You just looked funny for a second. You know, like you were gonna cry or something."

"Forget it, twerp," Danny says. He jumps off the counter and plants his feet on the worn linoleum floor. "I'm tired is all. And hungry. See what's in the fridge." Danny checks the wall clock. "It's quarter to six already, Joey. We gotta hurry up. The Yanks are on at seven."

"All that's in here is baloney and peanut butter. And some leftover rigatoni."

Danny sneers at the choices; then he reaches in the pocket of his jeans. "I got a few bucks. Let's go grab a pizza at Vinnie's and bring it home for the game."

"Pepperoni and black olive," Joey says, licking his lips and slapping his hands together. "We better feed Zoomer first."

"Well, hurry up," Danny says. He grabs the bag of dog food from the broom closet. Joey hands him Zoomer's dish. The dog whines as Danny fills his bowl. "Here you go, boy," he says, rubbing the dog's nose. Zoomer starts to eat, then pauses. His ears stand straight, catching the sound of a turning door knob and he scoots into the living room.

"He thinks it's Peanut," Joey says.

"Dumb dog. What the hell does he see in that little fart, anyway?" Danny says.

Dad's voice rises from the front door, "Down, boy. Go on, get out of here. Go."

Danny pockets his money and frowns. "Guess it's fish sticks after all, Joey."

"Shit. I thought you said he was working late."

"He must have gone to church instead," Danny says, defensively.

Every day, twice a day, Paulie Giovanni goes to church to pray the rosary. When he was younger, Danny used to tag along to sit in the pew and watch. He loved how Dad's calloused fingers cradled the black rosary beads. When he bent his head to pray, "Hail, Mary, full of grace," Dad's voice was soft in the quiet of the church. It was so different from the angry, rattling voice that fought with his mother. "The Lord is with thee," Dad prayed along each bead, and Danny felt safe and happy, as if God was right beside him at all times, protecting him.

When his father prayed, the holy hope of his heart seeped through his skin, until his face shimmered like St. Francis of Assisi's. Is he as selfless and forgiving as that saint? Or is he merely a pathetic martyr, enduring? What good is all that piety if he can't stop his wife from seeing Patrick? It makes Danny angry every time he thinks about it.

"You guys home?" Dad calls from the living room.

Danny tips his head and motions Joey to follow him into the living room.

"Hi, Dad," Danny says. He flips on the TV and flops onto the sofa. Joey drops down on the rug next to Zoomer.

"You guys got a broken arm or something?" Dad complains, scratching the back of his neck as he settles into his green recliner. He sifts through a stack of mail. "Why didn't you put the fish sticks in the oven?"

"We just got home a few minutes ago," Joey answers. "We were at the ball field. We thought maybe you were working late."

"Yeah," Danny adds. "We were just going to grab a pizza."

"We ain't got no money for pizza," Dad snaps.

It's a warning. Danny studies his father's tired face, the way his hands grip the edges of the envelopes before he tosses bills onto the small table near his chair.

"Besides, we don't eat meat on Fridays. Joey, go turn the oven on. And let that dog out."

Joey does as he's told. Just once, Danny wishes Joey would mouth off, tell their old man to piss off. Joey's too scared. Danny pushes his luck. He likes the rush of getting angry. He likes how it burns his veins. He gets into trouble more times than he can remember, but it's worth it to him. He feels alive.

On the TV, Walter Cronkite reports about some man in Chicago who murdered his wife after he found her in bed with her boyfriend. Danny turns up the volume.

"Can't even turn on the TV anymore without seeing that nonsense," Dad gripes. "Lower that damn TV. For cripes sake. Those people need to put God into their lives."

What's God gonna do about it? Danny says to himself. He sure as hell ain't helping you much. Out loud he says to his father, "Can't we have hot dogs or something besides fish sticks? I'm sick of that crap."

"Watch your mouth, young man. It's Friday."

"Yeah, I know it's Friday. It's kinda hard to forget that

one." Danny snaps. "Mom forgot to iron my shirt for work tomorrow."

"So iron it yourself. Sixteen is sure old enough."

"You never iron yours, and you ain't seen sixteen in a million years."

"Don't get smart with me, young man!" Dad yells. He raises his hand. "What's the matter with you?" He taps the back of his palm against the side of Danny's head. Danny ducks deeper into the couch. He braces himself against his father's stare. "I don't like your attitude," Dad says sharply. "You think it's a picnic, fixing you guys dinner every Friday night? Well it ain't. I can think of a lot of things I'd rather be doing."

Yeah, Danny thinks, like burying your head in a god-damn prayer book.

"Go on, get out of here," Dad orders. "Go wash up for dinner."

Danny narrows his eyes. He thinks about taking a swing at him, but his father's already heading away, toward the kitchen. "Goddamn son of a bitch, coward," Danny mumbles all the way up the stairs and into the bathroom. He squeezes a bar of Ivory soap, turns on the water and lathers up his hands. He thinks of the man on the TV news who killed his wife. At least he had the guts to do something. Joey runs up the steps and joins him in the bathroom.

"What's going on? Dad's slamming things around in the kitchen."

"Nothing," Danny says.

"You look really pissed off, too," Joey says.

"Watch your mouth, twerp," Danny snaps.

"What ya being such a creep about?" Joey asks, defensively. "Ever since we got home you've been acting weird."

Danny can't answer. He doesn't have words for how

his insides scream. He could tear the wall down. He just keeps rubbing soap suds all over his hands and between his fingers. "You think he could let up a little, once in a while," Danny finally says.

"You mean Dad? He's just sore about Mom and all."

"Yeah, and who isn't?" Danny tosses the soap to Joey. "Here, better get going before he calls us for supper."

He rinses the lather off his clean hands, then grabs a towel and rubs hard, wiping his fingers red. He pops the bathroom window open to let in some air. He sits on the edge of the bathtub and examines the creases in his palms. Except for a callus on the middle finger of his right hand, his hands are soft, almost tender. Priest hands, he thinks, remembering the smoothness of Patrick's fingers the first time he met him at dinner three years ago. Danny was thirteen then.

"So nice to meet you, Mrs. Giovanni," Patrick had said when Danny's father first introduced him to Marie and the kids. Dad had invited the new assistant pastor to dinner to welcome him to the parish. Father Patrick wore black tweed dress pants and a black dress shirt with his small white priest's collar. His blue eyes peered out from his serious face framed by neatly trimmed black hair cropped short around the ears and neck. His words flowed effortlessly from his mouth. Patrick was splendid, a man unlike any other man Danny had ever met. His dad, his uncles, the men in the neighborhood were nobodies in their khaki work shirts and jeans. Patrick was classy like Mr. Johnston, Danny's boss at the drug store. He lived across the canal in a big house on the rich side of town.

That first night at dinner, Danny gave up his usual place, next to his father, for the visitor. Danny sat on a chair across the table from the priest, watching him the whole time. How he picked up his fork. How he fingered his water glass. Danny studied his sophistication. All through dinner, he memorized the ways Patrick was different.

His dad plunged his fork into his plate and stuffed the pasta into his mouth. He slurped each swallow down with a gulp of water and started over again. Patrick ate like rich guys in the movies. Slow and deliberate. He presented his fork to his mouth as if it held precious gems. And he extended the pinkie finger of his right hand out and upward. He chewed his pasta politely, then dabbed first one corner of his mouth, then the other. He brought his water glass to his lips for a small sip. He balanced a slice of Italian bread on the rim of his plate and placed a pat of butter on the side of the dish. Dad tossed his bread on the Formica table top next to his plate and grabbed for butter from the dish in the middle of the table. The others were just as bad—Mom, Joey, the girls. Joey licked his fork and grabbed for more zitis from the serving plate. It was something Danny had done a thousand times himself without hesitating. But that night he kicked his brother under the table.

"Cut it out," Joey yelled, his mouth full of macaroni.

Danny's armpits itched. He snuck a quick glance Father Patrick's way to see if the fancy visitor had noticed. The priest was busy smiling at Danny's mother, complimenting her on the delicious dinner.

After supper, Peanut helped clear the table. She hung around for a bit before she left to take care of Rosa in the other room. Joey went over to Stevie Androzzi's house and Danny hung around the kitchen to check out the stranger a little while longer. He leaned against the counter, away from the others, trying to stay out of the way, unnoticed. While Mom made coffee, he listened to Dad and Patrick talk.

"What do you think about saying the Mass in English, Father?" Dad asked.

He grabbed a toothpick from the small glass holder in the middle of the table, and started sucking on it. Danny's hand jerked forward to yank the toothpick out of Dad's mouth, but he curled his fingers into his palm and pulled it back to his side. He wished, just once, his dad would show a little class.

"The Church has been excluding the common people long enough, don't you think, Mr. Giovanni?" Patrick asked. "And besides, it doesn't really matter, now does it? It's still the same old Mass."

"No it's not, Father," Dad disagreed. He flicked the toothpick between his front teeth. "Ya know, if they do away with Latin, what's next? Before you know it, they'll strip the powers from priests and bishops."

"It's time you stopped seeing the clergy as gods, Mr. Giovanni," Patrick said. He sat straight and kingly in the kitchen chair. "We're merely men, just like you."

Danny was so used to his father's stodgy views that he hadn't stopped to consider an alternative. Even as an altar boy, he fought to stay awake through the Latin gibberish. Maybe it could be different. Maybe priests were just ordinary guys, like him and Dad. But Father Patrick sure wasn't like them. Danny could tell right off.

"I think Father's right," Mom said, joining the conversation. She set three mugs of coffee on the table. "That John the Twenty-third is a breath of fresh air."

"He's a good man," Dad conceded. "But ya know, I'm afraid he may go too far. We still got to remember we're Catholics, not Protestants."

Mom laughed. "See what I've got to put up with, Father?"

Danny fidgeted. He agreed, but he didn't want her to talk about Dad that way in front of the visitor. Father

Patrick might get the wrong impression. Dad could stand some improvement, but he wasn't all bad. Just a little fanatic about Church stuff and a little hotheaded when it came to the way Mom spent his hard-earned money.

The priest smiled. "A staunch Catholic is a rare breed these days."

"That's right," Dad boasted. "Not many people respect the Church anymore."

"Paulie loves the Church," Mom said, "It means more to him than anything else in the whole world. It's all he ever talks about. Isn't that right, Paulie?"

Dad turned a mean eye towards her, then stared out the window. The room felt too small to hold them all. Danny wished the windows were open. He needed a slap of night air. His stomach knotted, and he blurted out, "My dad knows a lot about baseball, Father. He's a real Yankees fan, and so am I. I bet you don't know nothing about that."

Patrick turned toward Danny with a curious smile. Dad cocked his head, as if listening to play-by-play commentary on the radio. Mom exhaled a cloud of smoke into the air. "Why, Danny," she said, "I thought you'd gone off with your brother."

Their eyes fixed him in place. He stood nailed against the kitchen cabinets. The cool chrome handles carved a small space into his back. His embarrassment kept him pinned for a few minutes. The uneasiness between his parents settled into his belly. Remembering his manners, he excused himself and rushed out of the room. The last thing he saw was Mom's fingers resting on the table top inches away from Father Patrick's smooth hand.

***

"Danny, Joey, come and eat," Dad bellows from the bottom of the stairs.

Danny thwacks Joey playfully with the towel, and Joey swings back at him with his arm. "Let's go, ole buddy," Danny says.

"I'm so hungry," Joey says, "I'll even eat fish sticks."

The boys race downstairs and into the kitchen. They take their places at the table and eat without talking, spearing the tiny breaded pieces of fish with their forks. Danny glances at the empty seats where Peanut, Rosa, Winnie and his mother usually sit. He stares out the window, then at the pale-yellow paint chipping off the wall behind the stove. He kicks the chrome legs of his chair.

His father snaps, "For cryin' out loud, knock that off."

Danny looks across at Joey, trying to keep his cool. Joey smiles a fake smile back. His eyes tell Danny to cut it out. Danny smirks right back at him.

"What happened to the sugar bowl?" Dad asks.

Danny eyes Joey. His brother's mouth narrows and his cheek twitches. Danny's shoulders tighten.

"Zoomer knocked it off the table, Dad. We cleaned it up before you got home," Danny lies.

"What the hell was the dog doing on the kitchen table? Were you guys horsing around?"

"No, Dad. Honest," Joey picks up Danny's fib and takes off with it. "Zoomer just got excited because he thought we were Peanut coming home early or something. You know how crazy that dog is for her."

Dad shovels fish sticks into his mouth and nods. He buys Joey's explanation. Danny relaxes his shoulders and reaches for more tater tots and fish sticks. "What's for dessert?" he asks, thinking about his sisters sipping malts at Smiley's with Patrick.

"What do you think I am, a damn pastry chef?" Dad snarls.

"I didn't mean anything by it," Danny says, defensively.

"Hey Danny," Joey says, "Maybe Peanut will bring us home a milk shake."

Danny pictures his sisters and mother at that damn coffee shop in Cayuga, and he gets hot and tingly. "I don't give a good goddamn," he sneers.

Dad slaps the table. Danny swallows hard. He's crossed the line, pushed too far. Dad pushes himself back from the table, stands up and unhooks his belt buckle. Danny opens his mouth to scream at Dad, tell him to back off, but his throat tightens. His words stick to the back of his teeth. He watches Dad slide the brown leather belt from his pant loops. He holds the belt like a snake in his large calloused hands. He cracks it on the table. Bits of fish sticks fly into the air. "Don't you ever take the Lord's name in vain in my house, Daniel," he orders.

Danny tries to stand up. He wants to leave the room, but his knees buckle. He falls back into his chair. His throat loosens, and the words spill out. "What the fuck do you care, anyway? Since when are you the man of this house? You can't even make her stop seeing Patrick."

Danny throws his fork across the room. Dad's fingers twitch against the belt buckle. He slaps the table again. Joey jumps back. Danny smells the fear on his brother's skin. Joey crams the bottom of his lip into his shaking mouth. Danny wishes with all his heart that Mom was here right now. Joey's still young, still needs her around to make things alright. If she were home now, instead of with that bastard Patrick, Dad wouldn't be so riled up. Danny wishes even harder that Mom had never met that goddamn priest.

Dad hovers over the table. He stands without moving for a few moments, not saying a word. The silence turns against Danny; it is not a comfort now. He counts the seconds, holding his breath, praying Dad won't turn the strap against him. Finally Dad slips the belt between his pant loops and rebuckles. Danny barely breathes. He forces his hands still and sits straight back in his chair, eyes wide, watching, waiting. Did Dad ever want to take a gun and kill them both, like that man on the evening news? The thought races through his mind as he studies the deep lines in his father's face.

"So you want your mother back?" Dad finally says, nodding as if he understands. His voice is flat, sad, quiet now.

Joey nods his head yes, and Danny pleads, "Why can't you stop her, Dad?"

"Danny, Joey," he starts to say, "I wish…" but he turns his eyes away and his words evaporate. "It's out of my hands now," he whispers. He bows his head and leaves the room.

Danny stares at his back. The face of St. Francis haunts his mind. The bloody stigmata-hands hover before his eyes. "You son-of-a-bitch coward," he yells as his father walks across the braided living room rug, past the TV set and the statue of the Sacred Heart of Jesus. When Dad reaches the front door, Danny waves his fists at the quiet air. "Go on, go to church. See if Jesus can make it all better," he shouts. Dad pauses a second. He opens the front door and walks outside.

"You really did it this time, Danny!" Joey yells. "Now he's gone, too!"

"Shut the fuck up, you little asshole! What do you know about it?" Danny screams. He flies out of the kitchen, runs upstairs. He slams his bedroom door and rushes from corner to corner tearing things from the walls—a crucifix, a picture of Saint Francis, and a shriveled Easter palm. He tosses the collection onto the floor and stomps on the pile over and over again, until the palm shards pierce St. Francis' ripped paper eyes and the plaster arm of the crucified Jesus dangles on a thin wire, severed from its body.

He opens the bedroom window. The cool air trickles over his sweaty face. "Goddamn fucking God can go to hell," he yells to the streetlights, the rooftops, the neighbors' houses. He leans out the window, stares down the block at the steeple of St. Joan of Arc Church. God Almighty. God the Merciful. God the Avenger. Where the hell are you? He spits at the air and slams the window. The glass rattles in the pane. The Venetian blind cord sways like a rosary.

FIVE

Mama hasn't said a word since we drove away from Smiley's. I lay my head against the window. My stomach's spinning, and Mama and Patrick's voices are chasing around my mind. I think about how close we came to going to Happy Town tonight, and I get hot inside. I want to cry, but I know I better not. Mama's pretty upset. She lights one cigarette after another until the car is dusty with smoke, but I'm too afraid to open up the window. She just might jump at me. There's no telling sometimes what's gonna get her riled up, but the way Patrick walked back to his car might do it.

Mama stares at the road and hardly blinks. She lets the ashes on the end of her cigarette pile up gray and long, then she flicks them into the car ashtray without even looking. Sometimes she misses and the ashes land on the floor. She doesn't say a word, but I can tell her mind is working hard. Her lips twitch like she's getting ready to talk, but she doesn't. Maybe she really wanted to go, and I made her change her mind with all that stupid talk about me having to go to the dentist and Joey getting his baseball award. The quiet is everywhere, and it scares me.

Rosa and Winnie are asleep in the back seat. As soon as I knew we were free and clear, and Mama wasn't gonna change her mind and make us leave with Patrick, I jumped into the front seat. I wanted to be right next to Mama, in case she needs me. I watch and wait and listen to the car wheels hum against the highway, and I pray a special thank-you to the Blessed Virgin for pulling us through this time. One of these days my charm with the Holy Mother is going to wear off, but until it does, I'm glad to be going back to Pisa tonight. Amen.

Daddy says if you ask the Blessed Mother for anything, and if you deserve to have it, she'll make sure you get it. She just goes and asks her son, Jesus, and he says OK. It's a rule they have, I guess. If she asks him, he's got to say yes, because she wouldn't ask if it wasn't important.

Mama says she's sick of rules. She's sick of Daddy, too, and how high and mighty he gets about church stuff. She says she's tired of the bickering. She's tired of doing all the work around the house, cooking and cleaning and picking up. We make her so cranky she could just cry sometimes. Mama says her life isn't what she wanted it to be. I think she's still sad about the lost baby and about Patrick having to move so far away. That's why she wants to go to Happy Town. She says Patrick makes her feel like an angel flying into the stars. Someday we'll go. Not tonight. Someday. When Mama's ready, she won't change her mind. Whenever that day is, I want to be ready, too. Because I won't be able to come back for Zoomer or Amelia or anybody. I don't like that part, but Mama said so. "You'll make new friends," she told me. "Wait and see."

My shoulders pinch and I have to sneeze, the smoke's so thick in here. I crack the window, just a little bit, to let some fresh air in. Mama's humming softly now. She must be feeling better. She doesn't yell at me for opening the window, so I roll it down a bit more and take a deep breath. I hold it tightly and wonder how long I can go without breathing. Will I turn blue? Will I explode? Will Mama have to stop the car and call an ambulance? I let the air go out of my lungs and breathe the regular way now. My stomach growls.

"I'm hungry," I say to the quiet. I guess Mama must be listening because she answers.

"You should have eaten when you had the chance, Peanut."

I know, I want to say, but I was too worried that the cat family and all the other customers were listening to you and Patrick fight. I don't ever want to go back to Smiley's Coffee Shop. The cat family daughters can read my thoughts. They knew I was afraid. With their magical cat glasses, they could see underneath my thick hair into the center of my brain. They know. But they're just as scared as me. I can tell by the way their small eyes hardly open when they look at me. I think they want to be invisible too, but they're afraid of disappearing forever.

"Do you have any crackers in your purse, Mama?"

"I don't know. Check."

Mama sounds less cranky than before. I open her fancy handbag and rummage through it for some saltines. I find a tube of lipstick, Kleenex, house keys, a pack of cigarettes, a couple of quarters, a comb, but no crackers. I close the clasp.

"There's nothing in there," I whine.

Mama interrupts. "Don't start in on me, Peanut. I can't help it if you didn't finish your dinner. You'll have to wait 'til we get home now."

"Yes, Mama."

I don't want to get into trouble, so I decide to pipe down. I figure we gotta almost be home anyway. Maybe Mama will let me have a peanut-butter-and-jelly sandwich before I go to bed, if I make it myself so she doesn't have to bother. I think about how tired she looks, and I wish I knew how to drive so she could rest.

"Someday, when I'm older, Mama, I'll drive for you."

"You're such a sweet girl, Peanut," Mama says. "Even though sometimes you make me mad. Most of the time I don't know what I'd do without you."

Even in the dark I can tell she's smiling. Since Patrick, I'm the only one she can talk to. The girlfriends she used to have coffee with all stopped returning her phone calls. When they'd run into her at the grocery store or downtown, they'd make some excuse about being so busy with this and that or say their kids never gave them the phone message. After a while Mama gave up on those ladies. She didn't need them anymore. She had me. She knew I would love her, no matter what.

"Mama, are you and Daddy gonna get a divorce?"

"No, Peanut," Mama says in a hurry.

"But Patrick wants you to."

"Peanut," Mama snaps.

She puffs on her cigarette a long time, then breathes a cloud of smoke at the windshield.

"What are you worrying about stuff like that for?" she asks.

"I don't know," I say. I'm quiet a minute, then I ask, "When parents get a divorce, are their kids still their kids? Or do they get divorced, too?"

"I swear I don't know how you get some of your crazy ideas, Peanut. Only moms and dads get the divorce. Their kids stay their kids forever."

Mama's voice is shaky, so I reach over and touch her arm.

"It'll be OK, Mama. You don't have to get a divorce if you don't want."

I'm sitting there in the dark car, holding Mama's hand, thinking about how I don't want her to get a divorce, even if getting one means she won't divorce us kids. I figure if she stays married to Daddy, she and Patrick can't have a baby together. And if they can't have a baby, then the lost baby will have to stay away, maybe forever, or at least until I'm big enough to move away from home. But by then I guess maybe I won't care any more if the lost baby comes back. Then I get an idea.

"Maybe instead of getting a divorce," I say, "you should run away to New York City and be a Broadway star, and I could go with you and be your assistant."

That makes her laugh a little, but then she starts to cry, and I get worried. I grab a Kleenex from her pocketbook and hand it to her.

"Whatever made you think a thing like that?" She wipes her eyes with a Kleenex. "You're so silly sometimes, Peanut."

"No, I'm not. You always said in high school you wanted to be an actress. And remember that play you were in for the Mothers' Club? Remember how much you liked it? Maybe you should do it now. I could help you take care of Rosa and Winnie. And Danny and Joey could come to your plays, too. And if you didn't want to live with Daddy, then we could all just go visit him on Sundays and go to church, then eat supper, then go back to Broadway."

It's just make-believe, I know, but I like the idea, so I'm glad I said it. I imagine her on the stage in a shiny long dress, a skinny, younger version of Ethel Merman. Maybe she'll even get to appear on "The Ed Sullivan Show." It's one of my best ideas ever, and I wish I could tell Amelia about it.

"Peanut, you just don't understand. Grownups can't just all of a sudden one day pick up and move to the city to be an actress. It takes years of training and a lot of talent. And besides, that was just a foolish notion I had when I was a teenager. I don't want that any more."

I don't believe her. After that night when Patrick first came to dinner at our house, he decided that the Mothers' Club would put on a play to raise money for the parish. He picked *My Fair Lady*. He'd seen the real show on Broadway in New York City, seen Julie Andrews and Rex Harrison in person, before the movie version ever came out. He wanted to direct that play for the Mothers' Club, and he chose Mama to play Eliza Doolittle.

Mama says she won the part fair and square. That's not what Mrs. Tanturri and Mrs. Scalamassi said. They were mad and jealous. But they were always jealous of Mama, even before Patrick fell in love with her. And they were two of the first to stop returning her phone calls later on. "I sing better than her," Mrs. Tanturri complained. "She can't act her way out of a paper bag," Mrs. Scalamassi insisted. But Patrick gave the part to Mama. She told me all about it after she came home that night. We danced around the kitchen table and sang "The Rain in Spain" to celebrate.

Patrick was right. Mama really could sing and act. She was the best. Just like Audrey Hepburn in the movie version. She took me to rehearsals a few times. I sat in the front row watching everything. Singing along with the songs in my head. I knew every word. That's the first time I remember noticing her and Patrick. It was a little thing. He'd direct her in a scene, touch her shoulder, move her this way and that. And she never took her eyes off his. On opening night, he gave her a dozen red roses. She kissed him on the cheek and hugged him. It lasted only a second, but when they let go of each other there was a lonesome look in Mama's eyes, and her mouth tried to smile, but I could tell she wanted to cry.

Playing Eliza Doolittle made Mama happy. For those

few short weeks of rehearsals and all through the performances, Mama was a different person. The moody days stopped. She seemed taller and smarter and her long complaining face went away. After the play ended, she talked about trying out for other roles at community theaters in towns near Pisa. But she never did. Instead she spent more time helping Patrick with Mothers' Club stuff. Every once in a while, even now, when she reads about a local play in the newspaper a certain look comes across her face, and I can tell she wishes she were in it.

That's why my idea about moving to New York City is just as good as Patrick's idea of going to Happy Town. I don't understand why she thinks it's so dumb. If being an actress would make her happy, why doesn't she just do it? Why does she waste her time driving to and from Cayuga, Friday after Friday, dragging me and the girls along with her?

I think about this a lot, but I still can't figure it out. Maybe I never will. Even though Daddy hates it, we still visit Patrick. When he first found out, he shouted, "Stop it! Stop it right now!" Later, when Mama refused to stay, he yelled, "You have no right to take my daughters!" But Mama doesn't listen to him. She tells me all the time, "I love Patrick so much. I don't know what I'd do without him." She says she doesn't love Daddy, and she won't stop seeing Patrick. "I miss him so much, Peanut. I'm so glad to have you to talk to about these things. I'd go crazy without you."

I used to wonder why Mama stopped hugging and kissing Daddy. But now I don't any more. It's just the way things are. Some things about Daddy are pretty weird, I guess. He snores on the couch all night. He scratches his butt when he walks upstairs to clean up after work. And he wears his scapular day and night, taking it off only when he takes a bath. The small cloth pictures are all yellow and smell sweaty. But there are good things about him, too. He has a space between his two front teeth that whistles when he sings in church. He's got a nice laugh, and he's handsome. I think he could have been a movie star. He's tall and romantic-looking. I like to look at the pictures of him in his army uniform. That's how he looked when he first met Mama.

I know that story by heart. Mama used to tell me when I was little. She and Daddy met at a Knights of Columbus dance in 1945. It was a celebration for the soldiers coming home. Mama says Daddy asked her to dance and she said yes, because her girlfriends made her. She didn't really think he was good-looking. They twirled around the dance floor, under the sparkling ball. It sounds so romantic to me. I wonder, didn't she fall in love, then, even if just for a second?

Mama says they got married six months later, even though she never loved Daddy. She says she did it to forget her high-school sweetheart who'd gone away to college and found another girl. I think of Mama, with her chocolate brown hair, her fiery eyes, and I wonder how she could have settled for someone she didn't love. Did Daddy know? Why didn't he wait and find someone who loved only him? It hurts my heart to think about it all.

Mama's gonna leave Daddy and live with Patrick some day. There's nothing I can do about it except wait. I keep thinking maybe something will happen. Maybe if Mama becomes an actress, she'll be happy and won't need Patrick anymore. Or maybe Patrick will find somebody else to love. Maybe he'll get real sick, so he can't drive. Or maybe he'll die, and we won't have to go.

"Mama, did you want to go Happy Town tonight?" I ask.

She takes in a big breath, and her hands grip the steering wheel. My shoulders get stiff, and my eyes burn.

I wish I'd kept my mouth shut. Mama breathes out real slow.

"I don't know, Peanut."

She's quiet for a few minutes before she starts up again. This time her voice is soft and low and sad. "Someday I want us all to be together. But I wasn't ready. Not tonight."

Me too, I say to myself. Now I take a deep breath and let it out slowly. Then I say to her, "But someday, Mama, we really are going to Happy Town, aren't we?"

"Yes, honey."

"When?"

"I don't know."

"Do we have to go?"

She taps the steering wheel, three times, with her finger, then glances over at me. Her mouth is twisted at the corners. "Peanut, we've been over this a thousand times. Patrick and I love each other very much. We miss each other when we're away for too long. We want to be together, to be a family, all of us. You and the girls and your brothers, too. He loves all of you. He'll be a good father and a good husband."

I already got a father. I don't say this out loud. Mama won't understand. She'll think I'm being "difficult," and then she might decide to leave me behind. That makes me sick. Sometimes I think Patrick might be a good father. I imagine sitting on the couch next to him watching TV or telling him about my day at school, but my mind plays tricks on me. Daddy's face sometimes appears on Patrick's body, or Daddy's voice comes out of Patrick's mouth. The picture gets all jumbled. Besides, Patrick doesn't really want to be my father. He only wants to live with Mama.

"When we go to Happy Town, can I bring Zoomer?"

"Peanut," Mama snaps. "Give it a rest. We're almost home."

"But can I?" I push harder this time. I have to know. I can't go without Zoomer. Except for Amelia, Zoomer's my best friend. Who would I have to talk to? Who else but Zoomer can I tell the absolute truth to?

"Peanut, I don't want to discuss the dog now. I'm tired. It's been a long, hard day. Let me think about it. I don't want to make any promises I can't keep. Now hush up. We'll be home in five minutes."

Promises are important. If you make one, you better keep it. If you break a promise, you go straight to hell. My fifth-grade teacher, Sister Saint Joseph, says so all the time. "Jesus never lied, and we must all try, as hard as we can, to be like Jesus." I never break my promises, not even to Danny and Joey. It's my own personal vow. It's what separates a true heart from a rotten one.

"Mama, I keep my promises," I say, to reassure her.

"What are you talking about, Peanut?"

She's agitated now. I think about how I promised her I'd never tell anyone about our Friday night visits. We're buddies, in good times and bad, and Mama can count on me. I keep all our secrets tucked away.

"I won't tell anyone about Patrick wanting to leave tonight. I promise."

"I know you won't, honey." Mama's voice is softer. "I know I can count on you."

She reaches over and touches the top of my head. Her hand feels warm, and I smile. I sit there taking in the feeling for a few minutes before I realize she's steering the car into our driveway.

"We're home. Wake the girls, and let's go inside. Be real quiet, so we don't disturb anyone."

"OK."

I look at our rickety house with the slanted front

porch. It's dark and quiet. In a few seconds we'll go inside, turn the lights on and I'll hug Zoomer. After that, I'll help Mama get Rosa and Winnie upstairs to bed. Then I'll climb in too, and make room for Zoomer, right beside me.

I get out of the car, yawn and stretch. I suddenly feel very tired. I open the back door and wake the girls. "Let's go," I say. "We're home."

Six

On Saturday morning, I like to turn on "Tom and Jerry" cartoons and listen from the kitchen while we eat breakfast. That way I don't have to pay too much attention to Danny complaining about whatever it is he's gonna complain about. He's always bellyaching about something. I turn the TV up loud so we can hear it from the living room, but not too loud so it doesn't wake up Daddy or Mama. Daddy's still asleep on the good sofa in the front room. He sleeps in there on Fridays instead of in the living room, so we don't wake him up when we come home from visiting Patrick. Mama's asleep, too, in her bedroom off the kitchen.

I feel kind of weird today, like I've just woke up from some crazy dream that's got me wondering was it real or did I imagine it? Last night, I mean, and how Patrick wanted to go to Happy Town. Today, everything in the kitchen seems to stand up and shout at me. The toaster with the little white-and-yellow checkered cloth cover that Mama got at Woolworth's. The butter dish that Aunt Stella gave Mama for her birthday. It's made out of heavy glass and the butter sticks to its sides all thick and hard like dried mud. The cereal bowls with tiny apples painted on the inside. They're Mama's favorites. They match the apple-shaped sugar bowl that's always on the tabletop.

But today I notice it's gone. I check all the cupboards, thinking Mama put it away in a different place for some reason, but I can't find it anywhere.

"Anybody seen the sugar bowl?"

"No," Danny snaps. He's reading the newspaper and doesn't even bother to look up at me. "Just get some out of the canister."

I take the cereal out of the cupboard and poke around, still looking for the sugar bowl, but I don't find it.

"Hurry up, Peanut," Rosa complains. "I'm hungry."

Joey looks at me kind of funny. He mixes raspberry jam into his Cream of Wheat, making it all pink, then adds some milk. He slurps the runny goop, sucking it between the gap in his two front teeth. Sometimes Danny and I tease him and make him eat it at the counter or in the living room. That's just about the only thing Danny and I agree on; we both hate Joey's weird breakfast food. It makes us sick to eat at the same table with him.

"I want Sugar Pops," Rosa says.

"Coco Puffs," Winnie interrupts.

"We only got Rice Chex," I say.

"Yuck," Rosa says.

I put my hands on my hips, like Mama does when she's impatient, then I pour some cereal into their bowls and pull out a loaf of Italian bread for some toast.

"I want some sugar," Rosa says.

"I can't find the bowl," I say. "Eat it without, just for once."

"Peanut," Rosa starts to whine.

"For Christ's sake!" Danny yells. "Would you just put the goddamn canister on the table and forget about the fucking sugar bowl."

Now I'm really wondering what happened to it. "Did you guys break it or something?" I ask.

"Shut up!" Joey yells. Pink Cream of Wheat slips out of the corner of his mouth.

"You pig," I say. "Wait 'til Mama finds out."

"She ain't gonna find out," Danny says.

He stares at me, and I look away. I think about what he means, and I think maybe, just maybe, I'll tell Mama about her sugar bowl anyway. I don't want her to think I'm the one who broke it. Danny thinks he's so cool being such a bossy butt. I look back at him, and he's sitting himself down in Daddy's chair, at the head of the table.

"That's Daddy's chair," I say, real snotty.

"So?" Danny says. He puffs out his chest.

"So," I say right back. "You're not supposed to sit there."

"Who died and made you boss?" Danny sasses.

"Daddy's not gonna like it," I warn.

I can't believe he's being such a creep already. It's not even eight o'clock yet. He sits there, trying to act so grown-up, but he doesn't fool me—reading the sports section and sipping his coffee like he's the boss. He even started drinking his coffee without milk last year when he turned sixteen. I drink coffee too, but mine's half milk with two teaspoons of sugar—the way Grandma made it for us when we were small. I pour myself a cup and reach my spoon into the sugar canister, then I wave the spoon in the air—pretending it's a magician's wand. I want to poof Danny, make him disappear.

Next to Patrick, Danny gets me maddest of all. He's always getting himself into trouble. Sometimes I think he does it on purpose. He never stops at the first warning. He's no good at reading their voices. I can tell by the tiniest changes when it's time to back off. You can only go so far before something that starts out small blows up in your face. Not Danny. He likes to fight. It makes his cheeks red and his eyes shine. He's the oldest, and he's supposed to set a good example, but he doesn't, and it makes me mad. I try really hard to behave and I can't see any reason why he shouldn't try, too.

Joey's not so bad. He lets me read his comic books, and sometimes he lets me play ball with him. And Rosa and Winnie are OK. They're little and stay out of my way most of the time. Rosa loves her stuffed puppy, Binkie. She makes room for it on the chair beside her while she eats. And Winnie's always got her yellow blanket nearby. She likes to rub it between her fingers when she gets upset. It's ratty and old and nearly as thin as a Kleenex by now, but she won't let Mama throw it away.

Mama says being an older sister is important. You got to protect the little ones, like a guardian angel, save them from things that scare them or from people being mean to them. I try, but sometimes I'm mean to them, too. When my bad soul takes over, and my feelings boil up inside and set my temper on fire. Mama calls me a spark plug when I get mad. She says my forehead gets as red as my hair, and I explode.

I wish Mama was awake right now. She'd order Danny out of Daddy's chair. But I don't dare disturb her. She had a huge headache last night, and she told me she wanted to sleep in this morning. I'll tell on him later, if he doesn't stop being so full of himself.

"Can I have some juice, Peanut?" Rosa asks.

"Toast, toast," Winnie says.

I get up and take care of them. It's my job when Mama's asleep.

"The Yankees won another one last night," Danny announces.

"All right," Joey says. "I fell asleep in the middle of the eighth when they were down two to one."

"Yeah," Danny says. "I conked out in the bottom of

the ninth with two outs and two men on. When I woke up, "The Tonight Show" was on."

"Who cares about the stupid Yankees?" I say, as I put slices of Italian bread into the toaster for Winnie.

"Shows how much you know," Danny says.

I stick my tongue out at him. "I know more than you think I do."

"If you know so much, how come you still go with her every Friday?" Danny says. He cocks his head toward Mama's bedroom door. "Don't you know it's killing Dad?"

"You're just jealous you can't come," I say. I try to make my voice stop shaking, but I can't. I hate it when he starts in on me like this, as if I could make Mama stop. I feel achy, like I've got the flu or something. The red comes boiling to my face, just like Mama says, and I want to tell my brothers they should be glad we even came home at all last night. We could be long gone by now, if it wasn't for me.

"Shit. Jealous, my ass," Danny swears. He shakes the newspaper so it crinkles loudly and pounds the table with his fist.

Winnie drops her toast on her plate, and Rosa sets her juice glass down. Joey puts down his comic book. They all stare at me, waiting to see what I'll do. They know I tattle on Danny when he swears, but I decide to not say anything this time. If I open my mouth, I know I'll blab about last night. Then I'll get in trouble with Mama for breaking my promise.

It's quiet for a few seconds, then Joey starts in. "It's weird, you know." He stares right at me, and I feel like he has X-ray vision, like the guys in his comic book. "It ain't natural," he continues, "the way you guys trot off there all the time."

"Shut up," I say. But I know they're right.

"Peanut, you don't know your head from your asshole," Danny adds. "You think you're hot stuff seeing Patrick and all, but you don't get it."

"I get it," I say. "It makes Mama happy." I want to scream at them that they don't get it. I hate it as much as they do, but I don't want them to say stuff about Mama.

"So fucking what?" Danny says. His eyes are wide and angry. He glares at me.

"Yeah," Joey adds. "And what about Dad?"

"What about him?" I ask. I try to punch my words back at him.

"You never see him when he comes home on Friday night," Danny starts. "He pretends he's OK but he's not. He makes us fish sticks, then he takes off."

For a second, I imagine Daddy wandering around Pisa, crying, or going over to Rickey's Bar and Grille for a beer with his buddies. "I hate Friday nights," he moans and groans. "My wife takes off with my daughters and I get stuck with my sons." Maybe he borrows someone's car and drives off to spy on us. I can't really see Daddy doing either of these things. He probably just goes to church. But if I were him, I'd pick the crying part for sure.

Joey starts up again. His voice is prickly now. "Yeah, and what are we supposed to do? Our friends come over, and they know what's goin' on. It's embarrassing. They say things like 'How come your ma's not home, Joey?' But they know all along she's out with him."

Winnie throws her cereal spoon on the floor and starts to cry. "Quit yelling, you guys," I order. "You're scaring Winnie." Then Rosa moves closer to me and hugs Binkie until its eyes pop.

"When's it gonna stop?" Danny asks. He's real mad now. He's making his hands into fists and holding them tight against his legs.

"It's not my fault," I say.

I'm getting nervous now. My jaw is tight and I watch Danny closely, wondering if he's gonna pound the table or swing at me.

"Tell her not to go anymore," Danny demands.

"You tell her," I say. I stall, trying to sound strong, sure of myself.

"I tried. She doesn't listen to me," Danny says.

He sits back down in Daddy's chair and rubs his forehead. "Besides, you're the one she bends over backwards for."

"Tell her to take us too," Joey says. His voice is soft, like Rosa's when she wants me to take her with me to Amelia's.

My head spins around like I'm falling out of a tree. Then I feel Zoomer licking my finger, and the spinning stops. I stare at my brothers. They look as scared as the cat daughters at Smiley's. Their eyes are hardly open, and they have sad faces. Somehow, I think they know that Patrick doesn't want them to come to Happy Town. He would have left last night without them, if Mama hadn't changed her mind.

The kitchen feels stuffy, and I can't get enough air. I don't have the golden key to Mama's heart. I can't stop her. I'm just waiting, like they are, waiting for Mama and Patrick to decide. They think I can raise my hand and make it all go away, but one wrong move and I'll be left behind, too. My stomach knots. I grab for a chair and sit down as Daddy walks into the kitchen.

His messed hair sticks straight up from the right side of his head. Sleep lines run over his face, leftover marks from the good sofa in the front room. Bits of fuzz stick to the short bristly hair above his lip. With his eyes half shut he opens the back door and shoves Zoomer outside, then he scratches his butt and walks back toward the kitchen counter.

"For cryin' out loud!" he shouts. "What's all the racket about?" He doesn't wait for an answer, and none of us offers one. He pours himself a cup of coffee. Danny gets up out of Daddy's chair and moves across the room. "Give me the sports page," Daddy gruffs. Danny tosses it to him.

"The Yanks won again, Dad," Joey says. Daddy grunts then he sits and reads the paper in silence. In the far corner of the kitchen, Danny stares at him and tosses a baseball into the air, catching it with one hand. Joey stares at his comic book. I move my sisters into the living room to watch cartoons, then I come back in the kitchen and sit next to Daddy. Outside the back-door window, Zoomer runs circles in the side yard. I eat some toast and stab glances at Joey and Danny as I chew. No one says anything for a long while, until Daddy breaks the silence.

"Get me some more coffee, kiddo," he says to me.

I pour him another cup. He takes a sip and sucks it between his teeth, then he looks over at Danny. "Don't forget to put up the storm windows before you go to work today." He turns toward Joey, "You mow the lawn, and don't forget to feed that dog."

Danny and Joey say, "Yes, sir," then make faces at Daddy after he turns back to reading his newspaper.

I want to tell Daddy about last night, tell him to hurry up if he's going to keep us all together. When I open my mouth nothing comes out. Mama's secret's holding on to my tongue. Daddy concentrates on the sports page. His lips move slightly, forming words, connecting sentences. When I was little he used to read me bedtime stories. But he stopped after we started visiting Patrick. He spent more time praying after that. In church or in the front room he whispered the rosary. When I interrupted, he scolded, "Wait 'til I'm done. Then I'll read you a story." By the time he got through the long string of beads, I'd

92

already be asleep. I used to cry at first. And Mama would say, "I told you you couldn't count on him." Then she'd read to me. After a while I stopped asking for Daddy.

I want to ask him for a story right now, even though it's the middle of the morning, and I'm too old to be held. I want to smell his sour morning breath on my face, feel his calloused fingers brush the back of my hand as he turns the pages. But he keeps reading his paper like I'm not even here. I get up and clear the dirty dishes. As I scrape crumbs into the wastebasket, Mama walks in the room.

"A person can't even get any goddamn sleep around here," she mutters.

I pour some coffee and hurry to her side. "Mornin', Mama," I say, handing her the cup.

She lights a cigarette and grabs for the coffee.

"Who left the goddamn TV set blaring?"

My face feels hot. "I turned it up for Winnie and Rosa, Mama."

"Go turn it down," Mama orders.

She sits at the opposite end of the table from Daddy. She doesn't even look at him. I hurry out of the room, turn the TV down, then hurry back.

"Ma," Joey says. "Are you gonna come watch my practice game this afternoon?"

"I don't know, Joey. My head hurts so badly I can't even think straight. Ask me later."

Joey frowns. He looks down at the comic book rolled between his palms.

"Quit tossing that ball in the kitchen," Mama barks at Danny. "Go outside with it, for Christ's sake."

She still hasn't looked at Daddy, sitting at the end of the table. And he never looks at her. Danny hits Joey with the back of his hand as he catches the baseball one last time, and Joey turns around and socks Danny in the arm. Mama gets real mad, now.

"That's enough, now I mean it, go outside."

The boys don't leave. They lean against the back wall. Mama pours a glass of juice, snuffs out her cigarette and finally glances at Daddy. Danny tucks the baseball into his pocket and stands with his shoulders all stiff. Joey fidgets. I stand back a ways, in the doorway between the kitchen and the living room. I pray: Dear God, don't let them start fighting. Not now. It's too early.

"You got paid yesterday," Mama starts in. "I need grocery money. Don't be cheap this time. I want some decent food in this house for a change. I'm sick and tired of ground chuck and fatty pork steak."

She swallows the juice with one gulp and stands up to go back to her bedroom. I hold my breath. Daddy slowly raises his head, reaches out and grabs her arm as she passes.

"When'd you get in last night, Marie?"

Mama tries to yank her arm away, but Daddy holds on. "It's none of your goddamn business when I get in. You don't own me."

I rock back and forth against the wooden door frame. Joey hugs the wall near the back door. He squeezes his comic book. Danny stands like a soldier, waiting. His cheeks get redder and redder.

"When did you get in last night, Marie?" Daddy says again. His voice is icy cold.

"Let go of my arm, Paulie. You're hurting me," Mama says.

"I'll let go when I'm good and ready, Marie."

Daddy isn't yelling, but his voice rumbles, low. It builds slow, then explodes like thunder.

"I want you to stop it, Marie. Stop it for the kids, if not for me. Enough is enough!"

He loosens his grip on Mama's arm and stands in front of her, blocking her escape with his body.

"I'll never stop it, you son of a bitch," she says. She rubs her sore arm. "Give me a divorce. I want a divorce!" she screams.

"No!" Danny shouts. "No. No. No. No!"

He yanks the baseball from his pocket and fires it across the room. It skims the edges of Mama's hair, then bounces off the wall behind the stove and crashes to the floor.

"What the hell you doing?" Daddy yells.

I scream. Joey drops his comic book, slides onto the floor and buries his face in his knees. Rosa and Winnie run in from the living room. They wrap their arms around my legs and start to cry. Daddy slaps Danny's face. Danny doesn't even flinch.

"Hit me again," he says. "Go ahead. Be a man. A big shot, man."

Daddy raises his arm high to hit him again. "I've had it with your lip, young man. First last night, now today. Enough is enough." He shakes his head once and brings his arm down.

"I'm sorry, Daniel," he says. He reaches for him, but Danny moves away, closer to Mama. His face is on fire.

"You make me sick," Danny says. "Why can't you see what it's doing to all of us?"

"Don't talk to me like that!" Mama hollers. "I'm your mother!"

"Then act like my mother," Danny spits.

He whooshes past me, through the living room and out the front door. Joey jumps up and races after him. I peel the girls' arms from around my legs and push them back into the living room. "It'll be OK," I say, trying to comfort them. "No more fighting now. It'll be OK."

I got to throw up. I set my sisters in front of the TV. I

give Rosa her stuffed dog, Binkie, and hand Winnie her yellow blanket. I start to go upstairs to the bathroom, but I only make it as far as the couch. I bend over, and bits of mashed-up toast fly out of my mouth.

"Mommie, Mommie, Peanut threw up," Rosa shrieks, running back into the kitchen. Winnie steps back, closer to the picture window. She stuffs the end of her yellow blanket into her mouth and makes small sucking sounds.

Mama brings some paper towels to sop up the vomit and wipe my face. "Are you all right, honey?" she asks. She touches my forehead checking for a fever. Her hands shake. "Maybe you're coming down with something."

I moan and lean into Mama's waist. We should have gone last night. This thought spins over and over in my mind. We should have never come home. Patrick's right. They don't want us here. Danny and Joey and Dad just yell all the time. Why do they always have to fight? I want to go to Happy Town. I want to go right now. I wipe my eyes and nose on my pajama sleeve.

"Mama, I don't feel too good." The room spins. The floor can't steady my swirling stomach.

"Let's go wash off your face," Mama says. "You've got throw-up all over your mouth."

I grab her hand and follow her into the kitchen. We walk past Daddy, still sitting at the kitchen table. He's got his head in his hands, and he's rubbing his eyes. He whispers a Hail Mary. Mama leans against the edge of the sink. She drops my hand and covers her mouth.

"Mama?" I say. "Mama, are you OK?"

She hands me a wet dishrag and says, "I feel dizzy. I'm sorry, Peanut, but I've got to go lay down." She hurries off to her bedroom.

I pat my face with the wet cloth and start to cry. My tears mix with the water on the dish rag and soak through to my fingers. My legs shake, and I slouch against the cupboard door and close my eyes. Then I feel a hand touch my shoulder. I look up, expecting to see Mama, but instead it's Daddy. He takes the rag and wipes the vomit from around my mouth.

"It'll be OK, kiddo," he says. He bends down so that his tired eyes are even with mine. "It'll be OK," he says again.

I stare at him for a second. I don't know if I should lean my head on his shoulder or race off upstairs and shut my bedroom door. I'm disappointed that he's not Mama. I wish I could switch this morning off like a light. Switch last night off, too. I smell his musty, sweaty smell and I remember being smaller and it being easier somehow. The quiet wasn't so loud, the shouting wasn't so heavy. Then he reads my mind, and he hugs me with stiff cardboard arms. I hug back. From the other room, I hear the TV cartoons: Tweety Bird running from the big claws of Sylvester the cat.

SEVEN

Danny pries open the case of Clairol and restocks the shelves with cartons of Honey Red. "Don't forget to reorder more Crest," Sophia Marco says over his shoulder. "And we're low on Jergens' hand lotion, too."

The clerk circles to his right and stands beside him. Her sagging, suntan-colored nylons, rolled in folds around her ankles, are the first thing he sees. The brown snags match her sturdy tie shoes. He glances up at the hem of her flower-print dress and climbs the front of her pink smock, snap after snap until his eyes meet hers.

"You still haven't told me why you came in here today looking like a street cleaner had swept your face away."

She brushes back the strands of hair that dangle from her tightly-knotted bun and studies him. His eyes jerk away. The sweat rivers down his neck. His shoulder blades itch. He takes his time restocking, placing the boxes in perfect rows. He'd spent all afternoon evading her, first in the stock room, then down one aisle after another as he refilled the shelves.

"Nothing's wrong, Mrs. M.," he said. She had a mysterious way of reading his stone eyes, deciphering the secret code of his tight lips. Without a word spoken, she knew when things weren't good.

"You can't fool me," she answered. "Something's happened."

He stands up and unties his work apron. He wipes his hands on its heavy cotton edges. The thick seams scrape against his palm. After the fight with his mother this morning, he took off for the ball field and sat on the bleachers for hours, talking with Joey about ways to murder Patrick. Clean, quiet ways that wouldn't leave a trace. Just erase him from their lives forever. He bends over, folds the cardboard flaps into the Clairol case, picks the bundle up and heads toward the back room.

"Danny," Mrs. Marco calls to him.

He walks away, hoping she'll lose interest, forget about all her questions. Find somebody else to nursemaid. He tosses the empty box into the corner and fills out two order slips for Mrs. M.'s requests. When he's done, he hangs his apron on the hook in the pharmacy stock room. Working has dulled his imagination; he isn't up to committing the ultimate mortal sin any longer. Hauling shampoo bottles and hair rinse has emptied his heart. He can almost laugh, now, at wanting to snuff out the priest. He fills out his time card, grabs his jacket. Today's shift put him into overtime, and he needs an OK from Mr. Johnston before he goes home. He leans into the swinging doors and heads back into the store to find his boss.

"It's your mother, isn't it?" Mrs. M. says as he passes. She grabs hold of his shirtsleeve. Her fingers wrap around his arm, stopping him. He stares at the polished toes of his work shoes. "If you need anything, call me." She drops her hand, and he nods.

"Is Mr. Johnston still around?" he asks.

"He's up in tobacco with a customer."

Danny heads down the candy aisle, past the magazine racks to the cigarette counter.

"I bought a pack of Winstons yesterday. When I opened it, a couple of cigarettes were missing," old man Rossi complains.

Maybe you smoked some on the way home, you old fart, Danny thinks to himself.

Mr. Johnston leans over the counter. "Yes, yes. I understand." He hands Rossi a fresh pack. "Here you go. No charge." The old man pockets the cigarettes and heads out the door.

Service plus. That's Mr. Johnston's motto. He starts and ends every staff meeting with those words, like a prayer. Danny watches his boss rearranging the complementary Johnston's Pharmacy match books in the tin cup next to the cash register. Someday, I'm gonna own my own store. Make a lot of money. Be somebody. He's got it all. Wife and kids, a big home, a fancy car. He'd never let his wife make a fool of him. He's good-hearted, but he ain't stupid.

"Do I pay you to stand there like a statue?" his boss says.

Danny catches himself staring. "No sir." He stands up straight and pushes his time card toward Mr. Johnston.

"I need you to sign for my overtime."

"Overtime." His boss shakes his head. "If you keep working so much, your studies will suffer, Daniel. You can't get into college without good grades."

Danny looks away. Not today. I don't want a lecture. I just want your goddamn signature.

"I can help with a good recommendation, you know. When the time comes," Mr. Johnston adds.

"Thanks, sir," Danny says. He manages a smile, trying to make up for the angry thoughts he let race through his mind a second ago. He wants to get into college. He doesn't want to end up like his dad, sweating away his life in some rotten little town, making a few lousy bucks and having nothing to show for it but a rundown house and a wandering wife. He wants to make it. If he watches his mouth and doesn't screw things up, Mr. Johnston could help him out of this crummy hellhole of a town.

"Go, get on home. Your homework is waiting," Mr. Johnston says. "I'll put your time card back in the stock room."

Danny pulls his jacket over his shoulders, relieved that the lecture didn't last long. He leaves the pharmacy and heads home, pushing his face into the chilly wind. Dirt and pieces of litter from the sidewalk swoop up and sting his cheeks. He thinks about his father's hand hard against his face at breakfast. Maybe he deserved it this time. He shouldn't have thrown the baseball at Mom. He didn't mean to hurt her. Words slip out sometimes that he doesn't even know are inside him. His mouth opens, and they rush out like survivors fleeing a burning building.

I'll make it up to her tonight, he promises himself.

Danny crosses the bridge and heads towards home. He passes St. Joan of Arc's Church. Its thick stone walls and stained-glass windows look out of place next to the shabby houses in the rest of the neighborhood. When Danny was little the church was a magical, holy place where priests paraded down long gray slate aisles, cradling thick wooden crucifixes in their capable hands. Now his father has to drag him to Mass every Sunday. He sulks in the pew, never bothering to recite the prayers or kneel during the consecration.

He looks up at the ten-foot stained-glass window that towers over the front entrance—St. Joan in full armor, astride her steed, leading the cause for God and Right. Where has God gone? It really is all just a bunch of bullshit. People like his dad still believe because they have to. They hang on to the lies to keep from drowning in the sad sea of their lives. He pulls his jacket close around his neck and walks past the rectory. In the dusk, he spies his father pulling open the heavy wooden side doors. Dad slips into the church, quiet as a whisper.

A coldness spreads inside his chest. Go on, old man. Run to your Jesus. Pray for yourself. Pray for us all. He swallows hard and punches the icy anger down into his stomach. He feels sorry for his dad, sorry that he's duped himself into believing God can make a difference. Dad hasn't figured out yet that God's a million miles away, as far as the moon. Maybe even farther.

Danny walks swiftly down the few remaining blocks toward home. The house sits lonesome in the twilight. The two upstairs windows are sad eyes, watching the road. He steps around to the back door and stands outside the kitchen for a few minutes, wishing he didn't have to go in, see his mother, make things right between them. It's too hard to look into her eyes; they're a million miles away, too.

Through the window he watches her making supper. When he was a little boy, when Joey was still a baby and before Peanut or the littler girls were born, he spent hours with her. On Saturday afternoons they mixed meatballs. She crumbled the hamburger. He added bread crumbs. She minced garlic and sprinkled in oregano. He cracked the egg. She added the water. They rolled the meatballs and fried them in hot oil. But that was years ago.

He opens the back door and steps quietly inside. He sneaks behind her and nabs a fried meatball from the plastic bowl on the counter. "When's dinner?" he asks.

"Oh, Danny, you startled me," Mom says. "Five-thirty. We're having spaghetti. And keep your fingers out of there. I won't have enough for later."

"Ah, Mom," Danny teases. He kisses her softly on the hard arc of her cheekbone.

"So how are you, Danny boy?" she asks. Her voice is unexpectedly tender.

Maybe she's already forgotten this morning. He tried to apologize before he left for work, but she was still napping. Peanut warned him not to wake her. "Tell her I'm sorry," Danny told his sister.

"Did Peanut give you my message?" Danny asks.

"Yeah." She pauses a second, then adds, "How were things at the drugstore today?"

"OK," Danny says, stealing another meatball. She's not gonna bring it up. He decides to let it slide. Maybe she forgave him, maybe not. He isn't quite sure he cares. "The same old stuff." He grabs a milk bottle from the refrigerator and takes a swig.

"Daniel Giovanni, how many times have I told you never to drink out of the bottle? Get a glass," she says.

"You got eyes in the back of your head or what?" Danny teases.

"Never mind your back talk, young man. You may be sixteen but you're still gonna listen to your mother."

"Yeah, yeah." Danny smirks as he pours himself a glass of milk.

"So," he continues, "when'd you get in last night?"

It slipped out without him even thinking about it. He can't back off, give her a chance.

"When you gonna clean your room like I asked you to?" she says, ignoring his question.

"Mom, how come you don't answer me when I ask you about your Friday nights?"

He leans against a kitchen chair and folds his arms into his chest.

"Look, Danny, don't you start in on me. I expect it from your father, but I don't deserve it from you. This morning is history. Gone. Kaput. And anyway, what's the big deal? I've told you a million times, we don't do anything special on Friday nights. You and your brother always wanting to know. You'd think you were missing out on something."

It hurts, goddamnit, he wants to scream. You never invite me and Joey. What are we? Second-class, no-count bums?

His shoulders stiffen. "You always take the girls. How are we supposed to feel?"

She turns away from him and stirs the spaghetti sauce. "You must have more important things to do with your Friday nights than hang out with your sisters and me."

That's not the point, Danny thinks. He says, instead, to the back of her head, "I guess you're right."

"So how long you gonna keep seeing him?" Danny asks.

She turns off the gas burner, leaves the meatballs splattering in the frying pan, and pulls a chair next to him. She sits down and stares straight into his unflinching eyes.

"I take it all this questioning is you being mad still about this morning," she says. "I don't know what to say to you."

Her eyes pull him in, threaten to swoop him up, carry him far, far away. He looks away, stares at the flecks of yellow in the Formica tabletop. He thinks about his father, about his mother and Patrick. He imagines taking their heads in his hands and shaking and shaking until their eyes bleed. How can she love him and Joey and the girls and do what she does? She could make herself love Dad. Stop the fighting. The bickering eats away at him. He's willing to make a deal, barter his way to peace and quiet. He'll stop yelling if they do. He'll be sensible about this whole mess if they will, too. He's ready to surrender, but they've got to give in, too.

"Look at me when I talk to you," Mom orders.

He reaches for a chair, sits down and locks eyes with her. "You never even tried to work it out with Dad," he accuses.

"God as my holy judge I tried, Danny. Believe me, I tried."

Her eyes fill with tears. "I begged him to let me use birth control. I begged him to help me raise you kids. I begged him to be a better father. A decent husband. I tried to leave him when I was pregnant with Peanut, but my mother, God rest her soul, sent me back. 'Your place is with your husband', I can still hear her saying. So I came home. But I couldn't love him. You can't squeeze water from a stone, Danny. You tell me if that isn't so." She wipes her face with the edge of a dish towel.

He thinks about the times he's laid awake in bed listening, their angry words blistering his ears. Maybe Dad isn't the most perfect father in the world or the most wonderful husband, but he's the only dad he has, the only one he wants, and he hates that she can't resurrect whatever it was that made her marry him in the first place.

"I don't wanna talk about this anymore," Danny says. He stands up, back stiff, jaw set.

"Danny," Mom says, standing now, too. "I love you. I hope you know that. There's nothing more precious to me than you and Joey and the girls. Try to remember that, even if none of the other stuff makes sense. Maybe some-day when you fall in love, it will." She reaches over, touches his face and kisses his forehead.

"Sure," he says, offering no resistance. His face is empty, his eyes closed, shutting her out. "I gotta go get cleaned up for supper," he says.

***

After dinner Peanut and Rosa clear the table, and Mom cleans Winnie's face and hands. Joey feeds the dog. Dad reprimands Danny, "You didn't put up the storm windows."

"I'll do it tomorrow," Danny promises as he heads for the TV.

"You better not forget again, young man!" Dad hollers as he passes through the living room on his way to the front room. "Where's my book?" snaps Dad.

"It's on the TV," Danny says, pointing to his dad's copy of *Lives of the Saints.*

His father tucks the book safely under his arm. Danny rests his sneaker on the arm of the couch and watches him go. Holy holy holy, Lord. How'd he ever end up with all us kids? Goddamn freak of nature. He should have been a fourteenth-century mystic, for Christ's sake, the way he reads those saint stories.

He flips over, buries his face in his arms. Joey swats the back of his head. "When's the game start?" His brother's words aren't halfway out of his mouth when Danny overhears the girls and Mom in the kitchen.

"When you're done with the dishes, wash your hair, Peanut. Then do Rosa's."

"Can we watch 'The Jackie Gleason Show' when we're finished?" Peanut asks.

"Certainly."

"Shit," Danny moans. Saturday nights at home are the worst. Mom and the girls have to watch the June Taylor dancers and Ralph and Norton. He may as well kiss the Yankee game good-bye now.

"Hey, Joey. Wanna go watch the game at Androzzi's house?"

"Stevie's at his grandpa's tonight," Joey says.

Danny thinks about his friends. He could call one of them, but they'd want to go shoot pool or take in a movie, and he's out of cash until he gets paid next week. He already owes Mario Fratello five bucks from last weekend. Besides, it pisses him off that Mom automatically gives the girls first rights to the TV. She doesn't play fair. He wonders if Mrs. Marco is watching the Yanks. He's tempted to call her and ask if Joey and he can come over, but at work today she was in his face about his mother, and he can't stand the thought of her bugging him about it again tonight.

"We could go listen to the game on the radio upstairs," Joey suggests.

"Forget it," Danny gripes. He gets up and turns on the TV. "Let's at least see if anybody's scored yet."

"Don't get too settled," Mom says, as she and Winnie pass through the living room, on their way upstairs. "We've got first dibs on the TV."

"Shit. Why can't we watch the goddamn game, for once?"

"Don't give me any grief, Daniel. It's been a long day." She taps him on the shoulder. "I'll be back down after I give Winnie a bath."

"Let's get Dad and go down to Vinnie's Pizza. They usually have the game on in the back of the store," Joey says.

"Forget it, Joey. Dad's reading his holyholyholy books. Besides, the game's already started."

Danny turns the volume up and settles into the couch. Joey sprawls out on the living room rug.

"Jesus Christ, you'd think she'd give in sometimes. It makes me sick. She's always letting the girls have their way. 'Jackie Gleason.' Shit. Those morons always fight. Ralph and Alice. Jesus, you'd think she'd have enough of that crap with Dad."

"We're done, Mama!" Peanut yells. She and Rosa race through the living room with their wet hair all wrapped up in towels. "Can we have a candy bar now?"

"Shut, up!" Danny hollers. "Can't you see we're watching a game here?"

"Comb yourselves out, then you can have one," Mom says from the top of the stairs. "We'll be down in just a minute."

"Looks like our luck has run out, Danny," Joey says. "And it ain't even the fourth inning."

"Goddamnit all to hell," Danny mutters.

Peanut waltzes over to the TV and flips the channel to "The Jackie Gleason Show." "It's started, Mama. Hurry."

"Leave the goddamn TV set alone, Peanut!" Danny shouts. He gets up to change it back to the game.

"Shut up, pig. Mama said we could watch it." She plops herself on the floor near Dad's recliner. Zoomer snuggles in beside her.

"Mama," she calls. "Danny won't let us have the TV."

"Daniel, what did I tell you?" Mom's foot falls heavy on the last step of the stairs. Winnie's tucked in close, resting her head on Mom's shoulder.

She sets Winnie on the couch, settles in beside her and props her feet up on the worn ottoman. Rosa lays on the rug in front of the TV. She and Peanut munch Fifth Avenue bars. Chocolate rims their mouths.

"Turn 'The Jackie Gleason Show' on, Daniel," Mama orders.

Danny twists the knob and flips the channel. Then he swings around and pinches Peanut's leg with the toe of his shoe.

"Ma," Peanut complains.

"Daniel, leave her alone," Mom says. "Haven't you got something better to do than hang out with us on a Saturday night?"

"Yeah," Danny mutters. "Like watch the goddamn Yankees."

Danny grabs some candy bars from the bag in the middle of the rug and flops himself into a chair on the other side of the room. Joey stretches out near Danny's feet.

"I'll give you girls all my candy if you let us watch the game."

"That's enough, Daniel," Mom says. "Quit complaining. If it's that important to you, go watch it someplace else."

Danny taps his foot against Joey's head. "I can't see with this big sausage in my way."

"Cut it out, Danny!" Joey yells, swatting at Danny's leg.

Danny rolls his eyes at the June Taylor dancers as his sisters ooh and aah at the costumes.

"Wow," Peanut says. "It looks like a kaleidoscope. Someday I'm gonna dance on TV like that."

"Me too," Rosa says. "Can we take dancing lessons in Happy Town?"

"Shut up," Danny snaps. He tosses a wadded candy wrapper at his sister.

Mom shoots him one of her don't-give-me-a-reason-to-hit-you looks, then turns to Rosa. "How many times have I told you never to mention that in this house?"

About a hundred times, Danny thinks. Poor Rosa's too little to remember to keep her mouth shut. Look at her with her mouth flapping all over the place.

"Sorry, Mama," Rosa says.

"Where's Dad?" Joey asks. He sits up and looks around nervously.

"How the hell should I know?" Mom snaps.

"He's reading in the front room," Danny says. He peeks around the corner. His father's head is kicked back, his mouth flopped open, snoring. *Lives of the Saints* is propped on his heaving chest.

"He's sleeping," Danny reports.

"Figures," Mom says as she bites hard into a Fifth Avenue candy bar.

"Oh look, it's the Honeymooners!" Peanut squeals.

Ralph Kramden tries to squirm out of trouble by lying to Alice and having Norton back him up. But Alice is onto him and gets mad. Ralph threatens her with a shake of his fist. "To the moon, Alice!"

The girls laugh and wave their small fists in the air. "To the moon, Alice!" they shout.

Mom laughs, too.

Danny's head aches. Who needs Ralph Kramden? He can have yelling any night of the week in his own living room if he wants. All he has to do is open his mouth and mention Happy Town. That stupid make-believe land where Mom and Patrick want to take them all to live. Like one big happy family. He's heard that fucking excuse for a fairy tale before. He doesn't buy it for a minute.

"It's hotter than hell in here," Danny says, sitting straight up in his chair.

The back of his shirt is soaked with sweat. He looks at his mother, mesmerized by the TV program. Every now and then she laughs, and the corners of her mouth turn up softly. Maybe he has it all wrong. Maybe Dad isn't the problem after all. Friday nights with Patrick and Saturday nights in front of the TV like nothing's wrong. How does she do it, he wonders? How does she turn it off and on like that? Like the TV dial. Turn the channel until you find a program you like. One that makes you laugh.

"I got to get some air." Danny nudges his brother. "You want to catch the rest of the game down at Vinnie's?"

"No," Joey says. Joe the Bartender's on, now, and his brother's eyes never leave the screen.

"Suit yourself," Danny says, trying to sound as if it doesn't really matter. He stands up, walks across the room, switches off the TV.

"Ma!" the other kids yell in unison.

"What the hell you doing, smart ass?" Mom hollers.

"What the hell you doing?" Danny yells over his shoulder as he walks outside, slamming the front door behind him.

EIGHT

Last night, after Danny got mad, slammed the door and left, everybody was grouchy. Winnie started to cry. Mama picked her up and went into the kitchen to try and calm her down. Joey crabbed that the candy bars were all gone, and he kept eyeing the front door, waiting for Danny to come back. Rosa laid on the couch, over the spot where Mama had been, and pinched Binkie's legs. That's when the ache behind my eyes started. It stayed there all the way through "The Jackie Gleason Show," and I went to bed right after. Rosa came upstairs with me, but Mama let Winnie sleep downstairs, in her bed, the whole night.

All that awful fighting is worse than smelly perfume. It hangs in the air and makes you gag when you breathe. It's everywhere—behind the walls, underneath the bed, in the kitchen, the bathroom, the hallway. You can't get it off your clothes or wash it off your face. That's why I went upstairs. I got into bed, pulled the covers up tight and pretended I was floating high above all the stinky, stale air in the rest of the house. The pounding in my head started to relax, and I fell asleep.

This morning everything is still. Something came and ironed out the messy bumps and wrinkles. Today is fresh and clean and different. I can feel it. I take my time listening to the quiet. Nothing is better than the sound of nothing. I stretch and yawn. Rosa's legs touch mine under the covers. She slept real close to me all night, even though we had the whole bed to ourselves. I roll over on my side and stare at her. Her mouth's open in an O shape and Binkie is squished between her arms with his nose shoved into the yellow buttons on her pajama top. The quiet swims around her curly head. Zoomer nudges my feet. He throws his head back and yawns. His long ribbon tongue curls in the air. I reach down to the end of the bed and pet him.

"Good morning," I whisper. I'm careful not to wake Rosa up. I want it to stay peaceful for as long as it can. I prop my head up on my pillow and look around my room. The walls have long cracks and old wallpaper, and the curtains are faded. Our dresser used to be Mama's before she got married. The bottom drawer is missing and the top drawer doesn't close all the way, but I like it anyway. Especially today. The sun spills in through the windows, and the golden drawer handles look shiny and new. A picture of the Blessed Virgin Mary hangs on the wall across from my bed. Her arms stretch out in a friendly way. The light from the window falls all around her pretty face. Her halo glows. Regina. Queen of the World. That's who I'm named after.

I make the sign of the cross and pray. "Hail, Mary, full of grace."

Sister Saint Joseph talked about grace and forgiveness during catechism lessons last week. She was nice to me that day because I paid attention in class. She hates it when we let our minds wander. She calls us fallen angels when we answer questions wrong. But on that day I wanted to know about grace and forgiveness, so I listened. Sister said Jesus forgave everyone, even though they killed him. I asked her if his mama forgave everyone for hurting her son. She said, "Yes," but I don't believe her. I imagine Jesus and his mother fighting. "You're God, don't let them kill you," his mother yells. "You just don't understand," Jesus shouts, slamming the door behind him.

Grace and forgiveness are what you get from the beautiful Mother on my wall, not from the other Mother in the holy card on the dresser. That one's got on a long blue robe, and her heart sits on the outside of her dress. Seven arrows stick out of it. Tiny drops of blood drip onto the blue edges of her gown. Daddy says that's the Mother of Most Pitiful Sorrows. It's such a sad name. I want to cry every time I look at it. I try to push the Mother with the swollen heart out of my mind. It makes me think of leaving and not being able to take Zoomer.

"Holy Mary, Mother of God, pray for us sinners now and at the hour of our death. Amen." I finish my prayer and make another sign of the cross, push back the covers and get out of bed. The floor is cold, and I gotta pee. I whisper, "Come on, boy," to Zoomer. In the hallway I hear Daddy singing in the bathroom. "Fly me to the moon and let me play among the stars." It's his shaving song, the one he always sings when he's getting ready for eight o'clock Mass. The whole hallway is full of his voice and the creamy smell of his shaving cream. I listen for a tiny minute, then walk down the hall and knock on the bathroom door.

"Daddy," I say. "It's me. I gotta pee."

The singing stops when Daddy opens the door. His cheeks are covered with dots of shaving cream. Parts of his skin poke out here and there and his face looks like a jigsaw puzzle. He puts his hands on his waist and looks at me with impatient eyes.

"Hurry, I gotta get ready for church," he says. Then

he waits in the hall while me and Zoomer slip into the bathroom.

"I'll be quick," I promise as I close the door.

Zoomer lays on the floor near the bathtub while I pee. I flush, pull up my pajama bottoms and head for the sink when Daddy comes back in the room.

"Don't pull the plug now, Peanut," he warns.

I rinse my hands in the sudsy water and wipe them off as he watches.

"All done now, kiddo?" he says.

His voice is soft, like the towel, and I think about how nice he was to me yesterday when I got sick after breakfast. He cleaned up my face, walked me upstairs and tucked me in so I could take a nap. He smears the shaving cream dots together, covering his cheeks and chin with a smooth, even whiteness. He picks up his razor and starts to shave. I put the toilet lid down and sit and watch. Zoomer gives me a funny look. I whisper, "It's OK," and he curls up near my feet and closes his eyes. When I was in kindergarten, like Rosa, I used to watch Daddy shave every morning before he went to work. I used to think he was spreading whipped cream all over his face. I thought I could run my finger over his chin bone and scrape some off, like frosting from the bowl after Mama decorates a cake. I laugh about how silly I used to be.

"What's so funny, Red?"

I don't know if he sees my mouth flop open when he says this. I shut it quick and hide my surprise. I thought Betty, the waitress at Smiley's, was the one who gave me that nickname, but I guess I remembered wrong. It was Daddy. He hasn't called me that in a long, long time. He named me Red because I'm the only one of us kids with his hair. I was always the weird-looking one with pale skin and freckles.

"I thought Italians were supposed to have dark hair," I used to complain.

"You took after your father," Mama said. "His people have red hair."

I used to stand in front of the mirror trying to scratch the freckles off my nose. Every night I prayed for my hair to fall out and grow back brown. I worry that the part of Mama that hates Daddy gets sick every time she looks at me.

Daddy smiles. His eyes are sweet and delicious. His bright red hair lights up the room. I examine the tip of my red braid checking for brown hairs. Then I get this idea. It comes out of nowhere, and it makes my heart race.

"Daddy," I start to say. My heart is shouting now, but I make myself talk calmly. "I want to go to church with you today."

Daddy's razor stops, halfway down his sudsy face. In the mirror, his eyes get cloudy, then he says, "No, you're going with your mother."

"Why can't I go with you? I wanna go with you."

The words fly out of my mouth before I can stop them. I never go to church with him. I always wait and go to ten-thirty Mass with Mama. Every week she takes me and Rosa. Danny and Joey go with Daddy. Winnie's too little for church, so after Danny and Joey come home from early Mass, Mama makes them watch her until we get home.

But today, for some reason I can't explain, I want to go to Mass with Daddy. I chew on the tip of my finger and watch his face in the mirror, waiting to see what he says. He's quiet for a long time. While he's thinking, I am too. I think about how sometimes I get all mixed up about Daddy. Mama doesn't love him, so I think that means I'm not supposed to either. When he hurts Mama's feelings, I want to run as far away from him as I can and pretend he's not my Daddy. Sometimes I wish I could go to the store and pick out a new one, like a new pair of shoes or a new coat. That way I could find the one that fit perfectly. He'd read to me instead of praying the rosary, take me for walks instead of going off to church. And, most of all, he'd take Mama dancing and make her laugh in the middle of the afternoon.

Sometimes I watch Daddy out of the corner of my eye, at supper. He shovels food into his wide mouth and stares at his plate. His body's there, but his eyes have a faraway look, like the glassy eyes of the holy-card saint leaning against the statue of the Sacred Heart of Jesus on top of the TV. The saint's eyes are about to roll behind his eyelids and disappear into his halo. "He's in rapture," Daddy told me once when I asked him why the saint looked so funny. "He's found God." My daddy's found God, too. And he likes to talk with Him more than with the rest of us. Maybe God makes him laugh. Maybe Daddy just doesn't like any of us any more. Maybe it's my fault.

Daddy turns away from the bathroom mirror and looks at me, like his head hurts from thinking so much about me going to church with him. His face glows like a guardian angel. It makes me shiver, and I wrap my arms around my belly. Maybe Mama's wrong. Maybe Daddy isn't so bad after all.

"Well, OK, Red," Daddy says, finally. "You can go to church with me. But you better ask your mother first."

I want to twirl around the bathroom. I fly to my feet. Zoomer jumps up at me. I figure if I hurry, me and Rosa could be out of the house before Mama and Winnie even wake up. "We'll be ready in five minutes," I say.

"Your brothers are already dressed and downstairs, waiting," Daddy says. He scrapes the rest of the foam from his face.

"No," I say. "I mean me and Rosa. She's gotta come, too. Is that OK?"

"I don't know," Daddy hesitates. He wipes his face with a towel, then slaps some Old Spice aftershave on his cheeks. He reaches for his white Sunday shirt and the red-and-black necktie he hung around the doorknob. In his dress-up clothes he looks like Mr. Johnston, Danny's boss at the drug store. "Who's gonna watch Winnie if you two come with me and the boys?"

"Winnie's in Mama's room, Daddy. Please," I plead. "It'll be OK, honest."

"Well," he gives in. "What could it hurt?"

I race back to the bedroom with Zoomer right behind me. I don't have much time so I hurry to the closet. I search for my yellow dress, the one Patrick gave me for my birthday last July, but my fingers race past it and land on the purple one, further back. It's the one Daddy likes the best.

I tear off my pajamas, yank the dress from the hanger, and pull it over my head. I don't even look in the mirror, I just pat my messy hair, flopping my braid onto my back. Then I nudge Rosa out of bed. "Get up, we'll be late for Mass."

Rosa wakes up slow. She rubs her eyes and yawns. Binkie falls into the covers.

"Get a move on it, Rosa."

I dash to the dresser and check my wrist-watch. It's twenty-five to eight. Twenty-five minutes until Mass. "We gotta brush our teeth and get you dressed. Hurry."

Daddy walks down the hall, and his after-shave smell sneaks into our room. He heads downstairs finishing his song. "In other words, please be true. In other words, I love you." I smooth out the purple lace on the front of my dress. Zoomer nudges the back of my legs, then gallops over to Rosa. She's still half asleep and struggling with a clean pair of underpants.

"Here, let me help you." I pull her underwear up over her tiny butt, then I go back to the closet to get her a dress. "Which one do you want to wear today?"

"The green one with the pink flowers."

I snatch the right dress and hurry back to her. Zoomer follows every step I make. Back and forth. Back and forth. Until I snap at him, "I've got things to do, Zooms. You gotta be patient."

I yank the dress over Rosa's shoulders. "Ouch, Peanut. You're hurting me."

"Sorry. We gotta hurry, or Daddy will leave without us."

I finish buttoning her up, then I nudge her down the hall into the bathroom. "Here." I shove a toothbrush and a tube of Crest into her hand. "Brush your teeth." I brush her curly brown hair. The bathroom still smells like Daddy. I hold the spicy smell inside until my lungs hurt.

"How come we're going with Daddy?" Rosa asks as she spits toothpaste foam into the sink.

I stand back and inspect her hair. She looks OK, so I nudge her shoulder. "Let's go. Daddy's waiting."

"How come Mommy isn't getting ready, too?"

"Quit asking so many questions. Just follow me." I take the steps two at a time, with Rosa and Zoomer close behind.

"Hey, Peanut," Joey says when we hit the bottom step. "How come you're going to church with us?"

I don't have an answer. I can't explain about waking up in the quiet, about the glowing picture of the Blessed Virgin Mother, about Daddy calling me "Red." Something pushes from inside, something hot and blowing, until I

120

feel I could burst. I shrug my shoulders and say, "What's it to you?"

I sneak a quick look at Mama's bedroom door. It's still closed. I swallow hard. A burning feeling creeps into my throat. I got to get out of the house before Mama wakes up and catches me. I'll pay for it later. Mama will be crabby. She'll snap at me to set the table, watch the girls, get out of the way, be quiet, and a million other things. She'll probably even think I love Daddy more than her now. But it's not true. I just want Mama's face to laugh again, here at home, not just at Smiley's. I want Daddy's eyes to dance.

"Dad, the girls are ready," Danny says.

Even he looks handsome today, all neat with his hair combed and his tie knotted straight and crisp.

"Let's go, then," Daddy says.

I take Rosa's hand, and we follow Daddy out the front door. Danny and Joey lag behind. Zoomer barks as we head toward the church. I turn around once to tell him to pipe down. I don't want him to wake up Mama and Winnie. We march down the sidewalk, a parade of children following their daddy. Mama will be getting up soon, calling for a cup of coffee. I try not to think about what she'll do when I don't answer her. All the way down the block, I try to shove her from my mind. I concentrate on Daddy's footsteps on the sidewalk ahead of me.

"Good morning, Paulie." Dad's boss, Mr. Brown, waves from his front porch. "Fine-looking bunch you have there."

"Good morning." Daddy waves back. The sun catches the edges of his head, and his hair glows. Inside I smile a soft, sweet smile.

St. Joan's is crowded for the eight o'clock Mass. Daddy leads us to his favorite pew, third row from the altar. Whispers buzz all around as we genuflect and slide over the wooden bench. Mrs. Marco smiles at Danny. He nods hello. I see Amelia. She's wearing her new white gloves and she waves at me with her fingertips. Our neighbor Mrs. Brown nods at each of us. She studies our slightest moves. We settle in, and Daddy kneels down to pray right away. He makes the sign of the cross, closes his eyes, takes his rosary case from his pocket. His fingers rub against the black beads. His lips move silently, "Hail, Mary, full of grace." I kneel beside him, press my hands together, and point my fingers at the ceiling.

The altar looks like a shrine. A long white cloth lays over the marble top, and two candles sit like small white birds on either end. Behind the altar a huge crucifix dangles in the air. I like the podium best of all. It's tall, with wooden carvings all around the rim up near the top, where the priest stands when he gives his sermon. Before Patrick went away, he stood up there, too. The lace on his vestments shook when he pointed his fingers at the con-gregation. Every Sunday I sat next to Mama at his Masses. I hardly ever understood his sermons, but what he said must have been very holy because Mama listened to every word, and her eyes shined like the stained-glass windows.

I wonder if Patrick will still be a priest if we ever do go to Happy Town. Sister Saint Joseph said that priests get their fingers anointed with holy oil, and they stay priests forever. It's a sacrament. Nobody can undo it, except God. If Patrick and Mama get married, God will have to wipe the holy oil off his fingers, make them just regular like everybody else's. I wonder if Patrick will be sad about that.

My knees hurt from kneeling so long, so I sit back in the pew, next to Rosa. She flips through a hymnal, even though she can't read. Joey stares straight ahead. He looks bored. Danny slumps against the wooden pew. I smile at him, but he looks away. He's still sore about last night. I wonder where he rushed off to. Maybe after Mass I'll tell him everything is going to be alright. Mama decided not to leave on Friday because him and Joey weren't with us. He's got to know she didn't forget about them. Maybe then he won't get so hotheaded all the time. But then I remember I can't say anything. I promised Mama.

Daddy sits back in the pew now and folds his hands in his lap. We sit and wait for Mass to start. I get antsy, waiting. I close my eyes and think Mama must be up, getting ready for ten-thirty Mass. I can't keep my legs still. Daddy touches my knees. "Settle down," he whispers. I swallow hard and stare at the tops of my patent-leather Sunday shoes. A woman with frizzy brown hair rushes into the pew in front of us, and my heart jumps. But it's not Mama. It's Mrs. Johnston, Danny's boss' wife. She waves to Danny and settles in. I breathe out real slowly.

I look up at the high ceiling. Long lantern lights hang on thick chains and dance in the air. Colored light from the stained-glass windows dances off the lamps and falls on the stone floor. A small rainbow circle sits on the steps leading up to the altar. I imagine tiny, colored-light versions of the June Taylor dancers flitting in the air like trapeze artists dashing around the ceiling lanterns, sprinkling holy water over everybody. On the altar, Timmy Carelli and Michael Rossi wear their altar-boy dresses and light tall, white candles with long, thin, golden poles.

My mind flies this way and that with the imaginary dancers, in between the wooden pews, bouncing off the stained-glass windows. I can't catch it. Mama. Daddy. Patrick. I rattle off a hundred reasons why Mama doesn't love Daddy. Her voice shouts in my head. He doesn't make enough money. He's a lousy father. And a worse husband. He stinks when he comes home from work. He's lazy. He never lifts a finger to pick up after himself. He spits out the car window. He has a small heart. He's selfish. He never remembers to fill the gas tank on Thursday nights. He's a no good son of a bitch.

Maybe it's all the babies. If they only had me and Danny and Joey, maybe things would still be OK. I don't hate him, even if Mama does. My stomach gets hot when I think this. I want to scream. Mama's heart is gobbled up by Patrick and the lost baby. And Daddy's heart is gobbled up, too, with Jesus and the rosary.

Every day I pretend I'm happy so they'll have one less thing to worry about. Maybe if I pray hard enough, I won't have to pretend anymore. Maybe the Blessed Virgin Mother will sprinkle grace on us and make everything better. Sister Saint Joseph says grace and forgiveness will wash your soul clean, make you go straight to heaven, if you only let it. Most of the time I don't believe a word she says, but maybe she's right this time.

In the name of the Father, the Son and the Holy Ghost. Dear Holy Mother. Please make Daddy forgive Mama. Please make Mama love Daddy and not Patrick. Please make everyone stop yelling. And remember, my name is Regina, just like you. Amen.

The organ blurts out "Ave Maria," and everybody stands up. The priest walks down the aisle in a long, white, lacy robe. Timmy and Michael, the skinny altar boys, follow him. Daddy says the Mass is a sacred mystery, a sign of hope. I think it's a promise. Even though Jesus died for us, every Sunday we celebrate how he didn't really die at all. He came back, just like he said he would. The church is loud and bright. The stone floor glows red, blue, and yellow. The organ fills up my insides. I reach for Daddy's hand. He grabs back. I hold Rosa's fingers with my other hand. I wish with all my heart that Mama was here right now, too, on the other side of Daddy, standing beside him, holding his empty hand. It's up to you, Blessed Virgin, I pray. It's up to you now.

PART TWO

November 1966

Nine

Daddy's at church, saying a rosary, and Mama's in her bedroom, humming to herself. I try to concentrate on my homework, but I catch a whiff of Chanel No. 5 coming from her doorway, and I get nervous. Mama breezes into the kitchen and pats my shoulder as she passes. She's got her coat on, and her hair's all combed up real nice. She's got lipstick on, too, even though it's only Wednesday night. Something's up. "I'm going out for a while, Peanut," she says. "Watch your sisters."

"Where you going?" I ask, even though I already know the answer.

"I've got some errands to run," Mama says.

That's her code for visiting Patrick. Sometimes, during the middle of the week, she leaves after supper to see him alone.

"When will you be back?"

I try to sound calm, but I don't want her to go. I don't have time to babysit the girls. I've still got tons of home-work left and two tests to study for tomorrow. And besides, Mama's been acting weird since that night back in September when Patrick wanted to take off and go to Happy Town without so much as a good-bye to Danny and Joey and Daddy. She's forgetful about things. Last week, after she went grocery shopping, she left the car running in our driveway. Danny noticed it straightaway when he came home from work, and he turned it off. He brought the keys in the house and put them on the kitchen table.

"You forgot to turn the car off, Mom," he said. Mama looked at him like she was looking right through him—bones and skin and hair and everything. She's got a lot of things on her mind lately, only her mind can't carry them all. The ones that aren't so important slip off. If she sees Patrick tonight, maybe she'll forget to come back home. I press my fingers around my pencil and squeeze real tight. She better come back. She better.

"Can I go with you?"

"No, Peanut, not tonight. I won't be long. I promise."

Her going away nags at me. No matter what I do, I can't stop the pinching feeling inside me.

"I don't know when I'll be home," Mama says. "Don't wait up."

She fastens her coat button and slips out the back door. Danny and Joey are in the other room, watching TV. They don't see her go, but when the car pulls out of the driveway, Danny turns the volume up real loud.

I slam my book shut. I feel like the whole house is swallowing me up. I sneak into Mama's room and pull her music box out of her top drawer. I wind the golden knob on the bottom and open the lid. The lonesome music cries. "Somewhere my love, there will be songs to sing." I pull one of Mama's fancy Friday-night scarves out of another drawer and wrap it around my neck. It's full of her perfume, and I close my eyes and wish her close to me. When the music stops, I put the box back into Mama's secret drawer, fold her scarf and put that away too. Before I leave, I shut off the light and close the door. Back in the kitchen, I stare at my school books and think about the exams I've got tomorrow.

I haven't been doing good in school lately. Last year, the principal talked to Mama about keeping me behind a grade. Mama promised I'd do better this year. I can't mess up. I can't. Why can't Danny watch Winnie and Rosa, just once? It isn't fair.

"Danny," I yell into the living room. "Can you keep an eye on the girls for me so I can finish studying?"

"Get out of here," Danny yells back. "I ain't no babysitter."

Stupid pig. Can't even be nice for once. I go into the living room, to ask him to his face, thinking if I'm nice, maybe he'll give in this time.

"Please," I plead. "Just this one time."

"Ma put you in charge, Peanut," he yells without taking his eyes off the TV. "I ain't doing it." Then he looks at me with those crazy, mad eyes of his. "Where the hell did she go, anyway?"

I shrug my shoulders and turn away. "Goddamn Patrick," he says to my back.

I sit back down at the kitchen table, in front of my books, but I don't open them. My eyes feel heavy. A river wants to rush out of me, but I grab onto the edge of the table and press my fingers against the metal rim. I hold on until my fingertips get sore. I pull back my hand and look at the red marks I made. They beat like tiny hearts. The kitchen walls have eyes, and they watch me. "Leave me alone," I say.

"Peanut, will you read me a story?" Rosa comes up behind me with her little voice full of asking.

"I got homework, Rosa," I snap. "I'll read to you later, when I'm done."

She starts to cry, and her crying fills up the room. It's loud and high, and Danny starts to yell again. "For Christ's sake, shut her up. We can't hear the TV."

I go over to Rosa, thinking I'm gonna shake her 'til

131

she stops. My whole body's a bullet, flying fast at her. But her eyes are soggy, and she's got snot running out of her nose, and I can't yell at her. I grab a paper towel, bend over and wipe her face.

"What's the matter, Rosa? Stop crying."

She rubs her eyes on my shoulder and hangs on to me. "Peanut, where's Mommy?"

"She went shopping," I say. "She'll be back soon. Come on, I'll read you a story."

I take her hand, and we go into the living room. Winnie's sitting in the middle of the rug, wrapping a baby doll in her yellow blanket. Danny and Joey are still glued to the TV. They look like they're watching God or some miracle, how their eyes don't move for even a tiny second. Rosa and I flop onto the couch, and Winnie comes up next to us.

"Could you lower that stupid TV, so I can read a story here?" I holler at Danny.

He shoots me a look, but gets up and turns it down.

I read *The Cat in the Hat* five times. By the last time through, Winnie's sleeping with her head in my lap and her blanket knotted around her thumb, and Rosa's nodding off against my shoulder. I close the book and take the girls upstairs to bed. I should go study some more but I feel sleepy, too, so I get into my pajamas and snuggle in close to Rosa. She's nice and warm, and her face smells like the graham crackers she ate for dessert.

***

It's dark in the room when I wake up. I flip on the night light and check my Snow White watch. Her skinny arms point to two o'clock. I crawl out of bed and go over to the window to see if the car's in the driveway. It's there. Mama came back, just like she said she would. My mouth is dry and scratchy, and I need a drink real bad.

But I forgot to bring a glass up last night before I went to bed. I gotta go downstairs now, and I don't want to. It's creepy in the dark, all those tiny squeaks and moans that Mama says are just the house settling. She says I've got nothing to be scared of, but I can't help it.

I tiptoe down the stairs, feeling my way against the railing. By the bottom step, my eyes are used to the dark. I turn the corner without bumping into Daddy's chair, and head through the living room to the kitchen. That's when I notice something's different. Daddy's not there. His blankets and his pillow are all messed up, but the couch is empty. I figure maybe he's sleeping on the good sofa in the front room, like he does on Fridays so we don't disturb him when we come home late. But why'd he leave his pillow and blanket in here?

A crack of light shines from under Mama's bedroom door. I wonder if she and Patrick had a fight. Sometimes when she's upset and can't get to sleep, she reads all night. I sneak into the kitchen, get a glass of water and drink it in the dark.

I hear Mama snap, "No. Get out of here."

At first I think Zoomer's bugging her, but then I remember he's upstairs on the floor by my bed. Maybe Patrick came home with her. Maybe Daddy saw him and got mad and left the house and went to church. Maybe that's why he's not on the couch. But Mama doesn't sass at Patrick like that. Mama's bedroom door opens fast, then closes. I fall back into the kitchen darkness. I see Daddy creep back to the couch.

I blink a few times thinking I'm having a dream, even though I know I'm not. Daddy wouldn't have gone to church in his underwear. Then I smile. It was Daddy who was in Mama's room, not Patrick. Maybe Daddy's gonna get his pillow and blanket and go back. Maybe him and Mama will start sleeping in the same room again, like

133

Amelia's parents. But Daddy pulls the covers over his shoulders, turns his face toward the back cushions and settles in. It's quiet again, and Mama's bedroom light goes out. Everything is pitch dark, and I'm scared standing in the empty kitchen by myself. I set my cup down without making a sound and wait until Daddy snores. Then I sneak past him. I scoot upstairs, climb back into bed, and pull the covers up over my face.

Underneath it's warm, and the night can't get me. I try to fall asleep, but I can't. I put my hands over my ears and hum softly, so I don't hear the walls crying anymore.

***

In the morning, I wake up with my insides shouting, "No! No!"

I had that scary lost-baby dream again, the one about the little girl with the long black hair. Her arms were full of black-eyed Susans, and she was walking up to our front door, singing the song I like to sing to Mama— "Everything's coming up roses."

My heart races, and my forehead's all sweaty. Zoomer jumps on the bed and puts his cold nose in my face. I push him away and try to catch my breath. I pull the blanket up, tucking the edges under my chin to keep the cold air out. Zoomer hops on top of me. His warm body takes away the coldness in my arms. Morning light touches everything—the dresser top, the picture of the Blessed Virgin on the wall, the window curtains. I look around the room to make sure I'm not dreaming anymore. I can't get my heart to stop shivering.

The lost baby's coming back to snatch Mama away from me. To push her greedy face out of my mind, I stare at the ceiling and count the cracks around the light fixture. I hear a creak. I tell myself it's only Daddy getting up downstairs. I listen hard to be sure it's not the black-haired girl from my dream opening the door to Mama's room, crawling into bed with her. All I hear now are my sisters breathing in their sleep, right next to me.

Zoomer hops to the floor and stretches. I rub my face and wipe the sticky sleep out of my eyes. It's still too early to get up, but I do anyway. I don't want to fall back to sleep and hear the lost baby calling for Mama again. I reach over the edge of the bed to hug Zoomer's neck and grab some comfort from smelling his dog smell.

"I wish I could turn into a dog and stay home and play with you all day," I whisper. Zoomer licks my face. We'd run to our favorite spot by the creek and dance and sing until our feet ached. "I'd have a tail, too, Zoomer. A thick, red tail that wags and wags. We'd chase that ugly, bratty, lost baby down the block. She'd never come back again. Ever."

I make quiet little growling sounds as I get out of bed and get dressed for school. I grrr softly as I change into my uniform. I slip on my white blouse with the round collar. I grrr as I pull on my jumper and tie up my black-and-white saddle shoes. I'm as big and sharp and mean as pointed dog's teeth. No stupid lost baby's gonna come walking up our front porch, looking for Mama, with me and Zoomer guarding the door.

When I'm a famous Broadway dancer, I'm gonna have a house with a big stone wall and nobody will be able to come in unless I say so. Zoomer will live with me and Rosa and Winnie could visit sometimes. Mama, too. Danny and Joey can only visit if they're good and don't turn the TV set up too loud. I'll have a prayer room in the back for Daddy, so he won't have to leave to go to church. And I'd have hundreds of bathrooms, so I never have to wait to pee.

We slip into the hall and head for the bathroom. I gotta brush my teeth and wash my face. Mama won't let me out of the house for school looking like a bum. The bathroom door's closed. I knock, thinking Daddy's inside, getting ready for work, but he doesn't answer. I hear a weird moaning sound, like the way the walls cry at night, then another. I grrr and nudge the door open. Mama's bending over the toilet, throwing up.

"Goddamn son of a bitch," she says. She throws up again.

I cover my pointy, growling dog teeth and take a step back into the hall. I'm not a brave watchdog anymore. Mama's sick, and it scares me. Part of me wants to rush in, wet a wash cloth and wipe her face. Part of me says, "No, hurry back to bed, hide under the covers until it's all over." I try to call her name, but when I open my mouth only air rushes out. The vomit smell makes me want to heave, too.

Mama flushes the toilet, then stands up and opens the bathroom window. I close my eyes and lean against the wall. The little black-haired girl from my dream stares back at me. I catch a whiff of black-eyed Susans, and my insides feel creepy. My eyelids pop open.

"Mama, are you all right?"

She doesn't say anything. She pats her forehead with a wet towel. She sits on the toilet with her head between her knees and finishes wiping her face.

"Mama, are you all right?" I say again. I wait by the doorway. I can't go in, and I can't leave. Mama throws her head back and moans, again. Her face is blotchy. Her lips are chapped and cracked. Her eyes are scary.

The back of my neck feels prickly. I think about running downstairs, out the front door, down the block, over to Amelia's house. I grab the railing and race downstairs. At the bottom I catch my breath, then I hurry into the living room. I trip over Daddy's arm dangling off the couch. He's snoring loudly. I pick myself up and shake his shoulder.

"Daddy, Daddy wake up. Mama's sick."

"What the hell you doing?" he says.

He's half awake. I press his shoulder again.

"She's throwing up," I yell. "Was she sick last night? Is that why you went into her room?"

His eyes don't budge. I shake him harder. "Wake up."

Daddy pushes me away. He raises himself up and rests against the back of the couch. He rubs his eyes and yawns. "Settle down," he orders.

He's moving slow and everything inside me is racing. My skin could jump away from my bones and dance around the room all by itself. I stare at him, wishing he could fix it, make Mama better, take away the hot feelings boiling inside me. He finally opens his eyes all the way and looks right at me. The creases around his eyes relax, and he smiles. I give him a tiny, crooked smile back, thinking if I'm good enough, he'll help this time.

"Listen, kiddo." He puts his arms around me and tugs at my braid. "I don't know why your mother's sick. But you got nothin' to worry about. She's probably just got an upset stomach. You saw how much pizza she ate last night."

"Is that why you were in her room?"

Daddy's face scrunches up. "How did you know?" he starts to say, then he shakes his head and takes his arms off my shoulder. "No, Regina. That's not why. What were you doing up in the middle of the night, Miss Busy-body?"

"I couldn't sleep. I was thirsty." My mouth is dry again, as dry and scratchy as it was last night. I try to spit out the words, but they stick to my tongue.

"The next time you get thirsty, call for me. I'll bring you a glass."

I look real hard at his eyes. It seems like he means it, but I'm not sure. Sometimes he's extra nice to me, and sometimes he crabs for no reason. But I know he's sad about Mama and Patrick, too, so I think maybe he understands.

"Daddy," I ask carefully. "Do you think the lost baby can come back?"

"The what?" He screws up his face, again.

"You remember when the baby died, before I was born. Do you think it will ever come back?"

"Sometimes you say the craziest things, Red." His face goes back to normal, and he gets serious. "Your mother's not pregnant, kiddo. I'd know if she was. She's done having babies." He smiles a little then, and brushes my bangs away from my eyes. "Come on. Let's get some orange juice."

He takes my hand, and we go into the kitchen. The kitchen wall eyes see me holding Daddy's hand. I hope they don't tell Mama. A billion things rush through my head, but I'm afraid to talk. Can he really help? Will he try hard this time to change Mama's mind, before it's too late, before the lost baby comes back and makes Mama leave with Patrick?

I feel all jumpy again. I've got to sit down, or I'll fall in a heap on the floor. I push my butt into a kitchen chair. I sit up straight, like I'm in church.

Daddy puts two juice glasses on the table and pours us each a drink. He sets the orange-juice bottle down beside the salt and pepper shakers and swings the glass up in the air to make a toast. He winks at me and swallows in one big gulp. I raise my glass, too, but put it back down when I hear Mama's footsteps coming up behind me.

"Peanut, what are you doing up so early?"

I crank my head around and see her standing in the

doorway, wrapped in her worn blue bathrobe. Her hair flies out from the sides of her head in crazy waves. Her arms cuddle around her waist and she rocks back and forth, just a little. I glance back at Daddy. His head's buried in yesterday's newspaper. He never looks at Mama, but I can tell by the way his shoulders twitch that he knows she's there.

"I had a bad dream. Then I heard you throwing up, and I got worried. Daddy said you just ate too much pizza."

Mama makes a face. She walks over to my chair and stands behind me, resting her hands on my shoulders. "Your father thinks he knows so goddamn much. He don't know shit. He makes me sick. It wasn't no goddamn pizza." She exhales a long, hard sigh. It rushes down the top of my head. My shoulders lock, and I look across the table at Daddy.

"Lay off it, Marie," he says.

Daddy looks at Mama just once, then goes back to pretending he's reading the newspaper. Then it begins, the way it always does when they get mad at each other.

"I was only trying to calm the kid down." Daddy swings first. "She came racing down the stairs. She looked like she'd seen a ghost. What were you doing? Throwing up blood or something?"

"Shut up," Mama jabs back.

She leans into my chair. I don't move. I want to, but I can't get up. Mama's standing right behind me, Daddy's sitting right across the table. I'm caught. I fly, inside myself, to the tip-top part of my heart where I'm safe and they can't get me. It's tight, but I make myself smaller and smaller so they can't find me. Nobody can come in. Nobody is invited. Their voices rattle around me like the wind.

"For cryin' out loud, Marie, back off."

"You're the one who needs to back off, Paulie. You son of a bitch. What'd you think you'd get from me last night? You got a lot of gall."

Mama grabs the chrome rim of my chair. Her fingers brush against the back of my neck. They're hot. I flinch.

"Maybe I think you owe me something, Marie. The way you flaunt your dirty business all over the place."

Daddy stands up. He paces near the back door. If he wasn't in his underwear, he would have bolted outside. I wiggle deeper into myself. I watch everything.

"I don't owe you a goddamn thing, you son of a bitch. I'm warning you, Paulie. My room is off limits."

"What's with the attitude, Marie?" Daddy shouts back. His head pushes forward, and his eyes scream at Mama. His arms curl at his sides.

"I'm just telling you not to get any grandiose ideas about what you think I owe you, Paulie." Mama's arm shoots past my head; her finger points at Daddy.

"Quit playing with me, Marie. I don't like it."

Daddy lunges at the table, knocking over the salt and pepper shakers. White and black specks bounce over the yellow tabletop. I close my eyes, willing the mess to be gone. When I open them again, the salt and pepper are still there.

"I ain't playing with you, Paulie. That's the whole idea."

"So it's only when you want it, is that it, Marie? What kind of a woman are you, anyway?" Daddy shouts.

"A better woman than you deserve, you son of a bitch. I got needs, too, Paulie. But I suppose you've had your head in a goddamn prayer book so long you forgot about that."

Mama's really angry now. Her hands shake the back of my chair. She throws her arms in the air, shaking them this way and that. Daddy punches away, too,

140

batting at the air all around him. I want to scream, stop it, stop it, stop it, but my voice is dead.

"So, you got certain needs, Mrs. Hot Shot. Is that how you explain what happened a couple of months ago? What's the matter, that fancy boyfriend of yours not sexy enough anymore? You got to come running back to your husband after all this time?"

"What do you know about it, anyway? Maybe I just wanted to see if you remembered how to do it."

"Shut up, Marie!" Daddy shouts. He stabs his finger at Mama. "You're gonna rot in hell. You're playing with fire, and you're gonna burn. You'll pay for it. Mark my words."

The kitchen closes in on me. The cupboards shrink, the refrigerator blurs into the stove. The sink collapses full of dirty dishes. I shut off my mind. I hear them screaming. I see their arms flying around, their mouths twisted like tangled jump ropes. But I can't feel it anymore. My toes and fingers are numb. My legs and arms could fall off any minute. I fix my eyes on the wall behind Daddy. I stay that way until the shouting stops, until Mama and Daddy stare away from each other at opposite ends of the kitchen table.

"I gotta get ready for work," Daddy huffs. He kicks a chair. It hits the linoleum floor, bounces and skids to a stop.

Mama stares out the window at nothing. She doesn't even blink. Upstairs, above my head, I hear Danny and Joey getting ready for school. They'll be down for breakfast soon. I look around at the cold, messy kitchen.

TEN

Daddy charges upstairs. His footsteps rattle the ceiling. He runs into the bathroom, and the whole kitchen shakes below him. I think about getting up and grabbing the broom and dustpan, sweeping away the salt and pepper still spilled all over the table, but I can't move. Mama gets up, but she doesn't pick up the mess. She grabs a cigarette and lights it. She leans against the kitchen sink and looks down at the dirty floor. Above us, the ceiling shakes with noise.

"Get the hell out of my way. I've got to go to work." Daddy's voice rumbles through the walls.

"Dad." Joey's voice tumbles down the hallway, like he's being pushed from the bathroom. A door slams. I hear running water. A pause. A knock. Another pause. Joey's voice, again. He hesitates this time. "Dad, I gotta pee."

"Hold it," Daddy orders.

Quiet fills up everything for a second, then the bathroom door squeaks open. "OK, hurry up." Daddy's voice is nicer now.

Down the hall, the boys' bedroom door opens. Feet shuffle, and the floor creaks. Another knock on the bathroom door. Danny's voice this time. "You gonna be long, Dad?"

"For cryin' out loud, what's wrong with you guys?" Daddy booms.

The bathroom door slams. Daddy comes crashing down the steps. He plows through the living room, sending the Venetian blinds rattling. He opens the front door, then slams it. The car peels out of the driveway. Gravel hisses in the cold air.

"I wish they'd all just shut up, for once," Mama says. Her voice crawls out of the quiet and startles me. I turn and watch her without saying anything. "Why'd I ever have so many goddamn kids?" Mama complains. She blows her thoughts into the room with her cigarette smoke.

I stare at my saddle shoes. I might need boots today. I glance out the kitchen window to check if it's snowing. It's ugly gray November outside. Clouds and trees and ground all the same ugly color. Even the maple tree in the side yard looks cold. Snow collects on its branches. I close my eyes and think about snow angels and making snow forts. Soon. It will only be a little while longer before it really starts to fall. When it's thick and heavy, everything gets real quiet. That's the kind of quiet I like best of all—when nothing moves. It reminds me of the back of my closet. I hide there sometimes, under the skirt hems and pant cuffs dangling over wire hangers, and nobody can find me for hours and hours. I take a box of vanilla wafers with me and suck on the cookies until they melt on my tongue.

I stare at the cupboard and wonder if Mama bought vanilla wafers at the store yesterday. I want to grab a few, forget about school, crawl into the back of my closet and eat them right now. Mama flicks ashes into a metal ashtray and pulls a small saucepan out of the cupboard. She fills it with water and reaches for the Quaker Oats. She crosses over to the stove, and I follow her with my eyes.

144

My heart pushes against my ribs. It rushes into my lungs, up through my throat. It beats in my chin, my cheeks, my forehead.

Mama covers the pan and pulls out the toaster. She mumbles, "I'm a good mother. I make them breakfast every morning. Toast the bread. Make the cereal. Pour the juice. I love them all. They just never let me alone."

Mama cuts a piece of toast and lays it on a small plate. She drops the butter knife onto the floor. It clangs and splatters oleo onto my clean shoes. She stares at the floor, then she looks at my laces and finally right into my eyes. Her eyes are empty, like a dark and dangerous room. I look away, so I don't have to go inside.

"It's OK, Mama. I'll clean it up."

I grab a rag from the sink and wipe the oleo from my shoe and the floor. Mama nods a thank you, then sits by the window and lights another cigarette. She coughs, taps her fingertips on the table, takes a long drag off her Chesterfield, sighs and rubs her belly.

"Dear God...I won't. I can't," she mumbles. "Patrick, what are we gonna do?" She looks right at me. "Peanut," she says. She wants to say more but Danny and Joey and the girls rush into the kitchen and her words disappear.

"Mornin', Mama," they all say. Mama closes her eyes as they kiss her, one by one. I hang back, watching. I don't want to kiss her this morning. Danny and Joey grab a chair and reach for some toast. The kitchen is noisy again.

"What's burning?" Danny asks, sniffing at the air.

"Mama! The oatmeal!" I yell.

She doesn't move. I rush to the stove and turn the burner off. Mama takes another drag and watches. The smoke spills out of her mouth. I grab a pot holder, wrap it around the pan handle and dish hot cereal into Rosa and Winnie's bowls.

When I get to Danny's bowl he shoves my hand away. "I don't want any crummy burnt oatmeal," he snaps. He hogs three more pieces of toast. I want to slam the pan on his greedy fingers.

"Mama," I start to complain, but she's not listening. Her head's turned away, and she's facing out the window again. Smoke floats around her hair.

It's useless. She's not gonna help. I put the pan back on the stove and sit next to Rosa. I stab my spoon at the glop of oatmeal in my bowl. I don't want to look at Danny or the others. They act like nothing's wrong. They pretend they didn't hear the fight this morning, the awful shouting. Even if they were dead, they would have heard it. It would have shook the dirt off their graves.

My eyes slide back and forth between the table and Mama, checking to see if she's stopped staring out at the clouds. She's going away again. I'm afraid she'll burn a hole through that window, with all her looking, and slip away into the sky. My stomach is a bowl of small, twisted knots. I open my mouth to scream, but nothing comes out.

Mama stays like a statue all through breakfast. After we eat, I clear the table and put the dirty dishes into the sink. "I'll wash them when I come home for lunch, Mama." I don't know if she hears me or not. I send her I-love-you's with my mind. She doesn't say a word. She just keeps staring out the window and rubbing her stomach like she's gonna throw up again.

The boys grab their jackets and head for school. "See ya later," they call as they race out the front door. Rosa and I walk to school, too. Every day we pick up my best friend Amelia, who lives three doors down from us. Before we go, I wipe Winnie's face and hands with a dish rag and lift her out of her highchair. "Go in the living room. I'll turn 'Romper Room' on for you," I say. I pat her head thinking that will make her feel better. Winnie tugs at Mama's bathrobe. "Come on, Winnie, leave Mama alone," I order.

It's getting late, and I worry about making Amelia have to wait for us. After Winnie's settled, I grab Rosa's winter coat and bundle her up for our walk to school. I tuck her mittens in tight around her wrists to keep out the cold, just like Mama taught me. I pull out her red rubber boots and push them over her feet. Then I put on my own coat and boots and grab my book bag. I take one last look around the room to make sure I've got everything.

"Make sure Rosa keeps her coat on today," Mama calls from the kitchen. "It looks cold out."

"OK, Mama," I say.

She's come back. I peek into the kitchen to say good-bye, but she's lost in the window again. I wave to the back of her droopy bathrobe, grab Rosa's hand and head for the front door. "Let's go," I say.

Before we leave I give Winnie her raggedy blanket and kiss her forehead. "Be a good girl, now," I say. "We'll be home for lunch. Don't worry."

Rosa and I rush down the steps, down the block. The cold air slaps my skin. It makes me think of Daddy cracking his belt against the kitchen table. I squint as we turn the corner and head straight into the wind. I squeeze Rosa's hand.

"Come on. We're gonna be late."

"Ow! You're hurting me," Rosa cries.

"It's too cold to dawdle," I say. "And besides, Amelia's waiting."

Amelia rushes out of her front porch and waves hello as we get closer to her house. Most of the time I'm happy to see Amelia. Next to Zoomer, she's my best friend. I like her soft eyes most of all. They're blue-green, like a clear, clean lake in summer. But today I'm grouchy, and not even her summery eyes will make it better. All I can think of when I see her is how her mom and dad never fight. I've slept overnight at her house lots of times. I've eaten breakfast and dinner there, too, and never, ever, have her parents screamed at each other.

"Morning, Regina. Morning, Rosa." Amelia's lips are purple from the cold air. "What took you so long?"

I nod hello without answering. Her round pink face sticks out of the white flaps of her hat like carnival cotton candy in a paper holder. Sweet as candy, that's Amelia. She bounces along next to me and starts talking.

"What's wrong, Regina? You're so crabby. Are you hungry or something?" Every time I'm grouchy, she thinks it's because I'm hungry. That's the only time Amelia's crabby. She can't imagine any other reason for a sour mood. Amelia's silly like that. "Didn't you eat breakfast?" she asks. "My mom made me waffles. She said it's what you need on a cold day like today."

"I ain't grouchy," I snap. I don't want to hear about Amelia's breakfast or how sweet her mama is. "We're just late, that's all," I snap. I walk faster. "And we got to get to school."

"I'll say," Amelia huffs. It's as close to mad as she ever gets. "We got that math test today. Did you study last night?"

"Yeah," I lie.

Amelia wouldn't understand if I told her about having to babysit Rosa and Winnie while Mama went off to see Patrick. She's the youngest one in her family, and she never has to watch anybody but herself. Besides, I can't tell her stuff about Patrick, anyway. I promised Mama. Amelia buzzes on about our test and the *Sound of Music*

148

record she wants for her birthday. She says it has lots of great songs for us to learn. When she grows up, she's gonna play Maria von Trapp on Broadway. It's what she's always wanted. Her yakking is starting to bug me. You'd think she'd see that I'm not really listening. I say "Uh huh" and "Yeah" sometimes, just to throw her off, but she doesn't notice. She's too busy loving the sound of her own voice.

The snow falls hard now. The wet flakes land on our heads, the back of our coats, the top of our boots. We've got five more blocks until we get to school. I wonder if Amelia's gonna shut up before we get there. The cold air stings my ears. It feels good, like saying Hail Marys when you feel sad. My fingertips are numb from holding my book bag. All those heavy books I have to lug back and forth to school. I didn't hardly open them last night. I'm worried. I'm worried. I'm worried. The wind kicks snow in my face. It sticks to my hair and ices over. The cold starts to pile up in my lungs. My insides are cold now, too. Everything is frozen solid, like a pond. Amelia's voice slips off my ears. I grab hold of Rosa's hand to warm my fingers, but it's too late. My stomach rumbles. I think about the salt and pepper spilled all over the kitchen table. I think about Daddy's voice hissing mad and Mama's face, cloudy as the snowy sky.

Two more blocks and we'll be at school, far away from the screaming yellow kitchen walls. I'll sit at my desk, pick up my pencil, answer my test questions and push everything else away. One block from school now. I can see the big red brick building from here. I can read the letters, tall and friendly like a guardian angel: St. Joan of Arc Parochial School. I count my steps. One, two, three, four, five, six, seven, eight, nine, ten. And again, one, two, three, four....When I step off the curb my knees buckle. I drop my book bag and fall back onto the sidewalk into the snow.

"Regina, are you OK?" Amelia cries.

"I gotta sit for a minute," I say.

I concentrate on the front door of the school. Five, six, seven, eight, nine, ten. Rosa starts to cry.

"I don't feel too good, Rosa."

I pull my mittens off my sweaty hands. My fingers are white, as white as the wet, heavy snow falling all around. I think about Amelia's mom making waffles for breakfast. I think about Amelia's dad taking them sledding last week. I think about the lost baby and how her eyes are probably green-blue like Amelia's, always happy, always warm. I stare up at the tree branches. I want to climb to the top branch and jump off, fly away, never look down, never look back. Something funny pushes from inside. I drop my head between my knees and throw up.

"Regina," Amelia rushes to my side. I count the buckles on her boots. "You better go home and get into bed."

"No," I shout. "I'll be OK. Really."

I wipe my mouth with the edge of my mitten. "We're at school already. We've got that math test, and..."

"No," Amelia says. "You should go home. Let your Mama take care of you."

I shake my head. "I'm going to school, and that's that."

Rosa cries harder now.

"I'm OK," I try to reassure her. I pull myself up, wipe the snow off my butt, pick up my book bag, reach for Rosa's hand and stare right into Amelia's stubborn face.

"You're crazy, Regina Giovanni," Amelia says. She shakes her head. "Sometimes I just don't understand you."

Sometimes, I want to say to her, sometimes I don't

understand you either. You never want to scream until your head flies off. I stare at her pink, round, little kiss of a mouth. Maybe I could go to her house instead, have her mother tuck me in, read me a story, make me hot chocolate. Sing me to sleep. I can't stand it anymore. I wish I was a million miles away. I wish I was as big as a house and as loud as thunder. Sometimes, Amelia, I shout at her with my thoughts and my burning eyes, sometimes I wish I was you.

ELEVEN

Sister Saint Joseph eyes the room, spying for cheaters. She sits up straight against the back of her chair and looks around, first at Timmy Carelli, then at Filaberta DelaRico, then at me. Her right eye twitches. It looks like a cold, dead fish eye, staring at the sky. She's got a ruler in her hand, ready to thwack anybody who even looks like they might be thinking about cheating. She's on a mission to save her "fallen angels."

I sit in the third row from the window, right behind Timmy Carelli. Amelia sits kitty-corner from me, close enough to touch fingers when we swap combs and notes about Filaberta. She's the smelly, wrinkled girl whose mother never irons her school blouses. Mama says that's because Mrs. DelaRico can't afford to buy an iron. She even uses Ivory dish soap in her washing machine. They got it bad. Poor Filaberta. At least my Mama irons my uniform, even if she does it with sadness running down the side of her face.

We've still got half an hour to go before Sister collects our math tests. Timmy and Filaberta, Amelia and everybody else have their heads bent and their noses almost touching their papers. But not me. My brain's too tired to think anymore. All the spaces on my test paper where I'm supposed to put answers are bare naked, but I can't help it. I can't think of multiplication tables or adding and subtracting or anything. Mama's gonna be real mad when I don't pass my test. She's gonna want to know why, and I don't know why. It used to be easy to get A's. But my last report card was full of C's and D's, and Sister wrote "Doesn't apply herself," in the comments part. I guess I'm stupider than anybody expected. Stupider than even Filaberta whose uniform smells like Ivory dish soap. I'm the Queen of Sister's fallen rejects.

I turn my test over, stretch my arms and make sure my hands are away from my paper. I keep my eyes straight ahead, so Sister doesn't think I'm trying to peek at Amelia's answers. I can feel her dead fish eye watching me. I get up real slow and hand my test in. I stare at Sister, and she stares right back.

"You finished early, Regina. You must have studied hard last night."

She says it snotty. She doesn't believe I'm smart enough to pass her test, and I guess she's right, but I want to spit at her twitching fish eye all the same. I wonder if Filaberta's paper has as many blank spaces as mine.

"Yes, Sister."

I'm glad to be going home for lunch, just to get away from her creepy stares. I head for the cloak room and sneak a glance back over my shoulder at Amelia. She's still working on her arithmetic problems. I'm glad she's not finished yet. She won't be able to walk home for lunch with me and Rosa today. I won't have to talk about the math test or getting sick this morning or anything else I don't want to think about. My brain feels like a big brick wall. I wrap my scarf around my neck, pull on my boots, button the last button on my coat and head out the door.

All the way down the hall I say a little prayer that

Mama's in a better mood when I get home. I scuff my feet over the linoleum to make the bottom of my boots squeak. They sound like the plastic ducks Patrick gave Winnie when she was a baby, the kind that squeak when you press their little yellow bellies. I squeak my boots all the way to the kindergarten room. When I get there the door's closed, so I lean against the wall, wait for Rosa, and I think about all the dishes I left in the sink this morning. If Mrs. Infante lets her class out early, I can get home sooner and clean up the mess. That should help.

The door opens, and all the kindergarteners pile into the hallway, two by two. Rosa skips down the hall, holding hands with her best friend Lisa. I nab her on the shoulder when they pass me.

"Let's go," I say. I hurry away. Rosa lags behind and yells for me to wait. I slow down while she waves goodbye to Lisa and then races to catch up with me.

"Why you in such a hurry?" Rosa asks. "Are you feeling sick again?"

"I'm hungry," I say. I don't tell her I'm worried about Mama standing in the kitchen like a zombie. I don't like to lie to Rosa, but I can't tell her everything that's going on. She's too little, and she wouldn't understand. I take her hand, give it a little squeeze, and we head outside.

"Where's Amelia?" Rosa asks.

"She's still doing her test."

I'm in a big hurry now. I want to get home before Amelia finishes. I pull Rosa past the school crossing guard and yank her up the curb on the opposite side of the street.

"Peeaanuttt," Rosa complains. "Quit it, or I'll tell Mama."

I grab her shoulders. "Don't you be telling Mama anything, you hear? You bratty tattletale." I shake her once, real hard, and she starts crying. I feel bad. My hard-boiled hothead got the best of me again, that nasty old part of my twin soul. I pat her shoulder. "I'm sorry. I'm kind of grouchy. I didn't mean to hurt you. Just don't tell Mama. OK? And don't tell her I got sick on the way to school today. Understand?"

Rosa nods and wipes her nose and eyes with her coat sleeve. "OK," she says. I hug her and give her a little kiss on her forehead, then I put my arm through hers and say, "Let's go, now."

We head for home, stopping only once to make angels by the chestnut tree in front of the K of C. The snow's all fresh and fluffy, and even my grouchy self can't say no. We flop on the ground and wave our arms up and down, up and down, making perfect wings. Rosa giggles, and I start to laugh. I feel lighter inside. The angels have carried my heart into the air, shook all the dust off it, like a dirty old rug, and put it back inside, fresh and clean. When our arms and legs get tired, we stand up and take off for home. As we get closer, I brush clumps of snow off Rosa's coat and check to make sure our school uniforms aren't wet. I don't want to give Mama any excuses to yell at me.

I scoot Rosa up the front steps. "Take your boots off," I order. "We better not get snow on the rug." I think about the fight this morning and about how Mama looked before we left for school. My heart doesn't feel light any more. I wish the snow angels would come back and carry it away. I don't want to go inside. I stall as long as I can before Rosa complains about standing on the porch in her stocking feet. "I'm cold, Peanut."

"OK, OK," I say, finally opening the front door.

Winnie's still in her pj's, sitting on the rug watching TV. "Where's Mama?" I ask. She chews her blanket and looks toward the kitchen. I sniff at the air for smells of lunch, but I only catch a whiff of cigarette smoke. Zoomer barks hello and jumps up on me. I pet him and whisper, "What's goin' on here?" My stomach feels like a piece of yarn wrapped around and around in a tight little ball. I pull off my coat and scarf, throw them on the couch, and walk into the stuffy kitchen.

Mama's leaning against the window sill, still in her blue bathrobe, staring out the window like she doesn't care about anybody or anything except the wind, blowing and blowing. Her hands are folded over her stomach, just like this morning when we left for school. I wonder if she's been that way the whole time, until I notice the ashtray is full of cigarette butts and two crumbled-up, empty packs are on the floor at her feet. She must have moved once or twice, at least, to grab more cigarettes from the drawer where she keeps them. My eyes are sore from all the smoke. I rub them, thinking that if I rub them hard enough, when I'm done, Mama will turn around and smile. I open my eyes and nothing's changed. I move closer. "Mama?" I say. "Mama, are you OK?"

She doesn't move. I feel tiny and empty. It's beginning again, just like after Patrick moved away. Mama slipped behind a door too small for me to follow.

"I'm hungry," Rosa whines, pulling up a chair and settling herself at the kitchen table. Winnie's right behind her, dragging her raggedy blanket.

I look at Mama, then back at the girls. Rosa chews the side of her lip and stares at Mama. Winnie's hair's all messed up, and her face has dried bits of oatmeal on it from breakfast. I want to fall into a chair and let my arms and legs drop to the floor. They're so heavy I can hardly stand up.

"Be good girls," I order, "and I'll make you a sandwich."

I open the refrigerator and take out the bologna, the mustard, the mayonnaise. I grab the bread from the counter and toss it on the table. I walk past Mama to get a butter knife from the drawer. I brush against her hand, but she doesn't blink or move or nothing. Please, Mama, please don't go away again. I make the sandwiches. Every few minutes I glance over at Mama, hoping she's come back from the Sleeping Beauty spell she's under, hoping she's ready to sit down and have lunch with us. I'd make her a bologna sandwich, too, if it would only help. I pour the girls some cherry Kool-Aid and set their sandwiches in front of them.

"Eat now, girls," I say.

I plaster on my good-twin-soul smile, trying to convince them that there's nothing to be scared of. It isn't working. Rosa and Winnie eat their sandwiches, taking their eyes off Mama only long enough to take a swig of Kool-Aid and look at me for answers.

"What's wrong with Mama?" Rosa asks.

She looks worried. Winnie spits out pieces of bologna and stuffs the edge of her blanket into her mouth.

"She's just tired," I say.

My legs ache. I sit down and stare at Mama's empty face. Her mouth is a thin dark mark across her skin, like a crack in the sidewalk. "Step on a crack, break your mother's back," Amelia says. The last time Mama got this sad she stayed in bed all day, staring at the ceiling. Nothing Daddy or Danny or Aunt Stella said could make her come back. It was terrible. Grandma Giovanni watched Rosa and Winnie so I could go to school. After school I picked them up, walked them home, and then fixed supper. Sometimes Aunt Stella helped out, but she had her own family to take care of. She couldn't do everything. After the dishes, Winnie needed to be rocked to sleep, and I had to read Rosa a story. By nine o'clock, I went to bed without doing any homework. I can't let it happen again. I shout to Mama from across the room. "Mama, wake up."

Mama's eyes blink fast, like something from the sky fell into them. She turns her head quickly, startled by my yelling. I meet her eyes and hold them tight. "Mama," I say again. "Are you OK?" My neck pinches from staring so hard.

"Oh, you're home," she says. She stands up and stretches slowly, like she's waking up from a nap. "Did you get some lunch?"

At least she knows what time of the day it is. I relax my shoulders a little and walk over to her.

"I just fed the girls, Mama." I try not to sound scared. Maybe it isn't too late. Maybe she hasn't closed the door, leaving me behind. "I can make a sandwich for you, too."

"I'm not hungry," Mama says. She turns away with a funny look on her face and walks into the living room, leaving us girls alone in the kitchen. I tell my sisters to stay put, and I follow Mama. She pushes my coat and scarf away and sits on the edge of the couch. She pats the cushion next to her. "Come here, honey," she says. Zoomer comes too, and sits at my feet, leaning against my legs. I want to lean into Mama the way Zoomer leans into me, safe and happy. I want to bury my head in her lap, beg her to take me with her to the land behind the doors this time, but she sits with her back all stiff like she's in church. I reach over and touch the edge of her bathrobe. She pushes my hand away. I'm afraid of hearing those words again, the ones that slap my fingers, make me put them back in their place: "Don't touch me, Peanut. I can't breathe when you hug me so hard."

I wait and watch. I fold my hands in my lap, and I'm as still as I can be. I tell myself, just be quiet, just be good. I count to ten over and over again. Mama looks bad, as bad as I can ever remember. She's got big dark rings under her eyes. Her lips are stained from all those cigarettes. She coughs and says, "Peanut, I've got something important to tell you. Something you must keep a secret. Can you do that for Mama?"

I nod. "You can trust me." Zoomer moves in closer. Mama opens her mouth to tell me the secret, and she starts to cry. She rocks back and forth with her hand on her stomach again. I wish I could make her laugh and laugh. Her crying doesn't let up. She rocks faster and faster now. Maybe she's gonna be sick. Maybe I should get a wastebasket or a washcloth. Maybe something's wrong with her stomach. Maybe that's why she was sick this morning.

"Mama, do you have to go to the hospital, like Danny?" I ask, remembering the time Danny got his appendix out.

"No, Peanut."

She touches the top of my head. I close my eyes. My head's a sponge, sucking up all the goodness from Mama's hand. She touches the side of my face. Her hand is warm and smooth. Her touches soak into my skin. I float in a pool of Mama's touches. Then she takes her hand away, leaving a warm circle of skin where her palm had been. I shiver, and Zoomer whines. I can't hold back anymore. Mama's touching melted away whatever it is that keeps everything inside me. I start to cry.

"Peanut, don't cry," Mama says, "I told you I don't need an operation."

I try to stop, but I can't. I sniff and wipe and sniff again. Bad girls cry. Good girls don't upset Mama. Stop it. Stop it now. I stare at her hands. I want her to touch me again, make it all better, tell me she loves me and that nothing can ever take her away again. I shove my feelings back inside, behind where Mama touched my face. Zoomer pushes his nose into my hand, but I pull away and he slinks behind the couch. Mama reaches into her bathrobe pocket and hands me a kleenex. I blow my nose, and she starts talking again.

"Peanut," she says. "I think I'm pregnant."

At first I don't get it. I hear her talking, but her words don't mean anything. Then she rubs her stomach again, and stares out the picture window. "I'm going to have a baby," she says. I watch her hands giving their warm touches to her belly. The leftover patch of warm on my face where Mama touched me turns cold and spreads all over. The room is as cold as the snow outside. Even colder. The room is as cold as Siberia. Another baby will make her more tired, more cranky. Mama takes a deep breath and begins again.

"Patrick is the baby's father." She sighs, then sits back on the couch.

My head pounds. Mama's new secret moves through my brain, down my face, past my heart, into my stomach. I stare at her belly. It's in there, just like the other babies. Just like Rosa and Winnie used to be, tucked inside, so close to Mama. But this time it's different. He's done it. I don't know how, but Patrick found a way to pull Mama away from us. He gave her a baby. Just like he always said he wanted. Children of their own. But she's already got enough kids. Too many, she says all the time.

"It's the lost baby, isn't it Mama?"

"This is no time for crazy talk, Peanut. I've got a real problem here, don't you understand?"

I understand. The lost baby is coming back. Soon Patrick's baby will push me out, take my place. I cover my face and lean back into the couch. I want to ask God a thousand questions. Haven't I been good enough? Didn't I just make lunch for Rosa and Winnie? Doesn't that count? Will I have to stay at home on Friday night after Patrick's new baby is born? And what about Happy

Town? Will they still take me with them? I feel like the time Danny accidentally socked me in the stomach. "He just knocked the wind out of you," Daddy said. "You'll be OK in a few minutes." But I wasn't. I couldn't cry, and I couldn't breathe.

"Peanut, I told Patrick yesterday."

Mama tugs at some loose threads on the couch cushions. "I've been a little scattered today," she says. "I didn't sleep well last night. I don't want to worry you, but I do want you to know that I'll need your help more than ever now. Peanut, do you understand what Mama is saying?"

Somehow, I remember to say the things she wants to hear. "Don't worry, Mama. It'll be OK. I can help you. I'll keep Rosa and Winnie out of your hair when I come home from school, so you can take a nap. I'll even start dinner for you."

"You're such a good girl, Peanut. I'd be lost without you."

My eyes burn. Tears sneak out, and I brush them away before Mama sees. The girls come into the living room, asking for cookies.

"I'll get them," Mama says.

I flop over on my stomach and bite the cushions so I won't scream. I don't want to go back to school. What if Mama isn't here when I come home? Now that the lost baby is coming back, maybe she'll go away with Patrick this afternoon. I want to be little, like my sisters, so Mama will hold me and rock me, bring me cookies, fill me up with warm touches.

"You better head on back to school, Peanut," Mama says. She's standing over me now, tapping the back of my shoulder. "Be sure to come right home afterwards," she adds.

I roll over on my back and look up at her. She's holding my coat and I take it from her, grab my scarf, get up and walk toward the front door. Zoomer squirms out from behind the couch and follows me outside. The cold slaps me. I'm big enough. I can take care of the others if she leaves. The cold stings my eyes and more tears squeeze out. I wipe them away and look at my dog.

"Go back. Make sure they don't leave, OK?" He barks, then turns and runs onto the porch as I hurry down the block to school.

***

I'm late for my English test. I rush into the classroom, past Sister Saint Joseph writing the test questions on the board, past Filaberta DelaRico, smelling like Ivory dish soap, past Timmy Carelli, sitting with a stupid grin on his mean face, past Amelia looking at me with her blue-green lake eyes all worried.

"Regina," Sister calls. "I want to talk with you after class." She points a crooked finger at my desk. "Go sit down, child."

I slink into my seat, trying not to notice the other kids staring at me. The last thing I want is for Timmy and Filaberta to know I'm scared. I don't even look at Amelia. One glance from her, and I know I'll burst. I try to concentrate on the questions Sister chalks on the board, but all I can think of is what Mama told me at lunchtime. If Patrick comes for Mama before I get home from school, I'm gonna run away. I'll follow the railroad tracks behind our house until I find a place to hide. A place with no lost babies, no Smiley's Coffee Shop, no grouchy mothers, and no Patricks.

"Class, for the first part of your exam, take out your notebooks and write a theme on autumn," Sister says.

I open my theme book and stare at the thin blue lines until my heart slows down.

Autumn. I write the title in big letters across the top of the page. Then I begin. Autumn is my favorite season. I like the red maple trees best of all. We have one in our back yard. The wind blows the leaves, and they look like June Taylor dancers twirling to the ground.

Mama's sad face pokes into my mind. I see her hugging her stomach, and I squeeze the pencil between my fingers. I draw a thick, black line across the bottom of the page. Then more lines and curves until I've got a circle of June Taylor dancers making flowery shapes with their legs and arms. I put leaf hats on their heads, and I draw one dancer in the middle of the circle, with a pregnant belly. The other dancers kick her stomach. I lean back to inspect my drawing and the edge of Sister's ruler cuts into my shoulder. I drop my pencil to the floor.

"Fallen angel," Sister scolds. Her voice is hot and icy all at the same time. Her dead fish eye twitches. "Report to the principal's office immediately. And bring your theme book with you." Timmy Carelli snickers and Filaberta hides her blushing face behind her hands. Amelia looks away.

***

Fish eye, fish eye, big old ugly fish eye. Meaner than the devil, uglier than a dead baby's dead face. I hate you. I hate you. I hate you. I walk fast down the hall with my theme book tucked under my armpit. I hate the principal's office. It smells like new school books and old holy water. You sit in a chair in front of the principal's desk and you feel like you're in confession, except you can't hide behind a little screen or a big curtain. The principal sees right into your soul when she yells at you.

Stupid theme book. Stupid picture. Stupid principal. Now she's gonna call Mama and tell her I got in trouble, and I'm gonna get it good this time. Sister sent me to her office a couple of times before. Once when I punched Timmy Carelli in the stomach for calling my Mama dirty names, and once when I got caught cheating on my geography test.

"What brings you here this time, Regina?" Mrs. Malone, the school secretary, asks. She smirks, and I know she's gonna go home later and call up all her friends and say, "Guess who I saw in the principal's office getting yelled at AGAIN."

"I'm supposed to see Sister Mary Martha," I say.

Mrs. Malone stares at me from behind her big square glasses. She's trying to read my mind, see through the pages of the notebook, so she can report all the facts to her gossipy friends later. I hold my theme book close to my chest and stare right back at her. Finally she gets up, walks over to the principal's door, knocks and peeks her head in. "Sister Saint Joseph sent Regina Giovanni to see you again."

"Send her in."

Mrs. Malone smirks one more time as I pass her.

Sister Mary Martha stands by the window. She plays with the rosary beads dangling from her black habit. She motions me to a chair in front of her desk with one wave of her wide hand.

"Sit down, Regina," she says. Her eyes are deep blue, and her voice is calm. I think of a quiet pond with lily pads and I feel a little less scared. "Tell me why Sister Saint Joseph sent you to me this afternoon."

I rest my notebook on my lap. Sister Mary Martha taps her fingers against the window sill and then turns suddenly. She swishes past me. I hold my breath. She circles my chair and her black veil brushes the side of my face. I pull back, expecting a slap, but instead Sister sits behind her desk. My palms itch, and the back of my thighs stick to the chair. I glue my eyes to the floor and listen as the wall clock ticks and ticks like my heart beating faster and faster.

"I drew in my theme book," I confess, "during our composition exam."

"Why did you draw in your writing book, Regina? Don't you realize things like this upset Sister Saint Joseph?"

I don't have an answer. Sister gets weird about a lot of things I don't understand. Like the time Tony Marcelli threw up in the cloak room, Sister Mary Martha dismissed us early because Sister Saint Joseph refused to teach in a classroom that smelled like vomit. Or when Mary Margaret Piscatelli wet her pants because Sister wouldn't excuse her to go to the bathroom. The principal sent Sister Saint Joseph home for the afternoon, and Sister Agnes took care of our class for the rest of the day. But I don't know why drawing a picture of June Taylor dancers would upset Sister Saint Joseph so much.

"I finished my theme about why I like autumn then I just started drawing. I didn't do it on purpose." I try to sound sorry, like I do when I go to confession.

"Let me see the picture, my child," the principal orders.

I hold tight to the edge of my theme book. I don't want her to see the pregnant dancer. If she does she'll know about Mama's secret, and I'll be in even bigger trouble for telling after I promised I wouldn't.

"Regina, I'm not going to ask you again." Sister's voice gets cooler.

I look out the window, trying to think up a way out of this mess. I could throw my theme book out the window into a snow bank and then dash out of the office and head for the railroad tracks. I can move faster than Sister Mary Martha in all her robes. I start to get up, but Sister pushes against my shoulder and grabs the notebook.

She opens to the drawing and leans against her desk. She's only a few inches in front of me. I can smell the tuna fish she ate for lunch. I stare at her shoes, wishing I could get "beamed up" like Captain Kirk on "Star Trek." When he gets in trouble all he has to do is say the word, and Scotty swirls him into a puff of tiny atoms and dust, and he's swooped safely back into the Enterprise.

"Your essay is very nice, Regina. But you shouldn't have drawn in your theme book. It is very important to follow rules. Do you know what happens to little girls who don't?" Her voice is serious, like Father DiSante's when he's telling me to say five Hail Marys and two Our Fathers for penance after confession.

I imagine they lock little girls who don't obey in some convent and make them iron old nun's habits until their brain swells and they turn into Sister Saint Joseph. Or they make you write "I will obey Sister" one thousand times on the blackboard until your fingers ache from holding the chalk and your legs get sore from standing up so long. And then if you still don't get it, and you're still bad, they condemn you to burn in hell for all eternity. But in answer to Sister Mary Martha's question I shake my head no, hoping for mercy.

"Little girls who don't follow the rules grow up to be very bad mothers," Sister Mary Martha tells me. "And you don't want that to happen, do you?"

"No, Sister, I don't want that to happen."

"You wouldn't want your mother and father to think you didn't follow the rules, now would you, Regina?"

"No, Sister."

"Good. Now tell me, Regina," Sister Mary Martha's voice gets soft, like lily pads again, and she bends down and leans forward breathing her tuna-fish breath into my eyes. "Why would these nice dancers want to kick a pregnant lady?"

I stare into the blue circles of her eyes and try to think of something quick. Daddy says lying is a sin and if I die before I go to confession, I'll go to hell. Maybe a story isn't a lie, maybe it's only make-believe. Like *The Cat in the Hat* and all those other stories I read to Rosa and Winnie. They're not real either. Make-believe isn't a sin.

"That dancer's not really pregnant," I say. "She's got a pillow under her costume, and she's just pretending to be pregnant. She's tired of being a June Taylor dancer, and Jackie Gleason won't let her quit unless she's pregnant."

"I see," Sister Mary Martha says. "Being pregnant is a special gift from God, Regina. You must never lie about such matters. It's a sin. Is that clear?"

"Yes, Sister," I say, sounding as holy as I can.

"Good, Regina."

Sister stands up and motions toward the door with her head. "You may go back to class now." She hands me my notebook, and I head for the door. I'm nearly out of the room when she calls her final warning.

"The next time I see you in my office, I won't be quite so lenient."

I pray I never have to return. I walk fast past Mrs. Malone, out into the hallway, away from the principal's office. Everything inside me is wound up tight. I don't want to go back to class. I don't want to face Sister Saint Joseph's twitching eye, her crooked finger pointing at the tip of my nose, "I hope you learned your lesson, Regina." Timmy Carelli's eyes will smirk, "Na na na na na." Other kids will stare, too. At recess Timmy will say, "You're a stupid, no-good little fart-face, Regina Giovanni, and your mother is scum." And Amelia will want to stick up for me, but her eyes will get all scared, and I'll want to disappear. Only Filaberta will come stand by me with her sad eyes and her voice as soft as Ivory dish soap.

I wish I didn't ever have to go back to class. I want to

sneak out, run home. I could go so fast I wouldn't even need my coat or mittens. But what would I tell Mama? She'll want to know what happened to my boots and hat and coat. She'll want to know why I'm home so early. Sister Mary Martha will find out I skipped, and she'll call home. I'll catch hell. And my English test. I've already missed the rest of it, and I don't know if Sister will let me make it up. I promised to bring my grades back up this year. I promised.

I cover my face with my hands like Filaberta always does. My cheeks feel as hot and red as hers look. I lean against the wall, but the hall starts to spin. Then it feels like the ceiling is falling down, and the linoleum is lifting me off the floor. I slump down, put my head between my knees and cry, just like Filaberta does when she confesses to Sister that her Mama didn't give her a nickel for milk break. I cover my mouth so nobody will hear me. I'm an outlaw, just like Mama and Patrick. That's what I should have told Sister Mary Martha. Outlaws don't have to follow your dumb rules. And we have secrets and promises, and we never break them, ever. Even if one of us gets caught, like today. Outlaws stick together. I'm not gonna tell a soul. Mama can count on me.

After a while I wipe my eyes and stand up. I've got to head back to the classroom soon, or I'll be in even more trouble. If Timmy makes faces, I'll step hard on his foot when I walk by. If Amelia looks away, I'll pretend I didn't notice. And if Filaberta hides her eyes behind her small hands again, I'll bring her a shiny nickel for milk break tomorrow.

TWELVE

When the school bell rings I rush to the cloak room and pull on my coat and hat before Amelia even gets her boots on. I push past Timmy Carelli, bopping him a good one in the back and slip past Filaberta, trying not to notice her sad eyes staring at me. I race down the hallway, push the school doors open, and run all the way home, not stopping once, not even to make snow angels. I pray and pray Sister Mary Martha hasn't called Mama yet to rat on me. I pray even harder that Mama hasn't taken her lost-baby belly and gone off with Patrick.

My cheeks match my red hair by the time I get home. I fly across the front porch and rush inside. As soon as I open the door, I know it's OK. *My Fair Lady* is on the record player and Rosa and Winnie are coloring at the kitchen table. Mama's sitting right beside them, flipping through a magazine, humming to the music. She sips her coffee and takes a drag off a cigarette. Her hair's combed, and she's not in her bathrobe any more. She's wearing her usual weekday clothes, faded blue jeans and an old work shirt—no fancy Friday sweater, no lipstick, no perfume floating around her head. She didn't go. How I love her pushes up through my heart, making my face redder than before.

"What ya staring at, Peanut?"

"Nothing," I say as calmly as I can. There's no need to hurry now. Mama's home.

"Slow down, then, you're giving me a headache," she says.

"Sorry."

I walk over and pet Zoomer, sending him thank-yous with my fingers for not letting Mama leave. I hang my coat by the cellar door, and Mama says, "Go change your clothes and come have some cookies with your sisters." I nod OK and rush upstairs.

I whisper a thank-you to the picture of the beautiful Blessed Mother on my bedroom wall as I pull on a pair of slacks. "I'll light a candle for you soon," I promise Our Lady, then I head downstairs to Mama and the girls.

Mama puts Oreos and ginger snaps on the table and pours three glasses of milk. I grab a couple of cookies and sit down right next to her. I listen the whole time, waiting for the phone to ring, thinking any minute now Sister Mary Martha will call and tell Mama how bad I was in school today. Maybe I should confess right now, get it over and done with.

"Patrick called," Mama says. "Things are gonna be OK." She snuffs out her cigarette and grabs an Oreo. I think she's telling the truth. Her face isn't as sad as it was this morning, but she still has tight little wrinkles around the corners of her mouth that squeeze together when she bites into her cookie. "It's still important that you keep your mouth shut about this whole thing, Peanut. Understand?"

Mama leans closer to me. She tilts her head the way Rosa does when she wants something. Her eyes are as round and open as the centers of black-eyed Susans. Her soft eyelashes look like skinny brown petals.

I nod, once, and take a swig of milk. I think about Filaberta DelaRico and remind myself to take an extra nickel out of my piggy bank for her for milk break tomorrow, then I look back at Mama lighting up another cigarette. She blows smoke into the air and smiles at me. She doesn't look so sad any more. Maybe she won't be mad at me about Sister Mary Martha when she finds out I didn't tell her secret.

"It sure snowed a lot today," she says, staring out the window but looking at the yard this time, not the sky. "Why don't you give Amelia a call and go sledding? I won't need your help with supper for a while."

"Amelia can't play today," I say. I can't tell Mama that her newest secret still pinches my heart. I kept it from Sister Mary Martha, but I can't keep it from Amelia, too. If I even look at her, she'll know something's wrong, and I won't be able to tell her. Staying away is the only way I know to keep my promise. In a few days, maybe, when the pinching goes away, I'll play with Amelia again. But not now.

"How was school?" Mama asks. She takes another swig of coffee and flicks ashes off her cigarette.

"The usual," I say. I stare at the Oreo package, wishing I could turn one of those cookies into a speeding chocolate spaceship and fly away. Maybe the principal already called. Maybe Mama's just teasing me with cookies and milk and saying I should go outside and have some fun. Maybe she wants me to feel all good inside and happy that she didn't take off to be with Patrick, so she can make me feel even worse for getting sent to the principal's office. Maybe she'll stare with her mean eyes, point her finger in my face and say, "I didn't go to Happy Town today, just for you, and you repay me with getting into trouble at school."

"We had a math test and an English test, but that's about it," I say.

"So, how'd you do?" Mama exhales a stream of smoke

173

at my face and rubs her stomach. I think about all the blanks I left on my math test, and the picture I drew in my theme book. When Mama finds out, she'll give me a lecture on how important it is to behave. "I want them to think I raised you right," Mama always says. "No hoodlums in the Giovanni family."

"I did OK," I say. "It was a hard test."

"Did you study last night?" Mama asks. She snuffs out her cigarette, grabs a bag of potatoes out of the broom closet, and dumps a bunch into the sink. She turns the faucet on and scrubs the potatoes, one by one.

"Yes," I say. "I studied." I tried, anyway, I want to say to her, but I can't. Instead, my eyes whisper at the table top: after you left last night, to go see Patrick, Rosa was crying and Winnie fell asleep on my lap and Danny and Joey wouldn't help and Daddy was away at church.

"Well, I'm sure you did just fine," Mama says. She peels the potatoes. "Want to help me?" she asks. She wipes her hands on a dish towel and pulls a pot out of the cupboard. I shake my head no.

The kitchen wall eyes know I lied to Mama. They know I'm gonna get it when she finds out about what really happened today. I lean against the back door and look out the window. The snow's piling on the lawn. Mama doesn't say anything else. Maybe she's tired of talking, or maybe, even if Sister Mary Martha did call, Mama's forgotten all about it.

"I think I'll just take Zoomer for a walk."

"Good idea," Mama says. "You can help me later. There'll still be plenty to do before we eat."

"OK," I say.

"Can I go, too?" Rosa asks. Her eyes beg to tag along.

"No, you stay inside with me. Let Peanut take Zoomer by herself this time."

"Are you still gonna be here when I get home?" I ask.

"Of course, silly. Where the hell else would I be?"

I pull on my boots, grab my coat and hat and scarf and mittens. "Come on, boy," I say to Zoomer. He stretches, then follows me out the door. We plow through the snow and head down the block. At the corner, we cross the street and take the path behind St. Joan's church that leads to the creek. "This is my favorite place in the whole world, Zooms. I don't come to this part of the creek with anyone but you. Not even Amelia."

I scramble down the side of the hill to my favorite spot between two tall, white birch trees. "This is it. Just enough room for me and you," I say. I plop down into the snow and tap the ground. Zoomer slides in beside me.

The secret place is a frozen forest. Bare trees and ice and snow everywhere. The branches are long and strong like Daddy's arms, and the tips are like icy fingers. Sometimes I build a snow fort out of chunks of snow and ice and bits of leaves left over from before all the snow fell, and then I hide inside telling Mama's secrets to the cold walls. Most times I just sit, like now, snuggled between the tree trunks, listening to the wind. Here, I don't need words. I just think of what I want to say, and my thinking flies out of my head into Zoomer's ears.

I lean against the stiff bark and wrap my arm around Zoomer's neck. If God is so smart, why does he let Mama and Daddy fight so much? Grownups are so weird. Sometimes I think Mama wishes she didn't have a family at all. Then she could just run off and be with Patrick forever. She'd be happier. I wish I could be invisible, so when Mama doesn't want to have a family I could vanish and come back only when she wants us around. I wonder if it would be lonesome being invisible. It might be fun. I could spy on Danny and Joey when they stay at home on Friday nights. Or even spy on Sister Saint Joseph in the convent. I wonder if her dead fish eye twitches when she sleeps. Maybe you could be my invisible dog, and then we could go anywhere we wanted to and do anything we liked.

Zoomer barks his agreement. He jumps up and runs around the birch trees, circling me in a ring of paw prints. I brush the snow off my butt and chase after him. I race to the frozen creek. It's my snow-covered Broadway stage. I grab Zoomer's front paws and we slip over the ice. "You be Henry Higgins, Zoomer. I'm Eliza." I sing, "I could have danced all night, I could have danced all night and still have begged for more." We dance round and round and round until our legs can't twirl any more, and we have to flop into a snow bank and catch our breath. "Let's go. I'm getting cold." We take the path back the way we came. A half a block behind St. Joan of Arc Church, we step out of the woods, leaving Mama's secrets, and mine, in our special, private place by the creek.

The only car in the church parking lot is my daddy's Rambler. Zoomer and I make fresh tracks in the snow all the way across the lot up to the front steps of the church. "I've got to light a candle to the Blessed Mother," I say. I shiver, still cold from dancing down by the creek. I pull my jacket collar up and bury my nose in my scarf. Zoomer whines. "I'll sneak you inside with me," I say. "Even though Daddy says animals aren't allowed in church. He says dogs don't have souls, but I don't believe him. We got to be extra quiet, so he doesn't notice us. If we slip in through the front door, we should be OK."

I pull the heavy church doors with two hands, and we go inside. St. Joan's is quiet and dark, except for the row of vigil candles lighting up the back corner, near the baptismal fountain. I stare straight ahead at the bare altar. It's peaceful inside; the quiet soars up to the tall ceiling. The church smells sweet and smoky from the leftover incense. I genuflect, make the sign of the cross, and scoot into the last pew in the back of the church. I unzip my jacket and unwrap my scarf. Further up, three rows from the altar, Daddy kneels with his head bowed and his shoulders hunched forward. I listen hard in the quiet for his voice mumbling the rosary.

I bow my head, close my eyes. The wind rattles against the windows, but inside the church the darkness feels warm all around me. It isn't scary, like at night in our house, when I beg Mama to leave the hall light on. Here, nothing can hurt me. No shouting, no fighting. No principal's office. No twitching dead fish eye. I feel like a baby all snuggled up in Jesus' arms. Maybe that's why Daddy likes to come to church so much.

Zoomer pads down the aisle, stops at my pew and sticks his head in. "Ssh," I whisper. "Don't let Daddy see you." He slinks down low, out of sight, and sits at my feet on the stone floor. I pull off my mittens, tuck them in my pocket and kneel to pray. Dear God, I begin, but no other words come out. I try to ask, just like the nuns told me to. "Ask God, and if you are worthy, He will grant it." I press my hands together and look up at the dying Jesus on the cross behind the altar. If you're watching, God, make it all stop. Maybe you're too busy listening to Daddy. Or maybe you can't waste your time on fallen angels like me. I know you're busy, but please, if you get an extra few minutes, talk to your Mother. She has something to ask you for me.

Out of the corner of my eye, votive candles flicker in front of the altar of Our Lady. I tug Zoomer's ear, and he follows me out of the pew. I tiptoe over to the row of glowing colored-glass cups. The small candles flicker as I reach into my pocket to scrounge a nickel or a dime to pay for my offering. All I pull out is lint and a Kleenex. I grab a wooden taper anyway. "I'll owe you one," I whisper to the stone eyes of the Blessed Virgin. Her cold face warms in the candle flames.

I choose a red candle. Red is for important requests. I kneel and say a quick Hail Mary. Then I add my own prayer, the one I prayed twice before. Once when Mama was pregnant with Rosa and once when she was pregnant with Winnie. Please, Blessed Virgin Mother, tell your son Jesus to take Mama's baby back to heaven where it belongs. Then I remember that this time it's Patrick's baby, and he's a priest, so my prayer has to be even more powerful. The Blessed Mother will listen to a priest before she'll listen me. I'll do anything you want. I promise. I'll give up vanilla wafers. I'll be nice to Danny and Joey. I'll never make trouble again. Promise. Just grant me this. Amen. Zoomer nudges the back of my legs, and I push him away. He rubs against me again, this time on the back of my arm, and I shake my head no and shove my elbow into his side. He barks, a short, deep yelp.

"Who's back there?" Daddy yells. He turns and looks down the aisle. I cover my face with my scarf, grab Zoomer by the collar and hurry toward the door.

"Who's there?" Daddy's voice fills up the church. His footsteps slap the stone floor. I push my whole body against the heavy church doors and rush outside. I tear down the steps; my heart races to keep up with my legs. I chase Zoomer down the block, heading for home. "Regina!" Daddy shouts from the church steps. "Regina! Come back here!"

THIRTEEN

"We're gonna get it for sure this time, Zooms." I run hard, racing as fast as I can to get home. I leap up the front steps, burst onto the porch, close the door and lean against the side wall, trying to catch my breath. "Daddy's gonna ground me, if he doesn't kill me first," I say to Zoomer. "I never should have taken you to church." My neck's all sweaty, and my legs itch. We only got maybe ten minutes before Daddy gets home. Maybe even less time, if he's really as mad as he sounded. I can hear him now, yelling at me about how the church is a sacred house of God and not meant for dogs. "It's a sacrilege!" he'll shout. Then he'll take off his belt and thwack it to hell on the table. I jump, just thinking about it. I gotta pee real bad, from all the running and the excitement and the cold. I squeeze my legs together tight, so I don't wet my pants, and wait for the urge to go away so I can move again and go inside.

Zoomer can't wait that long. He paws at the front door, scratching to go in. Danny opens the door and leans against the door frame. "What ya doing, Peanut?" he teases. "Waiting for a special invitation?"

"Shut up, pig," I sass. "I was just getting ready to turn the knob and let Zoomer in myself."

179

I uncross my legs and push my way through the door, poking his stomach with my elbow.

"Knock it off, brat," Danny warns.

I tilt my head up like the fashion models in those magazines at the beauty parlor. Nothing can touch them. I hurry inside past Danny and almost trip over Joey, sprawled in front of the TV like a wrinkled old rug. From the corner of my eye, I see Mama in the corner, talking on the phone.

"Uh huh. Yes. I see," Mama's says. Her voice is sharp like broken ice. "I'll be sure to talk to her, Sister. No, I can't imagine why she'd do that. Yes, uh huh. Thank you for calling."

I squeeze my eyes shut, bite my bottom lip and make a beeline for the staircase. I still gotta pee real bad, and I can hardly hold it another second. If I don't hurry I'm gonna leak all over the living-room rug.

"Regina!"

Mama's voice slaps the air. My right foot plops hard on the bottom step, and I freeze.

"Come back here right this instant, young lady."

Hail, Mary, full of grace. I turn, slowly, and face Mama.

"Where have you been, Regina?"

She waves her arms at the air, screaming at me with her mad eyes.

"I took Zoomer for a walk. Just like I said I was gonna do," I stammer.

Danny and Joey make faces at me and mimic Mama from behind her back. I want to slap their ugly mugs.

"I expected you back an hour ago, young lady. Now get in the kitchen and set the table. If you don't start minding me, you're gonna be in big trouble, Regina. I've had enough." Mama's head's high in the air, and her shoulders are straight and in place. She means business.

"I'm sorry, Mama. I promise. I'll be better. I promise."
My head shrinks into my shoulders. I step back, closer to
the wall, trying to dodge her scolding.

"Get a move on it!" Mama shouts. She points to the
kitchen.

"OK, OK," I say.

That had to be Sister on the phone. Mama knows
about the mess I got myself into. She's whirling mad. I
squeeze my bladder and march into the kitchen. She'd
think I was only trying to get out of helping her if I told
her I had to go to the bathroom right now. I promise
myself I can go, right after I set the table.

I don't even stop to take my coat and boots off. I pull
on an apron, wrap the strings around the middle of my
jacket, then I grab the supper dishes out of the cupboard.
I walk around the table, putting each plate in its right
spot, extra careful not to set the dishes down too hard.
Mama doesn't like it when the plates scrape against the
Formica. It feels like I'm in some sort of crazy dream, and
I can't shake myself awake. My fingertips are numb. I go
through the motions: plates, silverware, napkins, all set
in order. Mama's shouting echoes in my head. Every time
I move, it burns between my legs. Zoomer tries to help
me. He rubs against my thighs and whines, but I shoo
him away. I don't have time for him. I've got to do what I
got to do, and be done with it.

"When you're done setting the table, I want you to
heat up the green beans."

Mama's calmer now, but she doesn't look at me when
she talks. She's still upset. The numbness that started in
my fingertips creeps up my arms, down my legs, around
my bladder. It squeezes into my bones and skin and hair.
It gets stuck in the corner of my eyes; they're empty and
dry.

"Mama, I'm hungry," Rosa says. She tugs the edge of

Mama's shirt. Mama pats her head, touches the tip of her nose with her finger. "Supper will be ready in a bit, honey." Her voice is sweet and thick. "Go play upstairs with Winnie. I'll call you when it's time to eat."

I watch Rosa leave the kitchen and think how lucky she is that's she still little. She can't get into too much trouble.

I put the last plate in its right spot and shove my hand between my legs to hold my pee in. I hop to the counter and scrounge in the cupboard for two cans of string beans. I open them, dump the beans into a sauce-pan and put the pan on the burner. I turn on the gas and look at Mama.

"Can I do anything else for you, Mama?" I try to smile. My lips tingle.

"You can tell me why you got yourself into a mess at school today."

Mama points her eyes at a chair. She wants me to sit down. I don't fight her. It's useless. At least it's finally out in the open. Sooner or later, I'd have to face the facts and take my punishment. I push my butt onto the kitchen chair, tuck my hands between my legs and stare at my boots.

"Regina, I know what you did. I just want to know why you did it."

Mama's eyes droop. The wrinkles around her mouth fall into a frown. I unfasten the top button of my coat, stalling for time.

"Well," I start to say, then I stop. It sounds so funny to say it out loud. I can't explain why I drew a picture of a pregnant dancer in my theme notebook. I wiggle around in my chair and push my hand tighter into my crotch.

"Mama," I say. "I didn't tell, honest."

Mama scrunches her lips together, and she looks at

me like I've got ten eyes and purple hair. "What in the hell are you talking about?"

"You know. The secret. I didn't tell about the baby," I whisper, leaning closer to her face.

She pulls back. My words slap her face. She turns away, lights a cigarette, then stares at me. "Don't you be twisting the truth, Regina. Sister was real mad at what you did. Don't be changing the subject, trying to get away with it, not own up to how bad you were. I want to know what all this nonsense is about. And I want to know now."

She leans in closer. I feel her breath on my cheek. I close my eyes and try to think. I dig through layers and layers, trying to find the right answer. All I can concentrate on is not wetting my pants.

"Goddamn it. Goddamn it." Mama slaps her hand on the table top. "Answer me."

I open my mouth, but nothing comes out. My tongue won't cooperate. There's no way to convince her. She can't see the most important part. I kept our secret. I did my part. Why isn't she relieved? I stare at the linoleum floor, trying to pull the right words out of my brain.

"I want an explanation, Regina," Mama insists. "Look at me when I talk to you, young lady."

Her eyes are as big as a mouth; she's gonna swallow me up.

"This misbehaving at school is getting to be a regular thing with you. It's time you shaped up. I won't tolerate this kind of behavior." She takes a long drag off her cigarette and smoke charges out of her mouth. "This better be the last time, young lady. Or else you'll be grounded for a month. No Amelia. No walks with Zoomer. Nothing. Understand?"

"Yes, Mama."

I'm sorry I got her so upset, but I'm mad, too. She

doesn't even say one word of thanks for me not telling. I could have told, just to save my own butt. That should count for something.

"Good girl." Mama pats the top of my head. Her hand rests on my cheek. My whole face tingles now. Little by little, the numbness goes away. I forget how mad I am at her.

"I wanna be a good girl, Mama."

She's not listening. She walks away, goes to the window, and stares at the dark sky. "It's gonna snow again tonight," she says.

"Mama," I call. "Can I be excused? I gotta go to the bathroom. Mama." My voice rushes at her. "Mama."

She's gone. Just like that. Staring at the snow as if it's the face of God. I steady myself on the edge of my chair, stand up slowly and walk toward the stove. The green beans are boiling on the burner. I stir them and turn the gas down. Danny shuffles into the kitchen and sidles up to me. "So, did you get a good talkin' to?"

I glare at him waving a wooden spoon in my fist. "Get lost," I snap.

He steals a green bean from the pan and circles around the table glancing at Mama. She's still staring out the window.

"What's with Ma?" he asks.

"Go get Joey and wash up. Supper will be ready in five minutes," I say, ignoring his question. I do little hops in front of the stove trying to hold in my pee.

"Dad's not even home yet, you little fart. Since when are you the boss around here?" Danny sasses.

Zoomer growls from across the kitchen. "Shut up, you dumb dog."

"Leave him alone," I holler. "And don't touch these beans. I gotta go pee. I'll be right back." I reach under my coat and yank my pants high and tight between my crotch and hop toward the living room. The front door opens and slams shut. I drop the wooden spoon. It bounces and lands near my feet. Zoomer fetches it.

"Regina!" Daddy yells. He's coming toward the kitchen.

"What the hell did you do today to get them both mad at you?" Danny smirks. He looks pleased and worried at the same time.

I eye the back door. I'm three full steps from freedom. I can open the door, race to Amelia's house and beg to be let in. But what will I say? I'll look weird if I show up at her door with an apron over my winter coat and my bladder ready to burst. I look at Zoomer, then step back against the stove.

"There you are."

Daddy stands right in front of me. The top of my head barely reaches his chest. His big face throws a shadow over my eyes. He unbuckles his belt. The leather swooshes through the cloth loops.

"How many times have I told you never to bring that dog to church? It's a sacrilege. I won't have my children disrespecting God."

He folds the belt twice in his hands and slaps at the air. He clips the edge of the stove with a solid whack. My eyes fall into my face. I lean into the burner knob. It bites into my back.

"Mama!" I cry. A stream of pee rushes down my pant leg, into my boots, onto the floor.

"For crying out loud. Look what you've done now," Daddy snaps. He points at the puddle at my feet. "That's disgusting." He slaps his belt against the back of a kitchen chair. It clanks to the linoleum.

I cover my mouth with my hands, hide my eyes behind my palms, like Filaberta. My pants stick to the inside of my thigh, wet and clammy. I see Danny out of

185

the corner of my eye. He's hiding out of Daddy's view, back between the refrigerator and the side door. He's got a funny look on his face. At first I think he's laughing at me for peeing on the floor, but he's not smiling. He looks like he's gonna throw up. He squints and screws up his face. "Mama!" I yell, but she's still lost in the window.

Daddy comes at me, waving his belt in his big hand. Zoomer jumps at him and growls. He swings around and catches Zoomer's hind legs, sending him flying across the kitchen floor. Zoomer yelps, and Danny bolts from his corner. He rushes at Daddy. "Cut it out, Dad."

"Get out of the way, or I'll give it to you, too." Daddy doesn't raise his voice. He doesn't need to; when he gets this angry, it fills the room even when he whispers. He throws the belt strap across Danny's arm. The slap stings my ear. "Ow! Shit!" Danny yells.

"Mama!" I holler louder. I step over my puddle of pee and shake her shoulder. She twitches, and pushes my hands away.

"What? What is it, Peanut?" Her voice is dreamlike.

"Goddamn asshole, leave us alone!" Danny shouts.

"Mama, please," I beg. She slowly looks around at Danny and Daddy. She raises her hand and her voice.

"Stop it, Paulie. Leave my son alone," she demands.

She reaches for Danny and swoops him into her long arms. I hide behind her and press my face into her back. I glue my hands to her stomach. I squeeze hard against her middle, trying to squash the tiny dot of baby growing inside her. Zoomer whimpers in the corner by the back door.

"Get out of my way, Marie. I've had enough of this disrespect."

I'm gonna burst into a million flaming-hot cells. I steady myself, holding onto Mama's waist.

"For Christ's sake, Paulie!" Mama shouts. "Lay off it."

She snaps at Daddy like she's gonna bite his nose off. "Cool down a bit. What could be so god-awful bad as to make you come in here flying off the handle like a mad man, frightening my children?"

Danny squirms out of her arms and steps back, behind the kitchen table, away from Daddy. His eyes dart around the room. He's looking for something to smash. Daddy paces between the stove and the sink. "Regina brought Zoomer into church this afternoon," he complains.

"Is that it?" Mama asks. "That's what got you so riled up?"

"It ain't right, Marie," he snorts. "She should know better than to do that. And it ain't the first time."

I loosen my arms from Mama's waist and grab hold of the hem of her blouse.

"I didn't mean anything by taking Zoomer into church. We were just praying, honest. We were talking to the Blessed Virgin Mother. Honest." My wet pants stick to my butt. I reach behind and pull the soaked cloth away from my skin. Mama pulls away from me and walks over to the stove.

"I've got dinner to finish up here now, Paulie. Go on, get out of my kitchen," Mama says, pushing at the air.

"Lay off it, Marie. I ain't one of your babies or your weak-kneed boyfriend. Don't tell me how to handle my children."

"Oh, don't give me any grief, Paulie. You've said your piece. Now cool that hot head of yours. Go on, get out of here. I'll talk to Regina. Now get."

The kitchen is quieter now. Zoomer chews on the wooden spoon. Danny pulls some ice cubes out of the freezer and rubs the red marks on his arm. Daddy stares at the kitchen sink a few minutes, mumbling something under his breath. He swings around and stares straight at me. "You listen to me good. If I ever catch that dog in the Lord's house again, there'll be hell to pay. Understand?"

"Yes, Daddy," I say. My voice catches in the back of my throat.

Daddy stares me down until he breaks my staring. "Clean up that piss before we eat supper," he orders. He re-buckles his belt and leaves the room.

"What the hell is he talking about?" Mama asks.

I grab a handful of paper towels and bend over to dab up my pee.

"Put that damn dog outside! I won't have him messing up my kitchen floor!" Mama hollers. "He should know better than to pee inside. What the hell's wrong with him anyway?"

I shoot a glance at Danny, then quickly look away.

"Daniel, let that damn dog out."

I don't want Zoomer to have to take the blame for my accident, but I can't tell Mama it was me, not him. I swallow the truth. I'll make it up to you later, my eyes promise. I'm sorry. I'm sorry. Danny opens the kitchen door and scoots Zoomer outside.

"Get the vinegar and wipe away that smell," Mama orders. "Then go get your sisters and wash up for dinner. Supper will be ready in a few minutes. And Peanut, take off that apron. And your coat and boots, too. You look foolish, child."

I grab the vinegar, clean up the smell, then head for the staircase. I take two steps at a time. I have to get out of my wet pants.

"Rosa, Winnie!" I yell all the way upstairs. The girls are playing Barbie dolls in the bedroom, on the floor by the closet. "Go wash up, dinner's ready."

"OK, OK, Peanut. Quit hollering," Rosa says.

I untie the apron strings, take off my coat, and pull

off my boots. I peel off my wet slacks and my dirty underpants. I wad them in a bundle and toss them in the laun-
dry basket in the corner. I grab some dry underwear and
a pair of jeans and a turtleneck. It feels good to be warm
and dry again.

Zoomer barks in the yard outside. I tuck in my shirt,
zip up my pants, walk over to the window and press my
face to the cold glass. He runs along the side yard up to
the door, down the sidewalk and back again. His tail flips
this way and that. He's mad and cold, and I feel bad for
letting him take the blame. Maybe Danny's downstairs
right now, telling Mama it was really me who wet all over
her kitchen floor. I can't ever be sure what he'll do. I
didn't expect him to stick up for me and Zoomer in the
first place. I wonder what he wants.

"We're ready, Peanut," Rosa calls from the hallway.

"Let's go eat," I say, with a pretend smile.

***

All through supper, I stare at my plate. I poke my
mashed potatoes with my fork. "More gravy?" Mama
asks. I shake my head no and push my fork deeper into
the lumpy mess. I'm not hungry, and I don't want to sit at
the table until everyone else is finished. It's one of
Mama's rules. No one leaves the table until everyone is
done. It could be a while. Danny and Joey take huge
helpings of potatoes, green beans and meatloaf. Rosa
picks at her supper. Winnie refuses everything but
graham crackers and apple juice. Only Daddy eats fast.
His eyes are half closed. He's in some other world, telling
God how awful I am to take Zoomer into church. Mama
leans her elbows on the tabletop. She folds her hands in
front of her tired face. She doesn't eat at all.

I think about the baby growing inside her, and I
wonder where she will sit after she's born. There's barely

room enough for everyone as it is. First there was Rosa to fit in, then Winnie. Now there's gonna be one more. When it's still little, we can put her in Winnie's highchair, right between me and Mama, but after she grows up, she'll need her own place at the table. It's pretty crowded already. Mama will make me sit in the other room. Or maybe she'll make Danny eat at the counter. Maybe I won't have to worry. Maybe the Blessed Virgin Mother will listen to my prayers this time. It died being born once, it could happen again.

"So how was school today, Peanut?" Danny says. His mouth is full of mashed potatoes and meatloaf.

I stare at him with mean eyes. I don't want Mama to yell at me again in front of everybody.

"Nothing special," I say. "We had some tests, that's all." I grab my glass and swallow down the shiver in my voice. I stare at the bowl of potatoes in the center of the table.

"My day was crummy," Joey says. "Social Studies was a total waste of time. And English was a real bore. Why couldn't gym class be four hours long?"

"Yeah, old man Anderson's a real drip," Danny agrees. "I used to fall asleep in his class, Joey."

"The worst is fart-face Flynn, my study hall monitor. A real loser if there ever was one." Joey snorts and reaches for more meatloaf.

"Watch your language, young man," Daddy snaps. In an instant, he's gone back to talking with God in his invisible hiding place of quiet. I say a silent prayer, thankful for Joey's chatter, and make plans for later. After supper's over and I do the dishes, I'm gonna take Zoomer upstairs and hide in the back of my closet; that's if he still wants to, after all the trouble I caused him.

"I hear you got sent to the principal's office today,"

Danny blurts out. "What'd ya do, kick Sister Saint Joseph?"

I hate him. He's worse than Daddy and Mama and Patrick all rolled into one. He doesn't let up.

"Mind your own business, Daniel," Mama snaps.

I smile to myself, glad that Mama didn't let this one get past her. Just when I'm feeling good about Danny getting yelled at, Mama turns to me and says, "This better be the last time, young lady. Or else you'll be grounded for a month."

"Ooh. Then she'll have to stay home with us on Fridays," Joey snickers. "That'll make her real mad."

"Pipe down, Joseph," Mama orders. "Nobody asked for your two cents worth."

A stinging marches across my eyelids. I grab my napkin, wipe away the wetness and bite my bottom lip until I taste blood. I won't cry. I won't. I hide my chin under the edge of my turtleneck.

"Mama, may I be excused?"

"No, Regina. Not until everyone is done."

"What's for dessert?" Danny asks. He's being a real creep tonight. He'll eat dessert real slow, knowing I can't stand to sit at the table one minute longer. He wants to make me cry. But I won't let him.

"No dessert tonight," Mama says. "This isn't a goddamn restaurant."

I smirk at Danny, satisfied. The kitchen clock ticks slowly. I watch its hands inch closer to the nine. Five forty-five. We should be done eating by six. Fifteen more minutes. The wait drags on. The clock's hands move toward the ten. Zoomer scratches the back door wanting to be let in. The clock's hands nudge closer to the eleven. Five more minutes. I stare at the second hand sweeping over the clock's face. Zoomer barks. He's been outside nearly an hour. At two minutes to six Mama says, "OK, Danny, let the dog in and feed him."

"Can I feed Zoomer tonight?" I ask.

"Why not?" Mama cocks her head at Danny, who's already let Zoomer inside. "In fact, Daniel," she continues, "Why don't you help me with dishes tonight?"

"I ain't doing that sissy stuff, Ma," Danny says.

"It'll do you some good. Get you ready for when you go to college and have to take care of yourself."

"No, Ma." Danny shakes his head.

"Don't you 'no, Ma', me, young man," she warns. She points her finger at his face. "Joey, you help him. Maybe its time the females in this household got a little break."

"I got homework to do, Ma," Joey insists.

"It can wait," Mama says.

"Dad," both boys plead. But Daddy's already heading out of the kitchen with his Catholic Digest tucked under his arm. He waves them away with the back of his hand. "Go on, do as your mother says."

"I don't want none of your bellyaching, boys." It's Mama's final order. "The more time you waste complaining, the longer it'll take you to get it over and done with."

Mama gets up slowly, wipes Winnie's hands and face and takes her out of her high chair.

"Can I go watch TV now, Mama?" Rosa asks.

"Sure, honey. But take Winnie with you."

I fill Zoomer's bowl. "Here you go, boy," I say. I pat his head. I bend over closer to his ear and whisper, "I'm sorry. I won't ever do it again, I promise." He licks my nose and rubs his face against mine. "After you're done eating, we'll go upstairs. Just you and me."

The boys clear the table and scrape the plates into the garbage can. "You little creep, Peanut. You think after what I did for you today, you'd have the decency to repay me," Danny snaps.

"You always get your way, brat." Joey complains.

I stick my tongue out at them and raid the cupboard. I sneak a handful of vanilla wafers into the pocket of my jeans.

"Hope the dish soap doesn't ruin your delicate hands," I tease as I slip into the living room.

Mama's lounging on the couch, watching TV. Rosa and Winnie are snuggled up next to her. "I'm gonna go upstairs and do my homework," I say. She nods. "I want you to do better in school, Regina. I don't need anything more to worry about."

"Yes, Mama," I say, lowering my eyes.

I twirl around and head for the steps.

"Regina," she calls.

Almost got away. I turn toward her. "Yeah?"

"You forgot your book bag."

"Oh, yeah. OK. Thanks, Mama."

I reach over the railing, grab hold of the handle and hoist the bag up to my waist. "See you later." I smile, then disappear up the stairs. In my room, I throw my unopened book bag onto the bed and flop down beside it. I close my eyes and feel for the vanilla wafers in my pocket. My head aches.

I lay still and listen to the TV downstairs. Every once in a while Mama laughs, and I try to imagine her face perfectly calm. I turn over on my stomach and bury my head into my pillow. My mouth opens up and everything spills out. I bite my pillow to stop the noise. Something as big as our house, as strong as the trees, as wide as the sky rushes through me. When it finally lets me go, I wipe my nose and eyes on the bedspread.

Zoomer nudges the bedroom door open with his nose. He comes over and lays his head next to my face. His brown eyes are forgiving. I hoist myself up and head for the closet. "Come on, boy," I whisper. "In here."

He follows me into the small dark space and sits between the closet wall and my left side. I swing my arm around his neck and pull him closer. I smell his warm smell. With my free hand I pull two vanilla wafers out of my pocket. I give one to Zoomer and shove the other one into my mouth. I bite down hard, shut my jaw tight and suck on the sweet cookie. I close my eyes, lean back into the hanging hems and pant legs until the vanilla wafer melts away, and all that's left is my tongue full of spit and cookie crumbs.

Fourteen

Riding in the back seat with Rosa is not my idea of fun, but I don't complain today. Mama's too cranky; practically anything sets her off. If I start crabbing about how Rosa's rubbing the bottom of her boots against my coat or how she's hogging all the room, I'll just get myself in trouble. Mama's been crying all day, and her eyes are puffy red pillows. I guess that's what happens when you're gonna have a baby. Everything makes you sad. Mama's got a hanky in her right hand, and she keeps dabbing at her eyes and wiping her nose while she's driving. This visit with Patrick is real important. Mama says she's got to talk with him about what to do, so I got to be extra good and be sure to keep Rosa and Winnie occupied, so she can hear herself think. I remember my promise to myself to love Mama with my whole heart, no matter what, so I agree. I figure if I keep everything peaceful while she drives to Cayuga today, that's a good start.

I wonder what Patrick thinks about the baby. He'll probably want to rush off to Happy Town tonight, like he wanted to do in September. I hope Mama doesn't go crazy and say yes. It's been a hard enough week already. I managed to make both Mama and Daddy fly off in a hollering fit. It must be a new record.

I've been watching and noticing and making sure I stay out of Mama's way, ever since. I could draw the way she breathes, the way her eyelashes blink, the way the color of her eyes change when she gets sad, then mad, then worried. I put on my best, good-baby soul like it's a fancy party dress, and I smiled and behaved. I've been polite and helpful. All week long. I did my homework, picked up my room, washed the dishes without complaining. I even watched Rosa and Winnie when she had one of her splitting headaches and had to lie down and rest. I hope Patrick's in a good mood so he can help cheer her up tonight. I could use a rest.

We pull into Smiley's parking lot, right behind Patrick's car. He honks and waves when he sees us. Now Mama's smiling a little, and a tiny sliver of tooth pokes through her cherry-red lips. Maybe it's a good sign, I'm not sure yet. It's better to be ready for the worst. I grab the door handle and flip it open. The cold air rushes at me. I grind my teeth and step out of the car. Mama hurries over to Patrick. Her wet hanky hangs out of her coat pocket and waves at me in the chilly breeze.

Patrick says, "Hello, honey." He's so close to Mama that his words cover her face. Mama wraps her arms around him real tight, and she starts to cry again. "Not here, not now," Patrick says. "Let's talk inside." He hands Mama his fancy handkerchief with the initials and holds onto her arm. "Everything will be OK, Marie. Don't worry." Then he turns to me and the girls. We've been waiting, patiently, in a line, with our backs against the cold fenders of our Daddy's car. "Let's get some hot chocolate, OK kids?"

Winnie runs up to Patrick, reaching for his free hand. Me and Rosa link arms and follow her. All five of us walk across the parking lot to the restaurant door without saying a word. I play a game with the traffic passing in the street. I count the blue cars that go by. One, two, three, four, five. One for each of us kids, Danny and Joey, the girls and me. Blue car number six cruises past, but I don't count it. The lost baby's not one of us. The cold makes my eyes water. When we get into the cafe, I wipe away the wet that snuck out without my permission.

I fill my insides with warm, greasy air. I wish I could bring Amelia to Smiley's sometime. I think she'd like the shiny chrome malt machine, the tube lights that look like long glowing tunnels, Betty's friendly smile. Patrick's still got his arm around Mama's shoulder. He picks out a booth and we follow him, one by one, like marching soldiers. I help Rosa and Winnie pull off their hats and coats and settle in.

"Three cocoas and two hot coffees, Betty," Patrick calls to the waitress.

"Coming right up," she calls back.

I slide across the booth, and Rosa and Winnie move in next to me. Mama sits right across from us. She scrounges in her pocketbook and pulls out a compact. She touches her swollen eyes with the soft, powdery pad. She clicks the compact shut and blows her nose in Patrick's handkerchief. I unbutton my coat and pull the bulky sleeves off my arms. Patrick settles in next to Mama. He reaches for her hands and wraps his fingers around hers. I shove my fingers into my pants pocket and try to warm the icy, numb tips. I shiver and sit back in the booth waiting for Betty to bring the cocoa.

Mama starts to cry again. I arrange the forks and knives on the table top. I pull some napkins out of the holder and push a couple toward Mama. She brushes her fingertips over the edges like she's gonna take them, but she changes her mind and uses Patrick's fancy handkerchief instead. Her tears mix with the powder she put on, and her makeup looks like pancake batter splattered on her cheeks. Her mouth is a red line of sadness, running like a squirt of syrup across her pale face.

It hurts to look at her. I stare at the clean, white paper napkins and think about snow and Christmas. Maybe this year I'll get a sled and Zoomer and Amelia and me can spend a whole Saturday afternoon at the big hill over by the school. I think about Christmas ribbon candy and Santa Claus. I don't believe in him anymore, but I like his kind eyes. Daddy says Christmas is really about the baby Jesus being born. I wonder if Mary cried as hard as Mama when she found out she was pregnant. I scrunch up the napkins and toss them into the ashtray.

"Mama, Mama," Winnie says. She fidgets at the end of the booth. She's trying to snatch some of Mama's attention. She doesn't know it's useless. When Mama's in one of her moods, nothing can drag her back. Patrick puts one hand on Mama's shoulder and stretches his other hand toward Winnie, touching her arm. I want to push his hand away, tell him I'm supposed to take care of my sisters, tell him to pay attention to Mama for awhile. That's his job, now that we're here. I can handle the rest. I reach over Rosa and grab Winnie's hand.

"Hey Winnie, look," I say, pointing across the restaurant. "There's that funny family again." I nod at the cat family in the booth near the window. They're wearing their funny glasses, same as always. "Don't they look like a bunch of kitty cats?" I move closer to my sisters and lean in front of their faces so they can't see Mama and Patrick any more. Winnie giggles a little and squeezes my hand. Rosa's eyes get real wide. "Meow," I tease. I'm just about to launch into a big purrrrr when Betty arrives at the table with our hot chocolate. The girls dive into the fancy swirl of whipped cream topping.

"Drink your cocoa, girls," I say, "but be careful, it's hot." I'm still working on keeping their attention. I mix the cream topping into my hot cocoa, then lick the spoon. "Good stuff, huh?" I say, nudging Rosa.

"Yeah," she agrees.

"Hey, Winnie, you want my cookie?" I ask, offering the triangle wafer that comes with the cocoa.

Winnie nods, and Rosa pouts, "I want it."

"I'll give you my extra pickles when I get my burger, OK?" I say, trying to keep her from whining and bugging Mama.

"OK," Rosa says.

It works. I try to find other ways to keep the girls' attention until Mama and Patrick finish their discussion. "Rosa tell Winnie that story Mrs. Infante taught you last week in school. The one about the little red hen and growing the wheat and making the bread." While Rosa talks, I sip my hot chocolate and eavesdrop on Mama and Patrick.

"I'm scared," Mama says. Her voice is tight. She lights a cigarette. The glowing end shakes between her nervous fingers.

"Are you sure you're pregnant, Marie?" Patrick asks. He tosses the wadded napkins out of the ashtray and puts it next to Mama.

"Of course I'm sure. I'm late. I've been through this enough times to know," Mama snaps. She sucks on the end of her Chesterfield.

"It'll be OK," Patrick says. He pats her hand and tries to look calm. He sips his coffee and sets the cup carefully back into the small ring of the saucer.

"What are we gonna do? I can't have this baby." Mama sucks in a sob and a breath of air. She flicks the ashes off her cigarette.

I don't understand grownups. Mama. Patrick. Even Daddy. They're like mixed up pieces of a jigsaw puzzle. I try and try to shove the edges together, but they buckle and bulge. And I don't understand all this stuff about babies; how they get born. If they come from God, maybe He could just decide one day to call them back home again. "Come on in, supper's ready," He'd say, and the baby soul would fly from its mother's warm belly back into the open gates of heaven, right up to the dinner table. Just as easy as that. Is that what Mama means when she says, "I can't have this baby"? Maybe she hears God ringing the dinner bell. I hope so. I hide a small smile under a mustache of whipping cream.

"It'll work out," Patrick says. His voice is toasty warm.

"What if Paulie figures it out?" Mama says. She starts to sniffle again. She sets her cigarette in the ashtray and leans into Patrick's shoulder.

"It means we'll just have to go sooner than we planned," Patrick says. "This time won't be like before. We should have left years ago, before it got so out of hand. I'm sorry I ever let you talk me out of it."

Patrick's eyes are watery. He swallows hard. I take a big gulp of my hot chocolate and burn the tip of my tongue. I reach for my water. My tongue feels raw.

"Don't get me started on that one, Patrick. You know as well as I that the first time we weren't in any position to get away. You were still in Pisa." Mama blows her nose hard on the embroidered "P" part of Patrick's handkerchief.

"Look, Marie, we did what we had to do back then. Now it's different. When Paulie finds out you're pregnant, he'll know it isn't his. He'll probably throw you out of the house anyway. It's time we left."

Mama pulls back from Patrick's arm and wipes her nose. She huffs like she's out of breath. "There's something I've got to tell you. It's about Paulie."

She lays her hands flat on the table and stares across the booth at me. I pretend I haven't been listening, but she knows better. Mama's eyes are calm and furious at the same time. My backbone tingles. I sit up straight and tall and return her stare with a serious one of my own.

"Honey, take your sisters to the bathroom."

I stop my urge to say, "But, I don't have to pee." All these years I realize I haven't been paying as careful attention to Mama and Patrick's conversations as I should have. There's a secret inside all the other secrets. I can tell by the way Mama holds her head in that stiff-necked way like she's crazy full of pain, and it won't go away. The burning on the tip of my tongue is nothing compared to the burning behind my eyes. I'm mad that after all these years of proving I could keep my mouth shut, she didn't trust me with some important detail. I bite my lip thinking about what she could have left out, but I come up empty.

"Peanut," Mama says. "I'm not gonna tell you again. Now take your sisters to the bathroom."

Her eyes mean business. I don't cross her this time. I push into Rosa's shoulder. "Come on, let's go."

"I don't have to pee," Rosa complains.

"Come on, I mean it," I say.

I nudge Rosa over the seat and poke at Winnie to hurry up, too. As we walk away I sneak a peek back over my shoulder at Mama and Patrick. Mama's resting her head in her hands; Patrick's hands are flying through the air. I'd hurry back there and lap up every word if it weren't for Mama's heavy eyes and Patrick's angry mouth going a mile a minute.

When we get to the bathroom I shove the girls into a stall. "But I don't gotta go," Rosa insists. "Try anyway," I order. "Winnie, go first." After Winnie pees, I wipe her with a wad of toilet paper. "You're next," I say to Rosa. When she finishes, I stall for more time. "My turn," I say. I pull down my pants and sit on the toilet seat, still warm from Rosa's butt. "Peanut, why is Mama crying?" Rosa asks. I pretend I don't hear her and finish wiping myself. I get up slow and pull the chrome lever on the toilet, like I'm handling some treasure and I've got to be real careful. "We gotta wash our hands now," I say.

"But you didn't answer me," Rosa insists.

"She's having a baby and she's scared." I figure if I tell only part of the secret Mama won't be mad. They'll find out soon enough. "But you can't tell anybody, not until Mama says it's OK to tell. Understand?" Rosa nods.

"Is she having it tonight?" Rosa asks.

"No. It takes a while," I explain. "She's having it later."

"When?"

"I don't know. And stop asking so many questions. Just wash your hands so we can get back to the booth. Dinner's probably there already."

Winnie whines as I push her hands under the luke-warm water.

"Be sure to use soap," I warn Rosa. "And don't get your sweater wet."

I check my wrist watch. Only five minutes have gone by. I wonder if that's enough time for Mama and Patrick to finish fighting. I can't stall these kids any longer. I wash my hands and look in the mirror. I've got dark circles under my eyes, and my braid is coming loose. I think of Amelia's summery green eyes, and I wish I was home right now, planning a Broadway show with her.

"We're done," Rosa says.

I line my sisters up and inspect their fingers and hands, first palm side up then palm side down. "OK, looks good," I say, then add, "Follow me back to the booth. And stay close, so the cat family doesn't get you. Meow," I tease.

The girls giggle. I take their hands, one on each side of me, and we cross the restaurant and head back to the booth. A few feet from our table I hear Patrick's loud whisper. "I don't understand how you could do something like that. Doesn't what we have mean anything to you?" He has big worry lines under his eyes. I think of how I looked in the bathroom mirror.

"I did it for us, Patrick," Mama says. "To buy us some time." She sounds like Danny does when he's trying to convince Mama that he shouldn't be grounded. "And I have to tell him. He'll figure it out. It's the only way. Who knows when we'll be ready to leave? I can't hide being pregnant, goddamnit."

"We're back," I say, real loud. Mama's lips tighten, and Patrick stares out the window. He's got circles of sweat under his arms.

"We'll finish this later," he snaps.

Their faces remind me of the scarecrow on the Wizard of Oz, stranded at the crossroads, his eyes blown one way, his feet and hands and heart every which way. If I were the powerful wizard, I could piece them back together.

I push my sisters back into the booth. I press against Rosa, trying to get her to move faster. "Quit it," she says, slapping at me with the back of her hand. Betty comes over and clears our cocoa cups. She comes back a few minutes later and brings french fries, burgers and colas. Rosa and Winnie slurp their sodas. They gulp down their burgers. I lay three dill pickle slices on Rosa's plate. She smiles at me.

I pat her knee then take a bite of my hamburger. I chew like a wild thing while my mind races. Patrick isn't doing his job. Mama's not happy. She looks worse than she did at home. The baby should make them happy. Isn't that what they both want? Now we can go to Happy Town. A million butterflies fly around inside me. Patrick still looks mad, and Mama looks guilty. Say something.

Please say something. Patrick, make Mama laugh. Make her eyes sing. Dear Holy Mother of God, tell me what I can do to help make it all better.

"You know," Patrick finally says. He pokes at a french fry, then bites it between his even teeth. He sounds better now, almost like his old self. The butterfly wings quiet down inside me. They wait to hear what he's gonna say next.

"I called my buddy Jack, in Madison, the other day. Things are looking good there. Plenty of jobs. Housing's reasonable. He has a few names for me and a place to stay until we find our own house."

Mama squints. Her eyelids are swollen tunnels. "You mean that friend of yours from seminary?"

"That's right. He's married now. Has a kid. He wanted to know when we were coming." Patrick bites into his burger. He chews hard and swallows. I watch the lump of food slide down his throat.

"What did you tell him?" Mama asks. She twists her mouth.

"I told him, soon. We'd be coming soon. He knows about the baby."

I stab at my hamburger with my fork. I imagine the lost baby's eyes. I gouge out pieces of meat and fling them onto the tabletop.

"Peanut, stop playing with your food," Patrick orders.

I don't even look at him. I shift my eyes to Mama to see if she'll make me obey. I want to tell him to shut up. I want to tell him I only listen to Mama and Daddy. He doesn't count.

"Peanut, do as he says," Mama says.

I stab my hamburger one more time then pull the fork out and lay it by my plate. I dig my shoulder blades into the booth and cross my arms over my chest.

"How far away is Happy Town, Mama?"

Maybe we should just leave tonight. Maybe it's better that way. Pack it all up, grab some sandwiches to go, and be done with it. All this bellyaching about his buddy Jack. And Mama never making up her mind once and for all. If Happy Town isn't too far, maybe I could still play with Amelia once in a while or visit Daddy and the boys. If it isn't too far, maybe things won't be that bad. I could come back for Zoomer. Zoomer has to come. He has to.

"It's a long way. About a thousand miles," Patrick answers.

"Is Happy Town as far away as the coffee shop?" Rosa asks.

"No, honey. A lot farther." Patrick smiles. "It's a big city, and it has a big lake for you to swim in."

I've never seen a real city. Cayuga's as big a town as I've ever been in, and I don't care for its smelly traffic, its ugly neon signs. All that concrete is as cold as the creek in winter and nowhere near as pretty. It reminds me of Patrick and how set he is on getting Mama and us to leave Pisa for some place we don't even know. It makes me shiver. Even though he's made it all sound so fancy and magical. Lollipops and cotton candy. Like a carnival or the county fair. Full of adventure and rides that make your heart twirl. No place can be that pretty. Not even a place called Happy Town.

"Can I still go to my school?" Rosa asks.

I imagine a big brick school building with a bright neon sign shouting, "Happy Town Elementary School."

"No, stupid. You can't!" My voice explodes. The cat family turns their eyeglasses to stare at us. Betty looks up from the cash register.

"Peanut, pipe down," Mama scolds.

I drop my eyes and close my mouth. I didn't mean it. The naughty half of my twin soul sometimes sneaks out and screams its ugly head off. If I could, I'd cut its tongue out, shove the red, hot nagging thing into the nearest wastebasket. I look out the window. Blue light from the coffee shop's neon "eat" sign blinks in the dark. I try to coax the good half of my twin soul to come out and finish supper. Be polite. Don't make a scene. Be happy about going to Happy Town. Keep smiling. Let them think you're with them all the way.

"I need you to be a good girl, Peanut," Mama says.

"Yes, Mama," I say. "I'm sorry. I'll be better. I promise." I stare into her muddy eyes.

"Apologize to your sister, too."

I turn toward Rosa. "Sorry." I pull the words out of my good-girl encyclopedia of how to be polite and forgiving.

"I'm not stupid," Rosa asserts.

"I know," I say. I pat her hand, trying to assure her.

"You girls are going to have to be on your best behavior," Patrick starts in on us. "Your mother's upset."

Rosa nods. I chew the side of my tongue and put my hands on my knees to keep my legs from swinging.

"Good girl," Winnie says through a mouthful of french fries.

Patrick smiles. He reaches across the booth and pats her fingers.

My knees jerk. They hit the underside of the tabletop, squashing my hands and toppling a water glass. My head sinks deeper into my shoulders. Water drips over the table edges into my lap. Rosa jumps toward to Winnie to escape the flood.

"Peanut!" Mama yells.

The girls laugh.

"Mama, I'm sorry," I say. "It was an accident." The cool water seeps into my crotch. I feel like I did when Daddy yelled at me and I wet my pants in the kitchen: cold and alone.

Patrick grabs extra napkins and sops up the rest of the water on the tabletop. Mama reaches across the booth, picks up the fallen glass and dabs the cuffs of my sweater. Betty rushes over with towels to clean up the mess.

"Looks like we've had a bit of an accident here," the waitress says. She smiles at me, and I think she can tell my heart's spilling all over my insides. "It's OK, Red. It happens all the time. Don't worry about it. We'll get it fixed up in no time."

Betty calmly wipes up the mess, then turns to me. "Why don't you slide out here, so your mother can wipe you off too," she says handing a towel to Mama.

I search Mama's face, looking for forgiveness. "Come on, let me dry you off."

I slide over to the edge and stand on the floor at the end of the booth. My corduroy pants are soaked through. The cat family daughters watch me from behind their black pointed glasses. I want to scratch their eyes out. I hang my head instead, wishing Mama would at least take me to the ladies' room to finish up in private.

Mama wipes my pant legs and hands me the towel. "Here, you get the rest." I stare at the floor and I dab my crotch with the towel until, at last, the corduroy is drier. When I'm done, I hand the wet towel to Mama. "Go give it back to Betty. And don't forget to thank her," Mama insists as she lights another cigarette.

I cross the restaurant, counting the black and white checkered linoleum squares. I refuse to look at any of the other diners. Betty meets me halfway. She pats the top of my head. "It's OK, Red. It's not the end of the world." I stare at her white waitress shoes, at the grease stains and the flecks of dried food stuck to the laces. I look up into her blue eyes and manage a small "Thank you."

"You're welcome, sweetie," Betty says, handing me a

chocolate mint. I hide the candy in my palm, then tuck it into my pants pocket. I'll eat it later, when I get home. Maybe I'll give half to Zoomer. I turn and walk back to my family.

Smoke hangs over the booth. Mama's ashtray is full of butts now. Patrick pulls out a pack and lights up one of his own. Then he starts making monkey faces at Rosa and Winnie, and they giggle. He looks stupid. Mama smiles for a second, too. They look happy without me. I think about ditching, pocketing Betty's chocolate and sneaking out the door. I'll find another family. Some place with a bed all my own and no other kids. Maybe some lonely couple in Cayuga wants a daughter. It's worth a try.

"Peanut," Mama calls, patting the spot in the booth right next to her. "Come here, sit by me."

I smile shyly at her invitation. I touch the candy mint in my pocket, for safekeeping, and settle in next to Mama. She slips her arm around my shoulder and kisses my forehead. "Everything OK now?"

"Yes, Mama," I answer. I close my eyes and lean into her hug. I breathe in her perfume. "Mama, I'm sorry," I say. I've never meant it more in my whole life.

"Hush, now," Mama says. Her words have round, soft edges. "I know you didn't do it on purpose. Things are hard now. It'll be OK. You'll see. It'll be OK."

She gives me a squeeze, then she pulls her arm back, lights another Chesterfield, exhales a puff of smoke into the air and rubs her belly. I reach for her hand and pull it towards me. My hungry fingers gobble up her arm, swallowing her whole from her fingertips to her elbow.

FIFTEEN

After church, there's usually nothing much to do. Sometimes I draw or listen to show tunes. Sometimes I play outside. But it's snowing and blowing today. Me and Mama hang out in the kitchen. She's getting Sunday dinner ready. I keep her company and draw in my notebook. She's edgy, as usual. After Mass, she yelled at me for dragging a leg when I stopped to say hello to Amelia. She was in such a hurry to get home. I didn't know she was supposed to call Patrick before noon. As soon as Daddy left to visit Grandma, Mama picked up the phone.

I put our favorite record on and sing along.

> All I want is a room somewhere
> Far away from the cold night air
> With one enormous chair ©

Mama joins me, "Wouldn't it be lov-er-ly."

I imagine Eliza Doolittle sitting on a flower crate in sooty London, her cold fingertips poking through torn gloves, her face dirty and beautiful.

Mama hums the rest of the song while she peels potatoes. I draw a picture of a London flower market and think about how Eliza's got it made. The handsome Professor Higgins is gonna snatch her from her sad life and plop her down in the middle of his fancy townhouse. "Wouldn't it be lov-er-ly." Mama's face gets dreamy, and I imagine her wishing Patrick could pluck her from our dreary kitchen and whoosh her off to Happy Town. Absolutely, blooming wonderful, it would be. For her.

I hold my notebook in the air. "Look, Mama," I say. "I drew you a picture."

She glances up quickly. "That's nice, honey," she says, before the potatoes grab her attention again. The phone rings, and I run to the living room to get it. It's Patrick. I tell Mama, and she wipes her hands on her apron. She rushes to the phone, turning down the record player as she passes.

She turns her face to the corner while she talks, and rubs her temples with her free hand. "No," she says. "Well, maybe. Look, I can't talk right now. I'll call you later. Tonight. After supper." She hangs up the phone and heads back to the kitchen. She picks up the paring knife and stabs a potato.

"Peanut, turn that damn record off," she hollers.

I pick the needle up and hang the arm on the metal prongs. I click the machine off and watch the record spin to a stop, then I slip it back into its jacket. By the time I finish, Mama's tearing into the potatoes. Peelings fly all over the counter top.

"Can I help, Mama?" I ask.

"No. Just leave me alone," she snaps.

Her eyes are as sharp as the edge of the paring knife. Her face reminds me of how Danny looked yesterday afternoon, when I came home from Amelia's house and found him sitting on the front steps with his hands shoved into his pants pockets. "What ya doing out here?" I asked. He snapped at me to shut up. Then he wadded a clump of snow into a icy ball and threw it at me, stinging the back of my legs. "I'm gonna tell Mama!" I yelled. He laughed, like a creature in a Saturday-matinee horror movie. I could have sworn his tongue was a black-and-red arrow shooting out of his bent mouth.

I ran inside, calling for Mama, but she wasn't there. I found Rosa crouched on the floor in the kitchen, between the refrigerator and the back door. Winnie was hiding under Mama's bed.

"Where's Mama?" I asked.

"She left," Rosa said.

"For where?" I demanded.

Rosa covered her face with Binkie. "They had a fight, and she went away in the car," she managed to tell me.

I wrestled the truth out of Danny after promising to make his bed for a week. But the truth didn't make me feel any better. He told me Daddy had been watching a Notre Dame game on TV and Danny was heading downstairs to join him when he heard Mama say, "I've got something to tell you, Paulie."

Danny watched the whole thing from the stairs. He said it was weird. Daddy got all antsy. He scratched his eyebrows the way he does when he's annoyed. "Dad asked her if she had divorce papers for him to sign," Danny told me. That's when Mama told Daddy about the baby. Danny said Daddy asked Mama if it was theirs. Mama looked mad and snapped back at him, "What do you think?" Then Daddy got all huffy. "I think a child is a gift from God, Marie. But you tell me what it means to you? Are you gonna settle down and be my wife again?"

Danny said Mama didn't answer him—just looked at Daddy with smouldering eyes. Daddy got mad right back. He said, "Maybe the baby's mine. Maybe it's not. I'll provide for it either way, because it's my obligation. But don't come crying to me that our marriage is no good. If you want a good marriage, try being a good wife and mother."

That's when it happened. Mama leapt off the couch and started yelling at the top of her lungs, "You bastard. So damn pious. So goddamn self-righteous. Did you ever stop to think that if you tried being a good husband, a good father, maybe I wouldn't need Patrick?"

Danny said Daddy just turned his back and walked away from her. She got so pissed she stomped out of the house, got in the car and took off. Danny had a big fight with Dad after that. Rosa and Winnie got so scared, they hid.

"That baby. It's Patrick's, isn't it?" Danny asked me after he told me the whole story.

I looked away, so he couldn't see the secret in my eyes. On top of everything else, Mama had taken off without any of us, and I didn't like that idea one bit. I tried to tell myself that Mama wouldn't leave for Happy Town without me or Winnie and Rosa. That was proof enough that she'd be back. But I didn't really believe it until she came home hours later. She made it back in time for dinner, even kissed me good night and tucked me and the girls in. Even her sour mood today can't take away the fact that she didn't forget to come back for us.

The kitchen crowds in on me. It's hot from the oven and Mama's temper. I go to the back door and press my face against the window. The wind is blowing its head off. "King me," Danny yells from the living room. He's playing checkers with Joey. Rosa and Winnie are in there, too, playing baby dolls on the brown couch. Daddy's still visiting Grandma. I wish I'd gone with him when he asked. It's snowing so hard you can hardly see the big tree out back. If it doesn't let up, we won't have school on Monday. I press my lips to the glass now, trying to breathe like a guppy in a fish bowl. I hope we don't get a snow day. Amelia thinks I'm crazy. She says I'm the only kid she knows who'd rather go to school than stay home.

"Mama, are there black-eyed Susans in Happy Town?" I ask, turning from the window.

"Don't be asking me a lot of questions. I feel like shit today." She slices potatoes into a kettle.

"Sorry," I whisper to the window, leaving a ring of breath on the glass. I go back to the table and turn my notebook to a clean page. I draw a long stalk, huge petals and a swollen black-eyed center. I draw a vase around the flower and add more black-eyed Susan's to the drawing.

"Why don't you put that damn pencil down and help me," Mama snaps.

She stabs another potato, digging deep into it. The knife slips, slicing into her finger. Blood drips into the white meaty part.

"Ouch, shit, goddamnit," she swears. She puts her mouth to the cut and sucks on it.

I jump up from my chair and run to have a look. Mama leans against the sink, turns the faucet on and runs her cut under the water. "Are you OK?" I say.

"Yeah, yeah. It's just a little nick. Grab me a Band-Aid, will ya?"

I scrounge in the side drawer, find a Band-Aid, tear the tiny red string down the side of the wrapper and turn to hand it to Mama, but she's not standing by the sink anymore. She's slumped into a kitchen chair. Her face looks like a peeled potato, naked and pale.

"Mama." My voice is so tiny I can hardly hear myself.

She bends over like she has a terrible stomach ache. She cups her hands between her legs. Her yellow apron is spotted with blood. The edge of the paper towel she used to dab her fingertip is soaked red.

"Mama!" I cry.

"Get your brother," she says, slow and serious. I run

to the front room. "Danny! Danny!" I race back to the kitchen to check on Mama.

Danny runs after me. Joey's right behind. "What the hell's going on?"

"Mama cut her finger," I cry. I point to the bloody paper towel bunched up in Mama's lap.

Danny pushes me away. He grabs a roll of paper towels, tears off a wad and presses Mama's hand to stop the bleeding.

"No, Daniel," she says. She pushes at him. "No. It's not my finger. It's the baby."

She motions him to come closer. He bends his ear to her lips, then he swings around and shouts at me. "Peanut. She's hemorrhaging. Get Mrs. Brown."

I can't move. My feet are heavy roots buried in the floor. I don't know what "hemorrhaging" means. She said, "It's the baby," and I see the blood and think it's the baby that's bleeding or Mama's bleeding, and the baby's gonna whoosh out of her on a river of blood any minute now.

"Help her, Danny," I beg.

"I'll be alright," Mama says. Her voice is tight, and I don't believe her. All the paper towels are bloody now. I don't know if it's from her finger or from the baby. Mama's going to die, and the last thing I'll remember about her is her twisted mouth.

"For cryin' out loud, Peanut, move your butt! Go get Mrs. Brown," Danny shouts.

Mama's hunched over now, holding onto Danny's arm. Joey grips a kitchen chair at the far end of the table. Rosa and Winnie are in the room, too. They hang back, by the refrigerator, and hold each other's hands. Zoomer runs around the kitchen, barking and barking.

"Shut that damn dog up!" Mama hollers. Joey grabs Zoomer by the collar and shoves him out the back door. Mama presses her cut hand against her temples. A line of blood drips down the side of her finger. I still can't move. I watch the blood trickle down, and I wait for her to collapse and her soul to rise out of her body, carrying the lost baby back to heaven with her, in her ghost arms.

Danny starts talking real fast now, firing out orders, left and right. "OK, you're gonna be OK now, Ma. Just hold on. Joey, call Dad at Grandma's. Tell him I'm taking Mom to the hospital. Tell him to meet me there. You little girls go sit in the living room and be quiet. Peanut will look after you until we get back."

He swings his arm under Mama and lifts her to her feet. "Goddamn it, Peanut, move your ass over to Mrs. Brown's and ask if I can borrow her car!" he yells.

Joey nudges my shoulder. "Get going," he urges. "I'm gonna go call Dad at Grandma's."

Joey's push loosens my feet. I push my eyes away from Mama and race out the back door. I slip and slide across the snowy street, up the back steps to Mrs. Brown's kitchen. "Mrs. Brown, Mrs. Brown!" I yell. My breathing is fast now. I'm being chased by whatever it is that's got a hold of Mama. I pound on the door.

"Open up! It's an emergency! My Mama's dying!"

"Dear God in heaven, child!" Mrs. Brown screams. Her back door swings open, and she flies past me. I follow her back across the slippery street up to our house. She pushes the kitchen door open with a wild swing of her arm. Her apron flutters as she moves though the maze of Rosa and Winnie and Joey. They step aside like turnstile spokes as she passes by.

"My God, Marie," Mrs. Brown says. She's out of breath from rushing and she puts her hand between her breasts like she's trying to stop her heart from running away all together. "Peanut said you were dying. I thought you'd be in a heap on the floor."

"I need to get to the hospital, Phyllis. I think I'm

having a miscarriage. It started early this morning. The cramps, the spotting. But I thought if I took it easy, it would go away."

"Oh, dear," Mrs. Brown says. "Let's get you out of here."

"I'm going with you," Danny insists.

"Me, too," I demand.

"No, Peanut, you stay here with Joey and the girls," Danny orders.

"No," I insist. "Mama, say I can go with you, too."

"It's better if you stay here and watch the girls, Peanut," Mama says. All her strength is sopped up in the blood drying on her apron. The angels will have to carry her to the car. Rosa and Winnie and Joey just stare at her. They're too scared to talk or even to cry.

"But Mama," I say. I start to whine until Mrs. Brown shoots me a look. "Now, Peanut, act your age."

"I'll be alright, Peanut," Mama says. "Just do as you're told."

I push my sneaker hard over the linoleum. Danny collects Mama into his arms and whisks her out of the kitchen, out of the house, across the street, and into Mrs. Brown's car.

Me and Joey and the girls chase into the front room after them. I pick Winnie up and we all press our faces to the picture window. Our eyes are taped to the glass, watching Mrs. Brown back her car out of her driveway and speed off. Zoomer chases them halfway down the block.

"Mama!" Winnie cries and taps her palm against the window.

"She'll be alright, she said so," I tell her, trying to sound as if I mean it.

"Danny will take care of her," Joey says.

"I wanna go too," Rosa whines. She yanks my sleeve.

216

I watch until I can't see the tail lights anymore. Poof. Mama and Danny and Mrs. Brown disappear into the snowy afternoon, leaving behind only clouds of exhaust from the car, clouds of worry in my heart. She wouldn't let me go. I'm the one who makes it all better. I'm the one who keeps her secrets tucked deep inside so no one can see or know what goes on in her heart. Me. It's me.

I imagine the emergency room, the nurses in white dresses, wearing white hats with pointed corners and white stockings. Everything is white and empty like the snow falling outside. They put Mama on a white bed and wheel her away down a long white hall into an even whiter room. They take off her yellow apron, stained with blood, and the lost baby slips out of her and lands on the floor in a pool of messy red clots. They cover her pink splotchy face with a white blanket, and Mama cries and cries, then disappears. They can't tell Danny where she went. They can't tell Mrs. Brown, either. They don't know. "We're sorry," they say, and Danny and Mrs. Brown put their hands in their pockets and shrug their shoulders. "I hope Peanut will understand," they tell each other. They close the door and head home.

I cry, and Joey walks away from the window, jumps on the couch and buries his face in the cushions. I set Winnie down and Rosa wraps her arms around my waist and hangs on tight. "Is Mama gonna die?" she asks. I cry harder. Winnie screams, "Mama, Mama!" I untangle myself from their tight fingers, run upstairs to my room and hide in the closet.

***

It's dark and warm and stuffy inside, back behind the dresses. I hear a car pull into the driveway, and at first I think it's Mama. My heart speeds up, and I get up quick to go back downstairs. I bump my head on the wall and sit back down. It stings clean down to my brain. The front door opens and slams. Daddy shouts, "Peanut, Joey?"

I hear Rosa and Winnie crying and Daddy trying to comfort them. "Slow down, I can't understand what you're saying. Where's Joey? Where the hell's Peanut? Is she with your mother? Why the hell'd she leave you little ones alone?"

Zoomer barks, and Daddy yells, "Settle down!" Zoomer doesn't listen, he runs around the living room. He barks first in one corner, then another and another. Then I hear Joey. He must be standing at the foot of the stairs. His voice floats up the steps.

"They took Ma to the hospital, Dad."

"Dear Jesus," Daddy says. "Joey, what happened?"

"Do you think she's gonna die?" Joey asks.

He sounds like he's gonna cry, and it makes the bump on my head throb even more. The girls are still crying. I open the closet door just a crack, so I can hear better.

"Joey, when you called me at Grandma's you didn't say nothing about dying. What happened to your mother?"

"They took her, Dad. They took her away, and there was a lot of blood."

"Dear God," Daddy prays out loud, "Don't let anything happen to her."

He pumps Joey for more information. "Where was the blood coming from? Did she cut herself on glass or something?"

"It was her hand, I think," Joey says. His voice is soft, and I think he really is crying now.

"Where on her hand?" Daddy shouts, as if it matters which finger got cut. Daddy doesn't know yet about the lost baby spilling out, leaving Mama's body with bloody wings. He can't see that it's my fault for praying to the

Blessed Virgin, for lighting the red votive candles, as red as blood. He doesn't know Patrick's baby is back in heaven. If he knew, he probably wouldn't be so upset. Joey's quiet now; he's probably sitting on the couch with his round face in his hands. Daddy walks over to the bottom step and yells up at me.

"Peanut! Peanut, come down here right now!"

I don't want to answer him. I want to pretend I'm lost in the closet. Swallowed up in the dark. I hear his footsteps on the stairs, and I know he's coming to get me. I don't want him to open the closet door, find me in my secret place. I crawl out and head for the hallway.

Zoomer rushes up the stairs past Daddy and jumps at me. He nearly knocks me over. He sniffs and sniffs. He can smell how scared I am.

"What, Daddy?" I say. I stare down the steps right into his eyes. He looks awful. In the shadows, his face looks dirty, his eyes swollen and worried.

"Come on down here and tell me what's going on." Daddy points at the bottom step. "Your brother's got his face crammed into the couch, and your sisters are crying up a river."

I tug Zoomer's ear and step carefully down the stairs. "It's Mama, Daddy. They took her away." I stop two steps above the landing. I don't want to get too close.

"I know they took her to the hospital, but can you please tell me why?" Daddy asks.

"She cut her finger, peeling potatoes," I tell him. I wonder if I should tell him everything. "And she said something about something else. Hemorrhaging. What's that mean, Daddy?"

The bump on my head starts to throb again, and I want to cry, but not in front of Daddy. I want to run into his arms and have him hold me and tell me everything is OK, but I can't. Something inside me holds back like a door with a rusty old knob. I turn and turn, but it won't open. I wait for Daddy to say something.

"The baby," Daddy says. He rubs his eyes with his long fingers. "When did they take her?" He checks his watch and heads down the stairs. I follow him.

"I gotta go check on her and the baby." He digs into his pants pocket for his car keys.

"Daddy. Wait," I call. "Is it gonna die?"

I want to kneel down on the living room rug and confess my sin. I killed her, Daddy, I have to say, so my soul will be clean and white again, like the snow falling all over the yard. Daddy isn't listening. He's picked up the phone, and he's dialing.

"Can't they fix it? Stitch Mama up and send her home?" I ask. I beg for him to tell me.

"For cryin' out loud," Daddy yells. "Shut up."

He pounds the wall. "That mother of yours is going to drive me to an early grave. And you too with all your questions. I haven't got time for all that now."

If the baby dies, I'm going to hell. I'm the one who prayed and prayed until my fingers ached from pointing. The bump on my head is just a tiny punishment for my evil wishes. Mama will probably die, too. Then God will make me see how bad I really am. Before, when I prayed about Rosa and Winnie, God didn't listen. I was a good girl then. Good girls don't want their baby sister to die.

"Go calm the girls, now," Daddy orders. "I'm trying to talk to the doctor about your mother."

Rosa and Winnie look so little and skinny on the edge of the couch. Their eyes droop and their mouths turn under. Their faces are pink from crying. Joey looks bad, too. His hair's all wet from sweating or something. He looks like he just woke up from a bad dream. He hangs his head when I stare at him. While Daddy is on the phone, I give the girls a hug and think about giving one to

Joey, too, but I don't. We all sit on the couch and wait to find out what the doctor said.

"Well," Daddy says, hanging up the phone. "The doctor said your mother is going to be alright. She lost the baby. But she's coming home. She didn't lose too much blood, thank God. But she's tired and weak, Peanut, so you'll have to help out around here until she gets back on her feet. They'll be home in a little bit."

I take Rosa's hand, and she holds Winnie's. Joey grabs on, too. We look like a string of sad pearls. We stare at Daddy as he holds his rosary and rocks and rocks in his recliner.

It's quiet a long time. Daddy's lips move over silent words, quiet as angels' wings, waiting for Mama to come back home to us. Is Daddy praying for the baby? For its soul flying back to heaven, back to God, unbaptized? Is it doomed to spend eternity in Limbo, God's eyes closed and quiet, not looking, not loving it ever? Or is he praying for my rotten soul, the one that prayed and prayed for the baby to stay lost forever, to never come back?

I did it. The doctor said the baby died. I asked, and the Blessed Virgin Mother listened this time. She scooped up my worries and wiped them away just like the nuns always said she would. When you need something so badly, something that no human can possibly give you, not even your mama or your daddy, just ask the Blessed Virgin. I believed. I feel like a horrible sinner. I'll have to go to confession. How will I tell the priest? "I killed my sister." How will I find the words to describe how awful I feel being a murderer, how good I feel to be finally free of the lost baby?

"Dear Jesus," Daddy prays out loud. "Help us to learn from your will and trust that you have called my baby's soul home to everlasting peace with you. May this burden make us a stronger family. Amen."

"Amen," I say. Joey and Rosa say it, too. "Amen."

Daddy curls his rosary back into its black leather case. The beads fall into the darkness and disappear. Oh my God, I am heartily sorry. I start a silent Act of Contrition, seeking forgiveness for my murderous ways, when Mrs. Brown pulls into the driveway and beeps her car horn.

"They're home!" Joey yells.

I drop Rosa's hand, rush to the kitchen and grab my drawing of the black-eyed Susans. Rosa and Winnie and Joey scramble to the front door and wait, with hungry eyes, for Mama and Danny to come inside. I can't wait. I push past the others holding out my drawing. I open the door, run into the driveway and wrap my arms around Mama's waist. "Are you OK?" The snow falls like tear drops on top of my head.

"Lay off it, Peanut," Danny says. "Give her a break, she's worn out."

"Do you have stitches, Mama?" I ask. I imagine a long line of thick black thread running up her belly, an evil kiss left by the lost baby before she slipped back to heaven.

Rosa and Winnie and Joey rush outside now.

"I wanna see, too," Rosa says.

"Me too," Winnie mimics.

"There ain't no stitches, girls," Danny says, shooing them away.

"Hey, Danny," Joey says, standing back from the commotion. He acts cool, as if his insides haven't been wadded up like an old Kleenex. "What was the ER like?"

"Pretty wild," Danny brags. "You'd like it. Maybe I'll be a doctor, instead of a pharmacist."

"Dad's home," Joey says.

"Yeah, I see his car," Danny says.

"Daniel, get your mother inside, out of this awful

weather," Mrs. Brown says, hurrying him along. "She needs to lie down and recuperate."

"Thanks for everything, Phyllis," Mama says. "You really helped a lot."

"Yeah, thanks, Mrs. Brown," Danny says, too.

"If you need anything, don't hesitate to call," Mrs. Brown says before she walks to her car.

I watch her go. Her back is strong and straight. Snow collects on her shoulders. I turn and follow Mama toward the house. My shoulders slump, and I bow my head, ashamed to look at her, afraid she'll see into my swollen heart and know it was me who killed her baby.

Daddy walks out onto the porch to meet us. He waves a thank-you to Mrs. Brown as she drives off, then he turns and smiles at the parade of all of us Giovanni kids helping Mama up the front steps.

"How you doing, Marie?" Daddy asks. "I was worried about you."

He offers a small grin, and his eyes smile, too. The wind goes through me, and I stomp my feet to shake snow off my sneakers.

Mama looks up at Daddy. "I guess I scared the kids a little, huh?" Her voice sounds small, like tiny stones dropping into a deep lake.

"She's gonna be OK now, Dad," Danny says. "The doctor said we got her there before she lost too much blood. She just needs to rest."

"You did a good job," Daddy says. He moves toward Mama, into the circle of us children surrounding her, and he takes her arm in his.

"I'm sorry about the baby," he says. "Come inside and rest now. We'll take care of everything. You concentrate on getting better."

He helps Mama inside the porch, out of the cold and the snow and the eyes of the neighbors. His kindness feels stiff, like a new winter coat that's tight under the arms.

"I'll help, too, Mama," I promise.

"I never finished supper," Mama worries out loud.

"Forget the pot roast, Marie. We can have hot dogs tonight," Daddy comforts.

"Just don't burn them, Paulie," Mama teases. A tiny bit of love dances between their eyes.

"Dad always burns them," Danny says. "It's his trademark."

"Never you mind. You're lucky to be eating anything for dinner with an attitude like that," Daddy says, swinging his hand at Danny's arm. Danny steps aside and misses the blow. He glares at Daddy. "Gotta be faster than that to catch me, old man."

Daddy reaches for his belt, but Mama interferes. "Please, just for once can't we have some peace and quiet?"

Daddy looks at the boys, then at Mama, then at each of us girls. I think we're quite a sight, all the Giovannis standing on the front porch together. Just like old times. He smiles at Danny and says, "You're getting more and more like your old man every day." Then, one by one, we all walk into the house, out of the snow and wind, away from the dead eyes of the lost baby.

PART THREE

March 1967

Sixteen

Mama's in the living room, laughing at something Mike Douglas just said on the TV. I want to watch too, but she won't let me. She says I've got to get my school work done, before any TV. I got a D in math and a C in English on my last report card and she got real mad, said I had to apply myself or else. I've been better, lately, about concentrating, doing my schoolwork. I figure I owe God a big favor. But it's still so hard to study with the TV set going, and Mike Douglas singing away.

"Mama, can I watch TV now?" I holler into the living room.

"Have you finished your homework?"

"Not all of it. But I can do the rest after supper."

"No, Peanut. You know how I feel about this." Mama gets up off the couch and comes into the kitchen. She looks right at me now. "And besides, after you're done I need you to give Winnie a bath before we eat supper."

This afternoon Winnie made mud pies and smeared them into her hair, right down to her scalp. Mama washed her face and hands but the stuff in her hair can't just be combed or brushed out; she has to be sudsed up and rinsed to get all the way clean.

"But Mama, can't Danny do that? Or Rosa?"

"Regina," she snaps. She points towards my books in that impatient way of hers. "I don't want to hear another word."

Arguing isn't gonna change her mind. An order's an order, and if I don't want to get on her bad side I better just give up this fight. Besides, God's keeping track, and I don't want to get Him mad at me, too. He might just send the lost baby back to punish me for my wicked ways. Without even complaining under my breath, I settle back in at the kitchen table, pick up my pencil and start my arithmetic homework again.

Things haven't changed much around here. After the baby died, Mama cried a lot. I felt bad for making her heart burst, but I also felt a tiny warm spot of hope. Maybe we wouldn't have to go to Happy Town after all. With his baby gone, maybe Patrick would change his mind and forget about us.

For a while it looked like that might just happen. We didn't go to Smiley's for a long time. The doctor told Mama she had to rest and get better. She didn't like that too much, but she obeyed him. I guess she was too weak to drive. She was sure too weak to do much around the house. She laid around in bed for days and days, and I brought cigarettes and orange juice to her. I fixed dinner most nights. Aunt Stella helped out with the harder stuff, like making meatballs and sauce. I could handle boiling the water for macaroni and most everything else we ate, like tuna sandwiches and potato chips and oatmeal, while Mama got better. Daddy made hot dogs and tater tots a few times. And fish sticks every Friday. I started to miss Smiley's and Betty. Even the cat family.

One morning Mama got out of bed and ate a piece of toast with the rest of us. It was a Saturday, and the cartoons were on like usual, but this time she didn't crab that the TV was too loud, and she didn't fight with

Daddy. Seems like there wasn't much to fight about, with Mama staying home and all. But I could tell she wasn't happy. Every now and then she'd ask me to get the music box out of her top drawer and play her that sad song. Then she'd cry a little and tell me how much she loved Patrick, and how she couldn't wait 'til she was all better and we could go see him again. "It won't be long," she told me.

The whole town knows about Mama's miscarriage. When Aunt Stella took me and Rosa to the beauty parlor before Thanksgiving, all the ladies asked how Mama was. I could tell they were just pretending to care. Their eyes were soft like they meant it, but their lips were hard and small like pebbles. Maybe they know it's Patrick's baby that was washed away in Mama's blood. I'm not sure, but when Amelia asked me how my Mama was feeling I told her "Just fine, thank you." I didn't tell her how my praying made the baby die. I felt too guilty. But even though I know I'll burn in hell for wishing that baby back to heaven, I'm not sorry.

That secret slipped away to God, but the other secrets stayed. Thanksgiving came and went, and Christmas too. Right after New Year's, we went back to school from vacation, and we started visiting Patrick again. He cried about the baby dying, right in the middle of Smiley's Coffee Shop. He blew his nose real loud into one of his fancy handkerchiefs. I thought for sure his heart had busted in a million pieces, each piece falling in a pure drop of water from his eyes. Mama put her arms around his sad shoulders and hugged him until he sighed and sat back with a tired look washed all over his face. Betty stayed away from our booth a long time, and when she finally came to take our order, she didn't look at Patrick or Mama. Her cheeks were pink, and she looked at the laces of her dirty waitress shoes.

The cat family daughters watched us the whole time. One of them started crying, and her mama had to put her arms around her and rock her quiet. It made me sad to see that little girl in tears, but I still wasn't sorry I killed the lost baby. I only hoped Patrick would never find out who did it. So far he hasn't said a word, and I guess Mama doesn't know either. She hasn't yelled at me for being rotten to the core.

***

Danny slams the back door and bops me on the back of my head as he passes. He grabs a swig of milk out of the refrigerator.

"What ya doin', Peanut?"

"Homework." I stare at the blur of words and numbers.

"Don't look like you're getting very far."

"I wanted to watch TV, but you know how far I got with that one."

"Couldn't get past the Enforcer, huh?" Danny shakes his head. He understands. He's sort of friendly, and it's kind of weird. He's been in the kitchen a whole minute, and he hasn't yelled at me or called me some nasty name.

"It'd be easier to stand on my head and spit nickels," I say.

Danny scrounges around looking for a snack. He grabs a bag of Oreos from the cupboard.

"I hate these stupid word problems." I drop hints. "I can never figure them out." If I asked for his help, straight out, he'd expect me to do his chores for a week just 'cuz he solved one stupid word problem. He fills his hands with cookies, then sits in the chair right beside me. I try not to look surprised.

"Want one?" He offers me an Oreo. I stare at the black and white cookie crumbs all over his mouth and grab a cookie. "So, Sister Saint Joe is piling on the home-work," he says. Sister was his fifth grade teacher, too. He must remember how she loads us up, especially just before a holiday break. Easter's coming up, and Sister loves to make life miserable.

"She's the worst," I say. "I always get in trouble with her."

He kind of laughs and almost chokes on his cookies. I wish I'd kept my mouth shut. He knows about my going to the principal's office. He knows about the time I hit Timmy Carelli during recess. He knows I'm not perfect. He likes to shove it in my face. I can't talk to him. He makes fun of everything I do. If I tried to tell him some-thing important, like how I killed the lost baby, he'd run and tell Mama just to get back at me. He's mean like that. Never nice just to be nice; he's got to have a reason. I stick to tame things, things that don't matter. I lie.

"Sometimes I talk to Amelia during lessons and Sister yells at me."

"She's a creep. Hell, ya'd think a kid would get enough shit dumped on 'em at home. They sure don't need it in school, too."

Danny gets all quiet and eats the rest of his cookie. I wonder what's going on, but I don't say nothing. I just keep staring at the far away look in his eyes. I wonder if he knows we're going to Happy Town soon. Losing the baby just made Patrick want to go all the more. He told Mama he's waited long enough, and she better get ready. He said he was gonna call his friend, the one who used to be a priest, and have him start looking around for jobs for him.

Maybe Danny's trying to butter me up, hoping I can convince Mama to bring the boys with us. He doesn't know it, but he could use my help in learning how to behave around Patrick, how to get on his good side and not upset him. Patrick won't stand for Danny's temper. Danny wants something from me. That's why he's being so nice this afternoon, offering cookies like they were kiss-and-make-up presents.

"What you starin' at?" Danny asks. He's finally noticed me gawking at him.

"Nothin'." I look away quick and pretend I'm reading my math problems.

"Lay off me, Peanut." It's the real Danny now, bumpy as a skating pond. "I wasn't doing nothing." I look away, real quick, and pretend I'm doing my arithmetic, but my mind is chasing around. I wonder how much Danny knows. Maybe he's being nice to me 'cuz he wants me to tell him stuff about Mama and Patrick. Maybe he's figured out we're going soon.

"Danny?"

"Yeah?"

I want to tell him, but I chicken out and ask a safer question. "Does Daddy ever get mad on Friday nights when we're all gone?"

He bites into his cookie and chews real fast. "What ya thinking about that for?"

"Jus 'cuz."

Me and Danny never talk about this stuff. We've got this rule, only we never say it's a rule. We both took sides, me for Mama, him for Daddy. He studies me for a long time. He thinks I'm Mama's favorite, and except for the lost baby, I think he's right. I'm a girl and Mama's a girl, and girls stick together—me and Mama and Rosa and Winnie. Just like in school, the boys hang out with the boys and the girls hang out with each other. It's the way things are.

"He's real strange on Friday nights," Danny says, finally. "Like he's edgy but calm at the same time. Sort of how the air gets real quiet just before a big storm. You can feel it coming in your bones, but it's peaceful at first so you think maybe it will pass. Maybe the sky won't explode with the wind and the rain."

"What do you do on Fridays?"

"What do ya mean?"

"Do you eat dinner? Do you watch TV? Does he take you some place special, just the three of you?"

Danny shakes his head and snorts. "It ain't fun and games. We don't do nothing. We eat burnt fish sticks, and me and Joey watch TV or hang out with our friends. Dad goes to church or somewhere. We don't always know. Then we go to bed. Sometimes he's home before we fall asleep, sometimes not."

He looks more and more like Daddy every day—worn-out eyes and a tired, sad mouth. Looking at him makes me want to cry.

"Did they ever love each other?"

"Who?"

"Mama and Daddy?"

"Hell, who knows? Who really cares anymore?" Danny says softly. He stares at the palms of his hand, as if looking at the creases will tell him the answer. After a few minutes he starts talking again. "I remember when he used to come home from work and give her a kiss each night. That was before you were born. I was real little. And Joey was a baby."

I try to imagine Mama and Daddy kissing. I stare at the lines in my hands, now, thinking it might help me picture something I can't ever remember seeing.

"Things weren't always this way, ya know," Danny says. "It could have worked." His voice gets small, and he turns his head and stares out the window.

"Do you really think so?"

"Hell," Danny says. "Things are far from perfect with them. Dad disappears into a church pew every chance he gets. And Mom's gone off the deep end for that damn priest. But it isn't too late, is it?"

His question melts into the quiet. Neither of us wants to believe Mama and Daddy can't get back whatever it was they once had. With every inch of skin and bone, I want Mama to be happy, and that means Patrick. But still, there's a sore part in my heart that wishes she could find it here in Pisa with our whole family.

"At first, when I heard her telling Dad she was pregnant, I thought, shit, how the hell did she wind up in a mess like this? Her and Patrick are such fools. But when I took her to the hospital and she ended up losing the baby, I was sort of glad, thinking maybe things might change. She might come to her senses and tell Patrick to kiss off. And after, when we came home, I thought maybe her and Dad could work things out. Remember how Dad was? How we all pulled together? Just like old times."

"Do you think Daddy still loves her?"

"Yeah. This whole thing tears him apart. Even a miscarriage isn't enough to make her stop farting around with that son of a bitch, Patrick."

I look away. I don't want Danny to see the truth in my eyes, how I prayed and prayed for the dead baby to go away.

"Peanut, do you think Mom's really gonna leave?"

My shoulders feel heavy. Piles of worries are stacked up on both sides of my head. "Yes," I say, and keep staring at my school book.

"Why?"

His words rush at me. He stands up, paces from the kitchen window to the table. I'm nervous, worried any second he's gonna explode all over the walls.

"Do you know when?" His voice tightens. "How could she do this?"

I follow him back and forth, back and forth with my

eyes. I don't know what to say. I want him to stop, sit back down, look at me. He's getting louder the angrier he gets. I don't want Mama coming into the kitchen to see what all the fuss is about.

"If we went, you'd come too, wouldn't you?"

His legs jerk to a stop, and he looks at me with furious eyes.

"I don't know, Peanut. I don't know if I could leave Dad. Besides, this is all just theory, isn't it? I mean, she isn't even getting a divorce, is she?"

"I don't know." I can't say any more. I shouldn't even have told him anything. Mama will kill me if she finds out I blabbed about the secret things they say at Smiley's. Patrick talked about divorce once, but Mama didn't like that idea. "Catholics can't get divorced," I think out loud.

"Don't be stupid, Peanut. The Church won't give them a divorce, but the state has to."

I picture Father DiSante with his back pressed against the front door of St. Joan of Arc's, his arms crossed over his chest, shaking his finger at Mama. Then Patrick runs up the sidewalk followed by a man wearing a hat that says New York State on the front of it. He's waving a golden paper in his hands and he's shouting, "The state said yes! The state said yes!"

"Do you have to have a divorce before you leave someone?" I ask.

"What's all this talk about divorce?"

Mama startles us. She caught me.

"What are you two up to?" she says. "Peanut, are you done with your homework yet? It's time to start supper, and I need you to set the table."

My math paper is still blank. "No, Mama," I say. "I still have lots left to do."

"Well if you'd been helping your sister, instead of

235

interrupting her, Danny, she could have been done by now," Mama snaps.

"I didn't do anything, Ma," Danny insists.

"He didn't, Mama," I say, trying to help him out.

"What the hell you been doing, then?" Mama asks.

"Talking, Ma," Danny says. His hands are nervous and he sucks in a belly full of air then blurts out, "Are you leaving?"

Mama's face gets all red. She looks at Danny, then shoots her mad eyes at me. "What have you two been talking about?"

"Don't get on her case, Ma," Danny says. "I brought it up."

I flip my math book shut and look at Danny. My eyes say, "We're gonna get in big trouble for this one."

"Sit down, Danny," Mama says. "If you have any questions, you ask me, not Peanut. Is that clear, young man?"

"Yeah, Ma," Danny says. He isn't apologizing. He doesn't look down at the floor or over Mama's shoulder at the yellowed wall by the sink. He stares right at her face. I sit quietly in my chair, hardly breathing, watching and waiting and hoping Mama doesn't get mad and decide to leave without me because I talked to Danny.

"Why you doing this, Ma?"

"Doing what, Daniel?"

"You know. For Christ's sake, you lost his goddamn baby, why you still seeing him? Can't you try with Dad again?"

Mama's face gets white and stiff. "How did you know.... " She stabs her eyes at me.

"I didn't say nothing, Mama. Honest."

Mama turns back to Danny. "There are a lot of things you don't understand," Mama says. She lays her hands on the table top. Her long fingers spread wide like a spider web. "I love Patrick. Maybe you can understand that. Maybe you can't. When I'm with him, I don't feel like a tired old bag of complaining anymore, like I feel around here. I'm more than just somebody's wife, somebody's mother. I'm me. Marie. With him I'm still young, still able to dream and laugh. He sees something in me I can't see myself anymore, something that I knew was there once. Something full of fire. He says he sees the world in my face. Can you imagine? All the places he's been to, all the things he's seen, and he still says he's found nothing that beats my brown eyes. Someday you'll love like that, Danny. Then you'll know why I can't stay here with nothing but nothing to keep me company."

"Are you getting a divorce?" Danny asks. His forehead is sweaty. His jaw is tight and stiff.

"No. I haven't filed for divorce." She closes her fingers around the salt and pepper shakers.

"Why not? How can you expect to leave him if you don't get a divorce?"

"In good time, Danny. It will all happen in good time."

"What does that mean?" Danny spits the words at her.

"Look, I know you're upset..."

"You don't know a goddamn thing," Danny says, standing up now. His temper fills up the room. "I'm pissed off that you gotta do it this way. Why don't you just leave if you hate it here so much? Get out of our lives. It would be better for all of us."

"Is that what you want, Danny?" Mama sounds calm, but her eyelids twitch. "You're just mad now. Don't say things you'll regret later."

"Bullshit! I want you out of this house! Out of my life! Now!" He slams his fists on the table top.

"Calm down, Danny. I refuse to talk with you when you're this way."

"You calm down. You stop cheating on us. You stop it. Mom. Please." His whole body shakes.

Mama reaches for his hand, then her whole face cracks open, and she starts to cry. "I don't know how to stop it, Danny. I can't anymore. I can't breathe in this house. I can't live like this anymore. It's hard on me, too. I know what this does to you kids. I see it in your faces, hear it in your angry words. Do you think it's easy? I want you to go with me. Will you do that?"

"No," Danny says. "No. I don't want to go. I don't want you to go, either. I want you to stay and be my mother, here."

"I can't. Your mother doesn't exist here anymore. She died a long time ago. You know that."

The kitchen wall eyes are crying, too, and inside I feel the burning, back behind my eyes, in that tender spot where the river starts. But I can't cry; my heart is dry. Danny cries. Tears rush down his red cheeks, and I can tell he's mad that he can't stop them. He keeps wiping them away, as fast as they fall, but more come, no matter what he does. "Ma, can't you see how much we need you to stay?"

They're both crying now. Mama and Danny. They look like Rosa and Winnie after they've had a big fight, and Mama tells them they got to make up.

"You need me to be your mother. I know that. Come with me, and you'll have your mother back again. I'll be your mother again."

"How can we leave Dad?"

"You and Joey need me more than you need him. He can take care of himself."

"No, he can't. You don't see him on Friday nights. He's like a zombie."

"He'll be OK."

"Take Joey. I'll stay here with Dad."

"No, you both come with me."

"Joey's littler. He still needs a mother."

"No. I want you both."

Danny looks like he's ready to give in, say yes to Mama, finally open up his heart and need her all the way, like I do, like Winnie and Rosa do. He cocks his head and squints at her through the tiny slits of his puffy eyelids.

"You could have all of us if you'd just stay here."

"Danny, don't start up again."

"I mean," he says, calming his voice down a little, "I mean you could still leave Dad. Just don't marry Patrick. Stay here in town."

"You're talking crazy, Danny." Mama shakes her head so hard, her curls bounce in the air around her face.

"No, I'm not. We could live with Aunt Stella and Uncle Tony. We could all be together and still be in Pisa. You'd never have to see Dad again if you didn't want to."

"Danny, I have no way to support all you kids. And besides, I want to be with Patrick. You'll understand in a few years when you fall in love with someone."

"I won't go if you go with him."

"Danny, don't ask me to choose between you and him," Mama says. "It isn't fair." He's pinching her heart, and she can't shake him loose.

"Just forget it. Do what you want. You don't care about me and Joey anyway."

Danny pushes his chair back. It crashes to the kitchen floor. He kicks it as he rushes out of the room. It flies against the bottom cupboard doors.

"Daniel Giovanni, you get your ass back in this room right now!" Mama screams.

From the living room, Danny screams back, "What the fuck do you want?"

It's a lonely sound. He's giving up. You can't fight Mama for too long. She wins in the end. It's easier to close the door to your mind, close out the hardness in her touch, the sad tears of her heart. If you wait too long, want too much, you end up being disappointed. It's just the way it is. Even though he's older than me, Danny hasn't learned that about Mama. You can't push her too far, or she'll go far, far away. You got to be willing to see things her way if you want her to love you. More than anything else, you got to be willing to love her more than she loves back; love her with everything inside of you, no matter what.

Mama follows Danny into the living room. Her hair flies straight out from the sides. She looks like a brown-haired devil. I scoot into the living room right behind her. Joey comes downstairs. "What's going on?" he asks.

"She's going, Joey," Danny says.

Joey gets all quiet. He grabs the back of Daddy's recliner and holds on tight.

"Tonight? Are you going tonight?" He pins his eyes on Mama.

"No, Joseph, I'm not going tonight." Mama turns her attention to Danny. "I expect you to listen to me when I tell you to do something." She's mad that he didn't stay put in the kitchen like she asked.

"What difference does it make anymore, Ma?"

"I'm still your mother, Daniel. I will always be your mother."

Danny swears under his breath, then collapses on to the couch. His shoulders fold into his chest; he rests his head in his hands. "Ma, I can't take it any more. Why can't you just quit it?"

Mama sits beside him, puts her arm around his waist and lays her head on his shoulder. "I love you, Danny. I wish I had an answer for all the hard questions, but I don't. I don't know why I can't have it both ways. If I could, God as my holy judge, I would." She looks over at

Joey, still hanging on the edge of Daddy's recliner. His eyes are soft and wet. She smiles at him and pats the couch next to her. "Come here, Joseph."

He wipes his nose with the backside of his hand and joins her. I stand back near the kitchen, watching. I see them all, but they don't see me. I'm like a ghost at a funeral, watching the live people cry and carry on.

Mama wraps her free arm around Joey and rocks her body slowly back and forth, back and forth. "I want to be a good mother to you boys. I know I haven't always been the best. But you got to believe me. I care about you. It hurts me more than it hurts you. You're my flesh and blood, and I can't stand to see you so torn up inside."

"Ma," Joey says softly. "Are you really gonna leave?"

"Well, honey," Mama whispers, "it's no surprise. Someday I'm gonna leave, but not now, not tonight. And you'll come with me, too. Won't you?"

Joey nods. "I wanna go, too, Ma. Don't forget."

She kisses his hair and squeezes Danny with a strong hug. "You boys are my pride and joy. My strong sons. My young men. I need you to be brave. Can you do that?"

"I'll try, Mama," Joey says.

"How about you, Danny?" Mama asks.

"I'm the oldest. I'll do what I have to do," Danny says to the rug. He hasn't looked at her since she sat down beside him on the couch.

"One more thing," Mama says. She stands up now. She's got something important to say, and she can't sit still to say it. "If, for some reason, I have to leave without you, I'll send for you later. OK?"

Joey checks Danny's reaction, but Danny doesn't even so much as blink. Joey swallows and says, "Yeah, Ma."

Mama looks at Danny for a quick second, waiting for a nod or a "Yes, Ma," from him, but he doesn't say

241

anything. Joey answers again, in case Mama didn't hear him the first time, "I will, Mama."

"Good," Mama says. "Now I gotta go get supper ready. I love you, boys."

Mama heads back to the kitchen. She touches my shoulder as she passes and turns me from a spying ghost back into just Peanut. "Come set the table," she says.

"OK, Mama," I say, but I wait a few minutes before I follow her. My brothers look like trees in winter, lonely bare branches shivering in the snow. It's a sight I hardly ever see, so I take as much of it in as I can. I know how it is to be feeling like the cold wind has blown off all your leaves, and you got nothing left to hide. It's not easy.

"Do you think you'll go with her, Danny?" Joey asks.

"I don't know. I guess I'll decide when it happens."

Joey bites his lip. "Me, too," he says.

He stands up and for the first time notices I'm in the room. He gets all embarrassed like I've caught him in his underwear and he walks by me and punches my arm. "What the hell you looking at, pig-face?" he says. I don't try to punch him back, like I'd normally do. He looks so silly and little, it wouldn't be fair; kind of like punching Winnie for sucking on the edges of her blanket. Danny's still slumped into the couch. Joey goes over to the window. He stares out at the rain, falling heavy now. The streets are wet and full of cars carrying fathers home from work. I imagine all the houses all over Pisa with happy families waiting to greet them; kitchens full of the smells of supper, pretty wives opening front doors kissing their tired husbands hello. Daddy pulls his car into the driveway. The car door shuts; I hear him coming down the front porch.

"Dad's home," Joey says.

"So what," Danny says from across the room. He stretches out on the couch and buries his face into the cushions as the front door swings open, and Daddy comes inside.

Seventeen

The clock on the wall behind Sister Saint Joseph's desk ticks and ticks and ticks. I can't think. I'm supposed to be doing math problems. Sister wants us to hand in our papers before we go home for lunch, and I'm not even halfway done. These word problems poke my brain like sharp stones and give me such a headache. It's quarter to twelve, almost time to leave. The problems stare back at me like they're going to wrestle me to the ground. I put my pencil down and say "uncle." I can't do it anymore.

The wind blows the trees outside the classroom window. They look like June Taylor dancers bowing to an audience of dead grass and dirty, melting snow. It's still too early for buds, but the tips of the branches have round brownish-red tops that swell like a sore. It won't be long now. Spring will be here, all the way, not halfway like now, with the wind still cold and the sun trying to be warm but it can't because it's still too far away. I like it when the wind blows loud and wild, like it has to, to blow away what's left of the snow, holding on for dear life with greedy icicle fingers.

Sister announces it's time to break for lunch. "Walkers line up near the cloak room and riders over here by the blackboard. Hand your papers to me as you leave."

Riders are kids who bus in from outside of town. They bring their lunch to school everyday. Walkers are the kids, like me, who live close enough to school to go home.

I get up, hand in my math worksheet and head for the walkers' line. "Regina Giovanni," Sister calls, "I want to see you before you leave. The rest of you are dismissed." Her voice is cranky. I'm in trouble. I hoped I could make it out the door before she yelled at me for not finishing. The other kids march out of the room; their footsteps echo down the hallway.

"You didn't even answer half the questions," Sister says, waving the paper in my face. "You don't even try anymore, Regina, and I'm getting tired of it." Her dead fish eye twitches at me. I look away at the floor, at the stringy edges of my shoe laces. Sister puts her hand on my shoulder. "Sit down, child." Her bony fingers are as hard as her voice. She digs into the side of my neck.

"I know things are not good at home, Regina, but you must try to apply yourself," Sister says, softer now. She's trying hard to be nice, even though she squeezes my shoulder blade. "If there's anything I can do to help you, you must tell me."

It burns where she pinches me, but I don't cry out; I don't even dare move away. Sister must have talked to the principal about Mama losing the baby. She knows I killed it, and how she presses on my shoulder blade is like a penance she owes me for being a fallen angel. Or maybe she knows more, maybe she knows about Patrick and Happy Town. About Daddy praying all day and all night too, now, at St. Joan's. Maybe she's seen him there in the late afternoon, when she goes to refill the votive candles, dust off the altar, arrange the clean white cloth on the wooden altar steps. Sister and the principal talking about those things makes me feel funny. They can see through my skin, past my bones, into my soul. And now she wants me to tell her if I need help. I want to scream at her, "I don't need anything, not from Sister Mary Martha, not from you, not from anyone!" but instead I say, "Thank you Sister, I can't think of anything right now." I watch her black nun shoes tap and tap against the classroom floor.

"I can't give you a passing grade on this assignment, Regina, and if you keep up the poor work you've been producing lately, I will have to make you repeat the fifth grade next year. Do you understand?"

"Yes, Sister." I try to sound like I mean it, like I'm in confession and the only thing that's standing between me and grace is an honest "Forgive me, Lord." But I'm too tired to even pretend to be sorry.

"Can I go now? My little sister is waiting for me to walk her home for lunch."

She lets go of my shoulder. "Go on," she says. "But I want to talk with you more about this, after school tonight."

I move away from her eyes that look through me, that know what my heart is whispering, and I walk slowly out of the room. I can't stay late tonight. It's Friday and I've got to rush home and get ready to go visit Patrick. When I hit the corridor, I run as fast as I can to the stairwell, then down the two flights of stairs to the heavy metal doors that lead outside. My body races to catch up with my heart. Rosa's crying on the cement steps outside the building. "Peanut," she says. "Where were you? I thought you forgot about me."

I put my arm around Rosa's shoulder and sit down beside her on the school steps. "I'm sorry. Sister made me stay behind so she could yell at me."

"Did you get in trouble again?" Rosa wipes her nose on her navy-blue sweater. "Mama's gonna be mad at you."

I pull a Kleenex out of my coat pocket and hand it to her. "Don't worry about that," I say. "She'll never know if we don't tell her, OK?"

Rosa nods, and I grab hold of her hand. The smallness of her fingers calms my heart, and we head home for lunch.

"Peanut, do you like school?" Rosa asks.

"It's OK," I lie. "How about you?"

"I like it a lot. I love my teacher, Mrs. Infante. She reads to us, and we learn songs and play games. I wish Mama did that, too."

I think about when we were younger and Mama had more time to read to us, tell us silly stories she made up. One time she invented a story, just for me, about a little girl with red hair who loved to dance and sing with the tree fairies. She fell asleep in the forest and was whisked away by bumblebees who made her their queen. I used to be afraid of bees until Mama told me that story. When Mama laughed and sang, I wasn't afraid of anything or anybody. When she smiled, my heart buzzed like bumblebee wings. Silly things like that make me want to be in kindergarten again. Mrs. Infante's smile is as warm as golden honey.

Half a block from our house, Zoomer sees us. He gallops down the sidewalk, wagging his tail. I let go of Rosa's hand and say, "Race ya to the front door. Ready. Set. Go." We tear off running fast and hard against the wind, Zoomer chasing beside us. I lag behind just a little to let Rosa pass me. She squeals, "I win, I win!" when she touches the doorframe first. Zoomer barks, congratulating her, and we both laugh. Rosa opens the front door and we rush in, pushed by the wind and a few leftover leaves, brown and wet from last fall.

"Mama, we're home!" me and Rosa yell from the living room.

"I'm in here," Mama calls from the kitchen.

We follow the trail of her voice and find her sitting at the head of the kitchen table, cigarette in one hand, a cup of coffee in the other. Winnie's in her highchair chewing on a few saltines, but the tomato soup and grilled cheese sandwiches we usually eat for lunch every Friday aren't ready. The table's empty except for an ashtray full of cold cigarette butts and a box of Nabisco crackers. I look at Mama, then at Winnie, then at the box of saltines. The wind isn't outside anymore; it's inside me, shoving things around and around.

"Sit down, girls," Mama says.

I take a chair, and Rosa sits next to me. Zoomer settles in between us on the floor. Mama's eyes are mean and scared and sad, all at the same time. She's been smoking all morning. Her fingertips are yellowed and her lips are chapped. She wets them with the edge of her tongue, from time to time, and stares at the wall behind our heads. She blows smoke into the air, and I think of volcanoes and wait for the hot lava to spill over and burn everything.

"Patrick called this morning." She takes another drag and exhales slowly. "He wants to go." The smoke hangs around her head. Now she looks like a sad snow angel who can't fly back to heaven because the snow is dirty and hard and the spring wind is blowing her wings to shreds. "Today." She finishes her sentence and turns her eyes on mine. "He says he thinks it's time. And I agree."

She presses the glowing tip of her cigarette into the cold pile of ashes in the metal ashtray. A trickle of smoke rises from the snuffed-out end and disappears into the still air. She starts to cry. And God starts to laugh. I hear it low at first, then louder inside my head, inside my heart, the full, belly-shaking laugh of God. His eyes are full of fire and He claps His hands together making a sound louder than any thunder I have ever heard. I want to run and hide, escape the slapping, the laughing that gushes out of his wide-open mouth. He's laughing and laughing at me for thinking that killing the lost baby would make Mama and Patrick stop wanting to go away. He's laughing at my foolish prayers, the votive-candle promises I made to swap my good twin soul for the death of the lost baby. He tricked me. God knows He's won.

"Who's going?" I ask. God laughs even louder now. I can only hope Mama isn't listening to Him, that she forgives me for making a pact with Him to make her lose her baby.

"What do you mean, who's going?"

"Who are you taking with you?" I ask the same question in a different way.

"You girls, of course. I won't go without you," Mama says, taking a swig of coffee. Her eyes are dirty brown smudges in the middle of her pale face.

I want to believe her, but I can't stop hearing God's powerful laugh. It's a test, I know. I'm not gonna pass. Maybe God told Patrick that the baby could come back as soon as he took my Mama to Happy Town. When we get there, God will let the lost baby live again and Mama and Patrick will send me back to Pisa, to be with Danny and Joey and Daddy. Dear Holy Mother of God, are you laughing, too?

"Can we take Joey and Danny with us?" I ask.

"No, we'll send for them later, Peanut, after we get settled."

"Why can't they come now?"

My questions are bugging her. She swats at the edges of her hair and rubs her eyes.

"They're at school and besides there isn't enough room in the car for everyone," Mama says. "Now don't ask so many questions."

"Can Zoomer come with us?" The question slips out and splashes onto the table.

"No!" Mama yells. "Regina, don't be silly. No dogs."

Zoomer whines. No dogs. No dogs in Happy Town. No dogs in Heaven. God laughs again. Then I hear a slam, but it's not in the house, it's not outside, it's in the back of my mind. I drag Zoomer inside my heart, hide him in the cracks between the light and the air. I squeeze in beside him and bury my head in his furry neck. I don't move. My legs will fall off if I try to stand up. My hands tingle. My head is full of mud and rocks and bushels of old, dead leaves. The nuns lied. Daddy lied. Even Mama lied. God isn't good and kind. God is mean. His heart is colder than the sun in winter, dim and far away. Even the Blessed Virgin Mary can't help me now.

If I can't take Zoomer, I don't want to go either. "Why didn't you tell me this was part of the deal?" my heart screams at God. His laugh is like Danny's, teasing me. He tricked me into thinking the baby had gone away for-ever. I stare at Mama hoping she'll hear Him too, hear how He teases me with His laugh. If she could only hear it right, she'd change her mind and let Zoomer come.

"Zoomer won't be any problem, I'll make sure of it."

Mama looks right through me. I'm made of air, thin and smoky and empty. If I beg her to take my dog she'll get mad, and she might change her mind and not take me either.

"I'm hungry, Mama," Rosa says.

"Peanut, fix her a sandwich, and make one for you, too. I've got to call Patrick back and tell him you girls are home now."

I move around the kitchen. My arms and legs belong to someone else. I reach into the refrigerator, but I can't feel the slices of American cheese I pull out. I walk over to the counter for a loaf of bread, but someone else's feet take me across the floor. I make some cold sandwiches, give one to Rosa, and stare at her, thinking about nothing at all. My mind is switched off. I watch her from the darkness. Everything inside me is still and quiet, like dead black-eyed Susans sticking out of the snow bank down by the creek, where Zoomer and me go to whisper Mama's secrets in our private, alone place. I feel scared and mad and worried all at the same time, and each one erases the others until there's nothing left, and I can't talk or cry or yell. Just the quiet crowding me so.

Winnie just sits in her highchair munching on crackers and slurping apple juice from a plastic cup. Her yellow blanket lies on her lap. She's too little to know what's going on. Rosa just eats her sandwich and stares at the kitchen sink. Her heart's all quiet, too.

"Rosa, what do you think?" I whisper.

"About what?" Rosa says out loud, her mouth full of mashed yellow cheese and soft white bread.

"About going to Happy Town today," I say, louder but still soft. I don't want Mama to hear me.

"We can have chocolate cake for dinner tonight," Rosa says. "Patrick said so. Remember?"

"Yeah. I remember."

But I don't want chocolate cake for supper. I want to know why leaving feels cold like winter in my bones. Then I think about Sister Saint Joseph's twitching, blue, dead fish eye. At least I won't have to face her this afternoon. All my life I've wanted to run away—leave the shouting and the smoky sadness that fills up our house, choking everybody. But now that I can, I don't want to.

Mama comes back in the kitchen, straight and tall. She's full of plans and purpose. "It's all settled. Hurry up and eat. I want you to get ready." She rummages through a drawer, and her hands shake. She pulls out a piece of paper and a pen, then grabs three A&P grocery bags and hands them to me. "Here," she says. "there's one for each of you. Put some of your clothes inside and help Rosa with hers. Don't forget to fill one for Winnie, too."

I never noticed before how paper bags smell like sadness. I hold the roughness in my hands and run my finger over the scalloped edges at the top. I bring the bag to my nose and smell. The brown seeps into my skin, and I tear the corner just a tiny bit.

"Can I bring the My Fair Lady record?"

"Can I bring my doll house?" Rosa asks.

"No girls, we're taking Patrick's car and there's not enough room for all that stuff. Now get a move on it."

I take Rosa's hand, and we go upstairs to our bedroom. I open our dresser drawers and pull out a few things. Zoomer circles around me like his fur is on fire. He cries and barks and looks at me with eyes that know what's happening but can't stop it.

"Go away," I say to him. "We can't take you." He doesn't listen. He rubs against my leg; he nuzzles his head behind my knee. It hurts to feel him touching me. I push at him. "Go away, I said. Go downstairs." I can't watch him. I want to grab hold of him, rush into my closet, slam the door shut and never come out. I stuff clothes into my paper bag and pretend I can't hear him whining.

"Please, Zoomer. Please go downstairs." My eyes meet his, and I try to tell him I love him without words. I try to send him special, secret thoughts to let him know I'll come back for him. I'll find some way. He races, like a dog of wind, down the stairs into the living room, then back up again, up and down, up and down, until at last I hear the back door open and shut and Zoomer yelping outside the house. Mama shut him out, but she can't quiet him. He barks and barks, shaking the neighborhood with his howling.

I finish packing my paper grocery bag. I stuff in my purple cardigan, a white long-sleeved turtleneck, my red corduroy skirt and my brown stretch pants. Rosa crams her yellow blouse, blue corduroy pants, black pullover sweater and her Snoopy pajamas into her bag. She reaches for Binkie. "I don't know if there's room for that," I say.

"I won't go without Binkie," Rosa says. She starts to cry, and I don't want her to get all upset and get Mama all riled up.

"Maybe you can put him on your lap," I say. She squeezes Binkie between her arms. "Grab some stuff for Winnie and don't forget some underwear for you, too," I remind her. I grab some cotton panties and some socks for myself and take a quick look around the room to see if there's anything else I want.

No sense in taking that junky old bedspread. Or the faded curtains. Or the holy card of the sad Virgin Mother with the swords stuck into her bleeding heart. The picture of the beautiful Mother with her arms reaching out for a hug would be nice in Happy Town. "Mama," I yell downstairs, "can I take the picture of the Blessed Virgin Mother?"

Mama shouts back up to me, "No! Just get your clothes and come down here!"

"But Mama," I start to argue, "It's the one I'm named after, my favorite! You can't make me leave it behind!"

"Peanut, come to the top of the stairs, this instant!" she orders.

I march over to the landing and stare at her staring back at me. One hand rests on her hips. She shakes her other hand at me. "Sit down for a second and listen to me carefully."

I plop down and set my grocery bag between my legs.

Mama's voice trembles. "Regina, I need you to cooperate. I want you to get yourself and your sisters ready. You can't be dragging a leg here. We're meeting Patrick in an hour. Take only what will fit in the trunk of his car. Nothing more. Do you understand?"

I nod and Mama says, "Good girl. Now get going."

I hop to my feet. I better not mess this up. This isn't just any regular Friday. We're going in Daddy's car to see Patrick, same as always, but tonight we aren't coming home. No Saturday-morning cartoons, no Sunday-morning church. No Pisa. No more. A little bit of what that means seeps into my brain. It feels sticky. I try not to think about it. My legs are heavy, and my feet move like they're stuck in a pile of sand. I look out the window at Zoomer racing up and down the side of the house. He's not barking anymore. His voice ran out of crying. Joey loves him almost as much as I do. He'll be nice to him until I can come back and get him.

I take the picture of the Blessed Virgin Mary off the wall and smash the glass with the handle of my hairbrush. I dump bits of glass onto the top of my dresser and slip the picture part out as carefully as I can. I blow glass dust off the Blessed Mother's face. Regina, Queen Mother, Holy Mother of God. Maybe you can make God stop laughing at me. I roll the picture up and stick it in my grocery sack.

"Are you ready, Rosa?" I ask.

"Yeah," she says.

"Then let's go."

I take her hand, and we run downstairs to the living room. Mama's in the kitchen, hunched over, writing something. I come up behind her and see Danny's and Joey's names on the outside of an envelope. "What's that, Mama?" I ask.

"It's a letter for the boys, Peanut. So they'll know I'll be sending for them soon," she says.

"Oh," I say. I imagine them coming home and getting a note that says something like "We've gone to Happy Town, see you later." It makes me shiver to think about them finding it. I hope they understand. I hope they aren't too mad at me. I hope Patrick and Mama send for them, and Zoomer, after we get to Happy Town.

"Get in the car now," Mama snaps at me and Rosa.

We walk outside, and Zoomer races up to us. I reach for him, but Mama grabs his collar and pulls him back inside the house. He howls now, behind the closed door. I shove my paper bag under my armpit and stick my fingers in my ears so I can't hear Zoomer. I swallow a scream.

One by one, we pile into Daddy's Rambler. Winnie sits up front, and Rosa sits in back, next to me. We put our A&P bags on the floor, near our feet. Mama shuts the house door, walks over to the car, and gets in. She pulls out of the driveway, checking the rear-view mirror for traffic. I watch her spy the Browns' house across the street, but Mrs. Brown isn't outside today. If she's peeking from her side window, we can't tell. Mama pulls the car onto the street and heads toward the highway.

No one says a word as Mama drives past the houses on Chestnut Street, past the playground where the boys play Little League, where I take craft lessons in the summer and learn how to weave yarn pot holders. We drive out of town without a sound except for the hissing of the tires against the road and the wind howling all around us. When we're on the highway, I break the silence.

"Where are we going to meet him, Mama?"

"In the parking lot at Ames', just outside of town."

"Are we just gonna leave Daddy's car there?"

"No. Peanut, quit asking so many questions. You don't have to know everything," Mama scolds.

Rosa starts to sing "Twinkle, Twinkle, Little Star," and Mama snaps, "Stop that."

"But Mrs. Infante taught us that song in school this morning, Mama. Can't I sing it just a little?"

"No!" Mama screams at Rosa.

"Mama's kinda nervous, Rosa," I say, trying to smooth her wrinkled feelings. "Let's play I-See-Something."

Winnie peeks her head over the back of the front seat, and smiles at us.

"OK," I say.

"Me first," Rosa says. "Um. I see something blue."

"Is it the sky?" I ask.

"Nope," Rosa says.

"Blue," Winnie says, pointing to the car seat.

"Nope," Rosa says.

"Is it the Blessed Virgin Mary?" I ask, pointing to the statue on the dashboard. Daddy put the statue there to protect us when we travel around town. When I said good-bye to him before he went to work this morning, I didn't think it would mean this kind of good-bye. He touched the top of my head and said "See ya later, kiddo." Something pinches inside when I think of his eyes. Will he be sad when he comes home from work, and we're not there? Will he miss us?

"Nope, it's not the statue," Rosa says.

"I know what it is," I say, but Mama interrupts.

"Girls, you've got to be quiet. I can't hear myself think, you're making such a racket."

"We were just trying to keep out of your hair," I say.

"Quiet!" Mama shouts, and we all fall back into our seats and stare out the windows. Winnie starts whimpering, and Mama says, "I'm sorry, honey. I didn't mean to scare you. Peanut, did you bring any of Winnie's books? Read her a story."

"I didn't remember her books," I say. I hardly get the words out, knowing how mad she's gonna be at me for forgetting.

"Goddamnit, Regina. I thought I could count on you. What the hell were you doing, lollygagging around again, like always?"

"I'm sorry, Mama," I say. The words are hot against my lips. It's hot in the car, it's hot on my head, it's hot all over. I'm sweating.

"Well, it doesn't matter now," Mama says. "We're almost there."

"Almost to Happy Town?" Rosa asks.

"No. No. To Ames' Department Store," Mama says. "Now girls, just shut up and let me think."

Mama keeps checking the rear-view mirror, like somebody's sitting on the back bumper. I turn around quick to check for myself. All I see are the yellow lines in the road falling behind us. Mama squints, even though it's cloudy out. She wants to cry or scream, maybe both. The lines around the corners of her eyes are deep like stick marks in thick mud, and her mouth is twisted. She's having a hard time trying to keep something inside. I lean against the back of her seat and touch the edges of her curls. "Mama," I say. "Are you OK?"

"Hush, now," she says. "We're here."

She pulls into the shopping center parking lot, drives past the other cars in front of Ames' and heads towards Patrick's red car, parked in the far corner of the lot. She pulls Daddy's car into the spot right next to Patrick's, shuts off the motor and turns around to look at me.

"Peanut, unload our stuff and put it into Patrick's trunk as quickly as possible. No fussing, no whining, no nothing. Just do as I say."

"OK, Mama."

Her face scares me. It's not the faraway look she gets

when she stares at the sky, waiting for the lost baby to come over the hill. It's worse. She looks old, all rough and knotted. She doesn't even smile when Patrick comes up to the car. He looks bad, too. His forehead is covered with sweat and his face is red and ready to explode. "Hi, Marie. How're you doing?" he says, leaning into the open window.

"As best as can be expected, I guess," Mama says.

"Got everything?" Patrick asks.

"I think so," she says. "And what we haven't got, I guess we don't need."

"It'll be OK, Marie," Patrick says. He opens our car door, and Mama gets out. She hugs him, and he kisses her, then he looks at me and the girls. "Hey, Winnie, how are you, sweetie?" He leans in and kisses Winnie on the forehead. "Rosa, you sure look pretty today." He touches the side of Rosa's face. "And Peanut, are you ready for an adventure?" He smiles at me. He tries to sound like he's not scared, but I can tell he is. His lips barely move when he talks.

Winnie crawls over the front seat and hops out of the car. Rosa opens the back door and runs up to Mama. I collect our grocery-bag suitcases and join them.

"Put those in the trunk, Peanut," Mama says. "Then get in the back seat." She points to Patrick's car.

"Come on, the rest of you, Rosa and Winnie, get in back with Peanut," Patrick says. Then he turns to Mama. "We'll follow you back, then pick you up two blocks from the house. OK?"

"Yeah," Mama says. She looks like she's gonna throw up.

"Are you going to be OK, Marie? Are you sure you want to do this?"

"God, yes. I can't take it anymore. It's time we were a family."

"OK. OK. Calm down. Can you drive?" Patrick says.

"Yes. Let's just get this over with. I'll be happier once we get out of this state."

Mama gets into Daddy's car, and Patrick joins us in his. "Where's Mama going?" I ask. I don't like it one bit. Rosa and Winnie look worried, too. "It's OK, girls. Your mama's just going to return your dad's car. We'll pick her up before we leave for Happy Town."

Mama drives off in Daddy's Rambler, leaving us with Patrick. I watch her pull out of Ames' parking lot, and I grab hold of the armrest in the back seat of Patrick's car. She wouldn't just forget about us. She wouldn't change her mind and go back to live with just the boys and Daddy. I hear God laughing again, and I scream.

"Peanut, shut up!" Patrick snaps. He slaps the back of the front seat and slams his car door. "You've got to keep quiet now. Your mother and I have got some important things to take care of. You can't be getting all crazy on us. You've got to be good. Look after your sisters. Understand?"

I nod, even though the only thing I understand is that I want him to start up his car and follow Mama. "Let's go get her," I say. "Hurry."

Patrick pulls out of the parking lot. Three cars pass us, and I lose sight of Mama. "Where is she? I don't see her," I say, careful not to scream it out. I pray to the rolled-up picture of the Blessed Mother stuck away in my grocery bag in the trunk. Please bring Mama back. I'll be good. I won't scream. I won't cry. I won't get in the way.

"Calm down, Peanut," Patrick says. "She's right up there. See? There she is, in that blue car."

"I see her," Rosa says. She points her out to me, and I feel better. "OK," I say. I relax my fingers, but I don't sit back in the seat. I can't rest until we get Mama back. We catch up to her again and follow her closely, the rest of the way back to Pisa.

Patrick drives past the playground again. I want to open the door and run into the fields, hide until sundown, then sneak back to Daddy and the boys and tell them Patrick tried to kidnap us, but I escaped. If I could pull Mama away with me, I'd do it. I swear.

When we get closer to our house, Patrick squeezes the steering wheel. He looks at us through the rear-view mirror and says, "OK, girls, I need you to do something for me now."

"What?" we ask.

"I want you to duck down in the seats so no one sees you."

Winnie giggles.

"Why?" I ask. He stares at me and says, "We'll play a game on your mama. You all hide until we go pick her up. When I say 'OK', that's your signal. You pop up and surprise her. It'll be fun."

He's lying. He's trying to pretend this is just a game, but it's not. I squint a mean look at him. He shoots me one right back. "Duck down," he orders. I scrunch down on the floor of the back seat so my head is below the bottom of the window, and Rosa and Winnie copy me. Patrick drives slowly, creeping down the street a few blocks from our house.

"Are we there yet?" Rosa asks.

"Shh," Patrick says. "I'll let you know when it's OK to come back up." The car stops all of a sudden, and the front door opens and slams.

"Let's get out of here," Mama says. Her voice shakes.

Winnie pops her head up, and Patrick snaps, "Stay down for a little bit more, girls."

We go a little ways longer, all bent up like cardboard boxes. My legs start to cramp up, and my head aches.

Finally, Patrick gives us the signal. "OK, you can sit up now."

Rosa and Winnie shout, "Surprise!" I undo my tangled legs and sit back in the seat. We pass the "Welcome to Pisa" sign. I don't look back to wave good-bye or to cry. Not even once.

EIGHTEEN

The wind blows steady, pushing at the branches outside the school door. The tips of small maple trees scrape against the brick like fingernails against cold, hard steel. Small piles of crusted snow and dirty patches of ice and decaying leaves, leftover from last fall, litter the school grounds, bleak and dull as a heartache. The chilly March wind is an annoying reminder that spring is still weeks away.

"Won't it ever let up?" Joey mumbles as he pulls the collar of his Yankees baseball jacket closer around his neck.

He's been staring out the window all day. He's been homesick, just waiting for the school bell to ring, waiting to get home, pick up his baseball bat and head for the field. He races away from the school, hustles down the block and heads for home. In a few weeks it'll be warm enough to start practice. He can hardly wait for the smell of grass stains on his jeans, the grime of home-plate dirt under his fingernails.

Maybe I can get Danny to hit a few balls this afternoon. It's Friday. There's no one to crab at me to hit the books instead of going to the ballfield before dinner. I wonder if Danny has to work today.

He glances back at the school, but he doesn't catch

sight of his brother. He tucks his geometry book under his arm, stuffs his hands into his pockets and heads into the wind. He crosses over the bridge, down Pine Street and past the church. He looks up at the stained-glass window of St. Joan, riding her mighty white horse. She sits proud and powerful. The way she holds her head up high, eyes staring straight into the wind and the cold, reminds him of his mother. He can't wait to tell her he got an A on his English exam. She'll be so proud of him, and her eyes will be warm and full of love when she hugs him. That's the best thing about Ma. Her hugs could melt that stained-glass window into a river of color.

He thinks of her sitting in the bleachers last summer, sipping a cola, watching him play shortstop, and he smiles as he rounds the corner and heads up Chestnut Street. Half a block from home he sees his dad's car in the driveway. Ma's still home. Maybe she's sick, or maybe one of the girls is. He picks up speed, then he thinks maybe he's got it all wrong, and he slows down again. If one of the girls were sick, she'd leave Peanut home to take care of them, and if it were Peanut who was sick, Ma'd still go. Peanut's old enough to take care of herself. Must be something wrong with Dad's car. Patrick must have swung by to pick her up. It's not too likely, what with Mrs. Brown being such a busybody and all, but who knows, it never pays to second-guess Ma.

He opens the porch door, expecting Zoomer to bark hello. Ma usually leaves the dog out here on Fridays. The wind must have blown the porch door open and Zoomer's off chasing squirrels or playing down by the creek. The dog will come home when he's good and hungry. Always does. Crazy mutt gets even crazier on Fridays when Peanut's gone.

Joey opens the front door and steps inside the house. It's stuffy and warm and smells like stale cigarettes. He unzips his jacket. Zoomer whimpers from behind the couch. His black paws stick out. "Hey, Zoomer. What ya doing back there, boy?" Joey asks. "How come you're still in the house? Ma must have forgot to let you out. She must have been in a real hurry today. Peanut probably dragging a leg again. Serves her right." Joey walks over and tugs at the dog's legs. "Come on, boy, let's get you a Milkbone." He helps Zoomer wiggle his way out from behind the couch. The dog sniffs at Joey's hands; once he's freed, he follows Joey into the kitchen.

Joey sets his schoolbook on the table. He opens the refrigerator and takes out a bottle of milk and a piece of leftover pizza. He grabs a handful of Milkbones from the cupboard and sets them on the floor beside Zoomer. "Here ya go, buddy." The dog refuses the treats. He whines and circles the kitchen table. He barks and jumps at Joey. "What the hell you doing?" Joey yells. He falls back and shouts, "Stop it, you crazy dog. You flipping out on me or something?" He opens the back door and forces Zoomer outside. "Get out of here, go jump at some squirrels or something." Zoomer stands in a patch of dirty snow, on the other side of the shut door, and barks louder. Joey narrows his eyes and looks at the dog, trying to figure out what's making him act so weird today. Maybe he misses Peanut. Damn dog and her are connected at the hip. He shouts through the closed window, "She'll be home later, don't get your sweat warm."

Zoomer circles the yard. He jumps at the kitchen door. Joey turns away, takes a swig out of the milk bottle and winces thinking about how, if Mom were here, she'd yell at him to get a glass. "What she don't know won't hurt her," he says, wiping the milk from his lips. He eats the pizza in three huge bites then goes to the cupboard, looking for some cookies.

He grabs a handful of Oreos and sits at the kitchen

table, stuffing them, one by one, into his mouth. His eyes rest on the clock above the stove. Where the hell is Danny, anyway? Not too much time left. It'll be dark soon. Too late to hit some balls. I'll go to the field without him. I need to practice. Tryouts are next week. Maybe Mom will let me play ball Sunday instead of going to church. If she's in a good mood tomorrow morning, I'll ask her. He shoves a few more cookies into his mouth, wipes the crumbs from his hands. His eyes fall on an envelope propped up against the salt and pepper shakers. "Joey & Danny" is written in his mother's handwriting. "Jesus, what chore does she want us to do now?" He picks up the note. Zoomer jumps at the door, startling him. "Knock it off," he yells back over his shoulder at the dog. He rips into the envelope and starts to read.

The stuffy, stale kitchen closes in on him. The air presses against his skin. It feels cold, like the wind biting his hands. It feels hot, like a fever biting into his bones.

> Dear Danny and Joey,
> I don't know how to say this, and I don't want you to ever think I don't love you. I've taken the girls and we've gone away with Patrick. By the time you read this note, we will be out of the state. I love you both, please remember that. I'll send for you soon.
>
> > Love,
> > Mom

"I will send for you soon," Joey repeats the words as if saying them will put flesh and bones on the vowels and make his mother come back. "I love you," he reads, as if saying those three words out loud will make the stinging in his heart go away, ease the terrible pounding in his brain.

His hands shake, and his legs have given up hope of holding the weight of his sadness. He drops the note onto the table and slumps into a kitchen chair. Zoomer barks and barks in the yard outside, his howling races out of his body. Joey opens his mouth to scream, but only silence races out, rushes into the room with a powerful quiet thud. He stares at the paper, at the ink, forming perfect letters on the page, telling him in perfect sentences that she is gone.

"No," he says. He slaps the table. "Jesus Christ, no, no, no, no!" He stands, twirls around swinging his arms at the air, at the walls, at his own fears. He punches the wall, screaming. "She did it, goddamnit, she did it! She walked out, that son of a bitch. How could she leave without me and Danny?!" He screams over and over as he punches and punches at the kitchen wall until his fist crashes through, bruising the wall, bruising his hand.

"Owwww!" he howls. "Look what you've done!" he screams at his mother's letter. He swings at the milk bottle, sending it crashing to the floor, a frothing sea of milk and broken glass. "Goddamn fucking asshole, how could she do this to us? How could she?" His arms are heavy from swinging, they fall loosely at his side, and he slumps into the corner by the refrigerator. He buries his face in his sore hands. Outside Zoomer whines and scratches at the back door. Joey mumbles, "Shut up, you old fool, shut up." He bangs his head against the wall as if knocking on the outside will kill the knocking inside. He doesn't hear the front dooropen, then slam shut.

"Joey? Are you here, Joey?" Danny calls from the living room. "Zoomer's acting like a maniac. Where the hell are you?" Danny yells. The dog sneaks in behind Danny and races past him into the kitchen. He runs up to Joey and licks the side of his head. "Jesus Christ, it's a fucking mess in here. What the hell did you do, Joey?" Danny says, standing tall and steady in front of Joey.

"She's gone," Joey says. He doesn't want to, but he starts to cry. He can't hold it back anymore, not even in front of Danny. He's too tired to pretend it doesn't matter anymore.

"What you talking about?" Danny asks.

Even with his eyes shut, Joey can feel Danny staring at his swollen face, his screaming, aching hands.

"It's all in there," Joey says, pointing to the note. "You can read it yourself."

Danny steps over the puddle of milk and broken glass and reaches for the note lying on the kitchen table. He reads it, rips it in half and tosses it on the floor. It floats like a leaf to the linoleum. Without saying a word, he turns around, bends over Joey, grabs his head between his arms and rocks him. The wind rushes through Joey's tired arms and legs, pushing through his gut and out his eyes. He can't stop the rushing any more. He leans into Danny's chest and howls like Zoomer howling at the back door. Danny holds him strong and fast and close to his heart. "All you need, you already got, Joey. Just remember that. You don't need nothing else."

When Joey stops crying, Danny grabs him some paper towels to blow his nose.

"Let's get out of here," Danny says.

"What do you mean?" Joey asks. "Should we follow her, make her take us too?"

"She don't want us, Joey. You better get used to it."

"She said she does. She said she'd send for us. You read it. You know what she said."

"She ain't gonna do that, Joey. She may think she is, but she ain't. And besides, Dad would never let us go. We're all he's got now. We got to be strong for him."

Joey's eyes are wet and wild. "I don't want to stay

here with Dad. I want Mom. Danny, you don't know nothing. She'll come back for us, you'll see." His shoulders stiffen; his whole body wills it to be true.

Danny shakes his head and turns away. "Let's go for a walk. This place is too stuffy for me. Zoomer, come on, ole boy. It's you and us, now. No more Peanut." Danny walks away toward the living room; the dog follows, his tail slung low between his back legs. "Come on Joey, let's go hit a few balls before Dad comes home."

Joey looks around the kitchen, at the stove where his Mom makes supper, at the sink where she sings sometimes when she and Peanut do the dishes together, at the ashtray on the counter, overflowing with old cigarette butts and cold ashes. This room is her room, full of her smells and her voice. Full of fights and yelling and angry fingers waving, sad hands slapping the worn edges of the old Formica table top. He swallows hard and eases himself up from the floor.

"Dad's gonna be mad when he sees the mess I made," Joey calls to the other room.

"We got time," Danny reassures. "We can pick it up after we hit some balls. Besides, he ain't gonna be happy no matter what, when he finds out she finally did it."

Joey grabs some ice, puts it in a towel and wraps it around his sore hand. "Danny," he asks, walking into the living room, "She ain't coming back, is she? She hates us."

"Don't matter now, does it?" Danny says, slinging his arm around Joey. "You sure got some punch in you, you son of a bitch. You put a hole the size of a basketball in that wall."

Danny smiles, and the hard center of Joey's heart softens just a little bit. He nods and grins a second, until the room feels too tight for him and his grin squeezes itself into a frown. "Danny, I'm scared."

"You can't let it get to you. She ain't worth it."

Maybe Danny's right. Maybe he's not. There's still that small quiet corner in the back of Joey's mind that won't give in. In there, safe and out of the wind, he pretends his Mom is just gone for the evening. When he gets up tomorrow, they'll all be there at the breakfast table: Peanut, Winnie and Rosa eating cereal and toast, just like always. And his mama will get up later and fix herself a cup of coffee and smoke too many cigarettes, and his dad will sit stone-faced, reading the morning paper. He can't picture it any other way. The note has to be some bad dream, a hoax his ma is playing on them. It isn't real. It's just her make-believe fantasy of how she wants it to be. She wouldn't choose Patrick over the rest of us. She couldn't do that. Joey knows. He knows in his heart.

Danny picks up a baseball and grabs a bat and glove, then the boys walk outside into the wind and the fading light. Zoomer tags along, a few steps behind them. "Spring training starts soon, Joey. What kind of team you think the Yanks will field this year?"

"We'll take the Series, you can bet on it," Joey says. He shivers and zips his jacket up. "Even Mom thinks so." It slips out, without thinking, tumbles over his tongue, as natural as the evening twilight. Neither one of the boys says another word as they walk to the baseball field.

NINETEEN

Mama complains about everything. First Patrick's driving too fast, then too slow. The car's too hot, it's too stuffy. Patrick opens a window. Then it's too cold. Her long face gets even longer. The wrinkle lines pinch her eyes and dig deep scars into the skin around her mouth. She picks at her fingernails for a while, then lights a cigarette. Patrick concentrates on the road. His face is serious and sweaty. My sisters are antsy. Winnie's slapping Rosa's arm 'cuz Rosa's inching over to her part of the seat, and Rosa pinches Winnie's leg and tells her, "Quit breathing on me." Every once in a while Mama yells, "Pipe down now, girls!" and I tell them to quit fighting or we'll get in trouble, but I don't say it too many times. They're just sick of being in the car. We all want to get out and get some fresh air.

"Mama, can we go home now?" Rosa asks. Mama looks like Rosa just spit in her face.

"We're going to Happy Town, Rosa, remember?" Patrick says, real quick.

"Happy Town. Happy Town," Winnie says in a singsong voice.

"How long will it take to get there?" I ask.

"A few days," Patrick says.

He talks to me through the rear-view mirror. His eyes are hard stones. I press my cheek against the window and watch the countryside whirl past, fast like the wind. It blurs and blurs until everything looks like everything else I just saw miles and miles ago; a river of gray sky and muddy brown snow. I feel hollow. All my guts are dumped in a heap on somebody's kitchen table, like a Halloween pumpkin, and I wait and wait for the knife to carve me a mouth, a nose, some eyes. I wait for the candlelight to spill out of my face, bright and shiny, eating away the dark.

I miss Zoomer so much I can hardly breathe. I close my eyes, and I see his scared face chasing around the living room. I open my eyes, and I see strands of his hair on my sweater. I touch his hairs, holding on tight to each flimsy piece.

The ride is long. Every time we hit a bump in the road, my head knocks against the back seat. The car stinks with cigarette smoke. I can't stand it. I think of Sister Saint Joseph's twitching, blue, dead fish eye and I wonder if she wonders why I didn't come back to school after lunch. She probably told the principal I skipped out, and she's probably calling our house right now. The phone keeps ringing and ringing. It must be driving Zoomer crazy. Now I feel like a smashed Halloween pumpkin, my orange skin splattered on the cold sidewalk.

Pretty soon Joey and Danny will find Mama's note. Maybe they'll feel smashed, too. They'll pick up the envelope with their names on it, and they'll know we didn't just go to Cayuga to visit Patrick. They'll know by the way Mama wrote the letters of their names, wiggly, like she was in a hurry and couldn't get her hand to stop shaking. Then they'll call Daddy at work. And Daddy will pray a rosary. He'll go to Saint Joan's, kneel in his

272

favorite pew, right up near the altar, bury his face in his hands and cry the rosary. God won't be laughing then.

Maybe Daddy will grab Uncle Tony and get in his car and come get us. I hope he does. I don't know if he'll know where to find us, but he better bring Zoomer with him. I hope he remembers to tell Amelia she's still my best friend, even though I couldn't tell her good-bye. Mama was in such a hurry, and besides if I said good-bye she'd want to know where I was going, and then I'd have to tell her all the secrets. It wouldn't be right to love her more than Mama. Mama comes first. Always.

Maybe Happy Town is too far for Daddy to even want to try to follow us. I looked up Wisconsin in the atlas at school once. It's four states away. Too far from Pisa to sneak out in the middle of the night and run home. Maybe once we get there, Mama won't like it, and she'll tell Patrick to turn around and take us back. "It's too cold," she could say, or "The people are grouchy." He could drop us back in Pisa, near the playground, if he was too scared to see Daddy. Then me and Mama and the girls could walk the few blocks home. I'd run as fast as I could, hollering for Zoomer all the way down the street.

Mama's head is tilted against the back of the front seat. The lines around her mouth are smoother, now. She looks calmer. Patrick's got his arm across the back, behind Mama's shoulder, and he's touching Mama's hair, rocking her to sleep with just his hand. "It'll be OK, honey," he says. "Now we're a family." Mama's eyes open and close like butterfly wings. They shut all the way now, and his hand rests near her face, warm as a blanket.

My eyes sting from the clouds of cigarette smoke in the car, and my throat is dry. I crack open the window to let in some clean air. Rosa holds Binkie tight and lays her head on my lap. I touch her hair, brush my fingers over her soft skin. Winnie's sleeping, all curled up by the other window, holding her blanket. She looks like a baby angel on her way back home to heaven. I shut my eyes and try to sleep, but I can't get comfortable, so I stare out the window. We pass towns with names like Bath and Hornell. We go farther still, and I don't know where we are, but I know we're a long way from Pisa. The air smells different. The buildings, the people, the streets, the trees look strange and new. It's getting dark out now, and the sky is lonesome without the stars.

I lock my car door. Rosa's asleep. She drools on my leg; it feels warm, like tears. All the times Mama and Patrick talked about going to Happy Town, I guess I never thought it would really happen. Deep inside, I hoped it was just make-believe, like when me and Amelia pretend to be famous Broadway dancers. We dress our mouths up with lipstick and put our hair up with bobby pins so we look beautiful and grown-up. We spray and spray hair stuff. The air around our heads shines like a halo. But after a while we get tired of being Broadway stars and go play checkers or ride our bikes. I guess Mama and Patrick never got tired of playing Happy Town.

Patrick fiddles with the radio, trying to tune in a station. He whistles softly, and I let the song carry me to a safer place.

"Patrick," Mama says. She's awake now, and her voice is soft like Patrick's whistling. I let it fill up the car, fill up my sad heart.

"Maybe we should stop for some dinner soon," she says. "The girls must be getting hungry."

"We can stop when we hit Pennsylvania. I don't want them to be able to come after us tonight," Patrick says. "It's only another 15 miles or so to Erie."

"OK," Mama says. "They're all asleep anyway."

I close my eyes, so she'll think I'm napping. We're really outlaws now. It's how he says it. He doesn't want them to come after us tonight. We're on the run from the law, from the sheriff's gun, from the eyes of God. God's not laughing now, not even at me. He's quiet and waiting for the posse to show up. Daddy and Danny and Joey with his baseball bat. Zoomer with his teeth, fierce and growling, ready to bite Patrick's face off.

"What are you thinking about, Marie?" Patrick says. His voice is heavy, like he wants to lay it down so he can rest awhile.

"Did we do the right thing?"

They talk in low, whispering voices. Patrick's quiet for a few minutes and all I hear is the soft music from the radio. Then he starts talking, and the words tumble out of his mouth like a sad song.

"When you lost the baby, I thought I'd go crazy. It made me realize how precious you and Winnie are to me." He stops for a second, like he's forgotten something, and he can't remember where he put it. "And Rosa and Peanut, too," he says, finally. "We're all family." I want to bite his cheek, leave teeth marks, small bruises, maybe even a scar, so every time he looks in the mirror he'll have to remember me and Rosa. Think of us, too. Not only Winnie. Always only Winnie.

"The boys must have gotten the letter by now," Mama says.

"What did you tell them?"

"I told them I loved them and that I didn't see any other way out. I told them I would send for them later, when we got settled. I said I hoped they'd understand and not hate me."

Mama cries. I want to jump over the back seat, push Patrick out of the car, turn it around and drive back to Pisa, but I sit real still, pretend to be sleeping and listen to their secrets.

"Marie, you did all you could do," Patrick says. "There

wasn't room in the car for everyone. We talked about it, remember? And we decided to do it this way."

"I know," Mama says. "But what if they don't come later? What if Paulie refuses to let them leave?"

"We'll cross that bridge when we get to it," Patrick says. His voice is regular now, not loud, not quiet. "Look, there it is." He gets all excited, and I crack one eye open and glance at the sign as we pass. Pennsylvania. It's too late now. Three more states to go, and we'll be there. And Patrick can have his family. If he was so lonesome, why didn't he find one of his own in Buffalo? Why'd he have to sneak into Pisa and steal ours?

"I think we're home free now, Marie."

I open my eyes, just a little, so they think I'm still sleeping. He puts his right arm around Mama's shoulder and squeezes her gently. We're home free. Just like in hide-and-go-seek.

He pulls off the highway and into the Erie Truck Stop Cafe. Mama reaches over the back of the front seat and nudges Winnie awake. Then she jiggles Rosa's leg and calls my name. I open my eyes all the way now, and Mama's smiling at me. "Are you hungry, honey?"

I stare at her lips, watch her teeth peek through like shy little girls. Patrick gets out of the car and stretches. "Boy, am I hungry," he says, patting his stomach. Then he nods at the cafe sign. "Just like old times, huh, Peanut? How about a burger and some fries?"

I open the door and get out, too, but I don't look at him. Rosa and Winnie yawn and rub their eyes awake.

"Are we there yet?" Rosa asks.

"Let's go, girls," Mama says. She waves her arms and herds the little ones to her. I hurry to catch up and throw my arms around her belly. I hold tight to the spot where the lost baby used to be. Mama hugs me back. I want to disappear into her coat, hide in her pocket, tell her I want to go home now. "What an adventure, huh, Peanut?" she says as she pats the top of my head.

"Yeah, Mama," I say. I squeeze her a little harder around the waist and whisper, "Holy Mary, Mother of God, pray for us outlaws, now and at the hour of our death, amen."

TWENTY

All things are possible if you just believe, and ask for it in God's name. Hadn't Dad said that a million times? Hadn't Danny prayed, too, until his praying was empty? Hadn't he begged God to stop her, make her stay in Pisa with them? Be a family again? In the beginning, Danny used to pray for God to give him ideas, new ways to stretch what little money his dad made. He even took a job, thinking if he helped out, it would ease the yelling, make the terrible shouting go away. With his help, his dad could stretch his paycheck, wrap it around Mom and bring her back, safe and full and satisfied. That's what he thought. But nothing worked. His mom still went back to Patrick, to his fancy car and his wallet stuffed with twenties. Danny spits his heartache onto the sidewalk. He coughs it up, pushes it out of his lungs so the cold March air can numb him.

He stares into the wind until it bites his eyes and he has to shut them. The stinging sinks into his cheeks, runs down the side of his face, rolls over his mouth, spills onto his chest, his arms, his hands holding fast to the end of a baseball bat. He walks into the evening, the light fading fast around him, around his brother and their dog, swallowing them into the belly of Pisa. This town will know, all too soon, that she left them a note, said good-bye, drove away into the dim, cold March afternoon.

They pass the Knights of Columbus hall, and Danny hands the baseball glove to Joey. Joey turns toward the ballfield. Danny yanks his arm, motions, "come on," with his head. "Aren't we gonna hit some balls, Danny?" Joey looks disappointed. Danny promised to practice with him, but his legs won't stop at the baseball diamond. They push on, taking him down the street toward the church. He thinks maybe his dad is inside. He thinks he better tell him God fell asleep. God's home snoring in the green recliner, feet propped up, mouth open wide and empty. He's not listening, Dad, Danny plans to tell him. All the asking in the world won't get you nowhere. You were wrong, and it's too late.

"No, Joey," Danny says. "We got something else to do. We can practice tomorrow. Come on."

Joey and Zoomer follow his lead. They head toward St. Joan of Arc's as the street lights blink on, one by one, in the early evening dusk.

The church looms in the twilight. Its spire pierces the sky, blocks out the tender moon. Danny opens the thick wooden door and goes inside. Joey and Zoomer slip into a pew in the back while Danny walks the stone floor, aisle after aisle, looking for his father. The quiet bothers him. It rustles like a terrible secret. He shakes his head to loosen its hold and searches the side altar for signs of Dad. He checks the stand of votive candles, but he's not there. Danny circles around to the other side of the church, but still no sign of his father. Maybe he's working a late shift. Of all the goddamn nights to pull a double. Danny can't hold his mother's leaving inside much longer. It pushes at him. The edges of his skin tingle. The hair on the back of his neck sticks out straight and sharp.

"He ain't here," he says to Joey.

"Where do you think he is?" Joey asks. He looks scared again, like he did in the kitchen, all folded in on himself, little and small. Danny can't stand to look at him. It scares him, makes him feel as if he's got to be as big as this church, as strong as the wind, to blow away Joey's hurting.

"I don't know, kiddo, but don't worry about it. I'm here." Danny touches Joey's arm and motions with his head to follow him outside.

Dirty leaves swirl around them as they leave the church. The wind moans and the branches on the maple trees near the rectory sway. "Where are we gonna go now, Danny? It's cold, and I'm hungry," Joey says.

"You wanna go home?" Danny says.

Joey looks at the ground and shakes his head no. Zoomer whines and brushes against Danny's leg. Danny walks down the steps, stands on the sidewalk in front of the church. He looks across the street at the houses, at the lights turning on inside, people coming home. He watches the cars pass by, headlights staring straight ahead, cutting a path through the dusk and the wind. His chest feels hard, like a baseball, a mass of stuff held together by stitches and leather.

"Danny," Joey says, and for a second Danny thinks it's his mother, calling from the kitchen, telling him to go wash up and get ready for supper. The mass in his chest rattles against his ribs, a tightness rolls down his arms until his fingers ache. He grips the end of the bat, swings the wood into the air, straddles the sidewalk. He reaches into his coat pocket and takes out a baseball. He holds it in his hands, feels the cold stitches against his palm. He tosses it into the wind, swings through the dusk and sends it crashing through the tall church window. God's faithful St. Joan rides to her death. Stained glass rains from the sky, glittering like jewels, all around them on the cold sidewalk.

"Jesus, Danny!" Joey yells. "What the hell'd you do that for?"

The rectory door flies open, and Father DiSante rushes into the evening, yelling, "Who's out there? Daniel. Joseph. What's going on?"

"Let's get out of here," Danny says. He drops the bat and they tear off down the block.

"Dad's gonna kill you when he finds out, Danny," Joey huffs when they finally stop down past the grade school.

"Who the fuck cares?"

Danny leans against the school building and catches his breath. His mind is flying now, trying to figure out what to do next. He can't go home. He can't run away, not with Joey and the dog. Where would they go? Who would take them in? He thinks of Mr. Johnston, but he'd be pretty pissed if he found out about the stained-glass window. He's not the kind to let his anger get the best of him. He wouldn't understand. Maybe Mrs. M. would let them spend the night, just until he could figure out what to do next. He could tell her he had a fight with his dad and he got kicked out of the house. But how would he explain Joey and Zoomer? Maybe he wouldn't have to.

"Come on, Joey," Danny says. He takes off again, running fast into the wind.

"Where we going now?" Joey shouts.

Joey runs hard to keep up to Danny's stride.

"Shut up," Danny snaps. "I'm gonna get us something to eat, OK?"

Two blocks down, he slows to a walk. He stops in front of a brown, shingled house and soaks the sweat from his face with his jacket sleeve. He stuffs his belly with air and goes around to the side of the house. He knocks hard on the aluminum storm door. Mrs. M. opens the door, and Danny offers a smile, trying to act as if they were out for a stroll and just happened to drop by. "Well, hello, Danny," the woman says. "What brings you here on a Friday night?"

Her gray bun is loosened, and her hair falls softly over her shoulders. She looks at Danny, then at Joey and the dog, then back at Danny. "Um," he starts. "We were taking a walk, and I was telling Joey about your Yankees scrap book, and he said he wanted to see it, and I said I didn't think you'd mind."

"Are you all right, Daniel?" she asks.

The baseball he used to break the church window feels like it's stuck in his throat. Danny swallows hard to push it down into his stomach. "Sure," he says. "Can we come in?"

Mrs. M. steps aside, and Danny and Joey and Zoomer walk into her warm kitchen.

"I was just having a little macaroni and cheese," she says. The table behind her is set with a single plate. A steaming casserole dish sits nearby. "Can I get you boys something to eat?"

"Sure, that'd be great," Danny says politely, like his mother taught him. Joey nods. "Put your mitt over there, then take off your coats and grab a chair," Mrs. M. tells them. She scoops some supper on a plate for each of the boys and sets it in front of them.

"So you're a Yankee fan," she says to Joey. Danny picks up his fork and shovels the macaroni and cheese into his mouth. Joey stuffs his bruised right fist into his lap and tries to balance his fork in his left hand. The macaroni falls off it onto the tabletop.

Danny's jaw tightens. He looks at the mess his brother made, then he looks at Mrs. M, who doesn't seem to notice or care about the clump of yellow plopped down

283

beside Joey's plate. She sips her coffee, pushes her empty dish to the side and says, "What's wrong with your hand, Joey?"

"He hurt it playing baseball," Danny says. "He nabbed one of my line drives and it bruised his palm."

"You should try to be more careful, Danny."

"Yes, Ma'am," Danny says. He nods softly, like a little boy, and reaches over to comfort his brother. Joey sets his fork down and stares at the plate of food. Zoomer whines at his side. Danny gulps down a glass of milk. This wasn't a good idea. They're gonna mess up my plan. Joey's being weird, and that damn Zoomer keeps pestering us.

"Have you two boys gotten yourself into some trouble?" she asks.

Danny hides behind innocent eyes. "No. We haven't done anything wrong."

"I've never known a boy Joey's age to pass up food," she says. "My son practically ate me out of house and home. And he never passed up macaroni and cheese."

Danny looks at his brother, hoping he won't crack. He can't tell her. It will be all over then. "Maybe we should go," Danny says, pushing away from the table.

"Aren't you going to even tell me why you stopped by?"

"I told you, we were taking a walk," Danny says. He's in a hurry to leave now. He stands up, reaches for his coat.

"I know what you told me, Danny. I want to know the real reason."

Her eyes stop him from going. He drops his coat and slumps back in his chair. He kicks the floor with the tip of his sneaker. Joey starts to cry, and Danny jumps up to put his hand over his brother's mouth. "Daniel, leave him alone," Mrs. M. cautions. Zoomer barks, and Mrs. M. points her finger at him to be still.

"What's bothering you, Joey?" she says. She puts her arm around Joey's shoulder and bends over him.

Danny holds his breath. Don't Joey, don't, he prays.

"She's gone," Joey says.

"Who? Who's gone, Joey?"

"Ma. She left, and she didn't even take us."

Danny thought he could pretend it never happened. Go on like nothing changed, as long as he didn't say the words out loud. He thought he could go to sleep and never wake up, leave town and never look back. He thought he had a chance until Joey opened his mouth and spit the words into Mrs. M.'s kitchen. The awful truth splatters all over the table. He can't clean up the mess. He can't wipe it away; the letters are smeared all over the Formica, clogging the cracks between the table leaves. Dirty words plopped down in the middle of the kitchen table. He can taste the messy grief on the tip of his tongue. It won't let him be.

"He don't know what he's talking about," Danny starts to say, but the bitter taste of his brother's confession stings his mouth and he sits, hands open in his lap, staring at Mrs. M.

"Your mother left?"

Joey nods. "There was a note," he says. "She said she'd bring us later." He talks as if his soul is crying, but his eyes are dry. His mouth opens and closes and the terrible words slip out. Danny wants to cram his fists into his brother's lips, but his hands lay open, too weak to tighten. Zoomer whines. The dog's high, sharp cry hurts his ears.

"Joey," she says. Her mouth stays open, like a question, but Joey doesn't say anything else. Danny fidgets in his chair, stares at her. "Danny, talk to me," she says.

He starts slowly, trying to find his way to the right words. He tries to tell her what happened without telling her how he feels about it. "She took off. You know, with Patrick. Hell, everybody in this godforsaken town knows about her and that asshole. Well, she finally did it. She finally left. I guess we must really piss her off or something. She didn't wait for us, to take us with her. Joey's really upset about it, but I told him we're better off without her anyway."

The words slip off his tongue. He looks past the gray strands of Mrs. M's long hair. He looks past the kitchen walls, past the plaster and beyond that to the two-by-fours, and then into the cold evening. He stares at the dark comfort of the night sky and closes his eyes. In the dark he can't see Joey's pale face, his mouth turned down, his eyes fat with tears. In the dark he can't see Mrs. M.'s brown eyes reaching out to touch his own sad face. In the dark he can't see her quiet hands closing in on his shoulders. Her fingertips are warm against his shirt, soft like his mother's brown curls.

He brings his hands to his face and presses against the stabbing behind his eyes. He folds his palms around his eye sockets and cradles his face in his hands. He rocks slowly. He feels Mrs. M.'s arms around him now, folding his small aching scream of a heart into her apron. His head rests on her breasts. He smells the sweetness of comfort on her breath. He grabs hold of her waist and the darkness rushes through him, pushing out of his eyes, his nose, his mouth. She gathers Joey in her arms, too, and Danny feels his brother's chest heaving, hears his tears rushing all around. Danny buries his face deeper into Mrs. M.'s apron so Joey can't see his own eyes, red and swollen. Zoomer leans against his leg and buries his face in the crook of Danny's knee.

Danny stays still for a few minutes, wrapped in Mrs.

M.'s arms, trying to catch his breath, calm his eyes. He waits until Joey is empty and quiet before he pulls away. He sits back in the chair without saying a word. Zoomer licks his hand. Joey wipes his nose on his shirt sleeve, and Mrs. M. reaches on the table behind her for a paper napkin and hands it to him. She offers one to Danny, but he refuses.

"We gotta be going now," he says.

Joey shoots him a panicked look that Danny tries to quell with a stare. "I ain't going, Danny," he says.

"Don't give me any grief, Joey," Danny says. "We gotta go see about Dad."

"It's best," Mrs. M. says. Her eyes are tender and firm. "Your place is with your father now. He needs you."

Danny nods. He grabs his coat and their baseball mitt, then nudges Joey and Zoomer toward the door.

"I'm here if you need me," she says. "Anything I can do. Just let me know."

She touches the side of his face. He backs away from her offering.

"Sure," he says. "Thanks."

He opens the storm door, and he and Joey and Zoomer step into the night and walk home.

✳✳✳

Halfway down Chestnut Street, Danny spies a black Lincoln parked in their driveway, right next to his dad's blue Rambler. "Jesus H. Christ," he mumbles.

"Who do you think it is, Danny?" Joey asks.

Danny drops his mitt on the driveway. The walk up the front steps, down the length of the porch and into the house is slow and quiet. Danny doesn't remember to breathe until he opens the front door. The living room is dimly lit. Two priests Danny doesn't recognize sit with their hands folded in their laps. Dad sits on the edge of his green recliner, shoulders hunched over. His hands shake. He stares at the braided rug, mumbling, "She's taken my daughters. Dear God in Heaven, she's taken my daughters." The priestly messengers don't say a word. The older one stares at his hands. The younger one stares at Danny's dad. He tugs a few times at his stiff white collar. There's something familiar in the way the priests hold their heads, as if God is whispering in their ears. Father DiSante sits in a chair by the TV. Danny's baseball bat rests against his leg.

Shit. They've come because of me, because I busted that goddamn window. "I'll pay for it, don't worry," Danny says. His voice is hurried, his eyes remorseful. He puts his hands in front of his chest to ward off the reprimand he assumes is coming. The visitors turn their heads slowly, finally noticing Danny and Joey standing by the front door.

"Come in, Daniel. Come in, Joseph," Father DiSante says. He motions them toward the couch near the staircase. "Sit down, boys."

Danny scans the room. Nothing's changed. Somehow he imagined coming home to a house torn to bits by his father's sorrow. He expected the furniture to be piled like an altar to the ceiling, the statue of the Sacred Heart of Jesus centered in the middle of a mountain of sofa cushions, his father kneeling on the braided rug, knees digging into crumbs and dog hair and leftover popcorn. But the room is as still and as quiet as a church. The priests' black shirts absorb the silence and whisper darkness back at him. A coldness creeps under his skin; his bones ache from carrying the wind inside him all these long hours since he read his mother's note. His father sits, the quietest of them all. Even though he has every reason to be a cyclone whirling around the room, stabbing the walls with his eyes, kicking the living shit out of the memories that scream from every corner of the house. Danny sits on the couch, down from the well-dressed priests with their quiet, clear eyes. But his father doesn't move. Not a hair on his thick, red head is out of place. His hands hang limp between his legs like a dog's tired tongue.

Zoomer nips at Father DiSante's ankle and the priest shoos him away. "Come here, boy," Danny says. Zoomer goes to his voice, curls up on the rug beside him and bares his teeth at the strangers. Joey follows him and leans against the wall, near the bottom of the staircase. The room smells of sweat and holy water. Priest smells, Danny thinks. It makes him sick to his stomach.

"These are Paulie's sons," Father DiSante says to the men in black. "Danny, Joey, this is Monsignor Hatch," he says, motioning to the older man with white eyebrows and green eyes, "and his assistant Father O'Brien." Father DiSante nods at the young man with black hair and blue eyes.

Like Patrick, Danny thinks. His hands collapse into a fist. He concentrates on relaxing his fingers. Back behind the Monsignor's head, Danny eyes the messy kitchen: milk and glass bits still in a puddle on the floor; the hole Joey punched into the wall, still screaming.

"Your father has been very worried about you," Monsignor Hatch says. "He thought perhaps something had happened to you, with the kitchen torn up so."

Danny rubs his eyes. He wants to re-live this after-noon, turn the clock back and come home from school early. He'd have stopped her. Changed her mind. Or begged her to take him and Joey with her. Anything to change what's happening now. He stares at the Monsignor's impatient eyes, then turns toward his father. Dad's eyes are far away, maybe on the road out of town, driving to overtake them, bring them back.

289

"Dad," he says. "I'm sorry."

His father doesn't move, his eyes a distant point on some imaginary horizon where God takes his hand and makes it all better. The room is hot, and the wind rattles at the windows. Danny wants to open one up, blow the house to shreds, breathe some fresh, cold air into the stifling, hot quiet that separates him from his father.

"Mr. Giovanni," the Monsignor's assistant says. "I'm sure you are aware of the unfortunate circumstances that have precipitated our visit." His face is clean and the words slip off his polished, practiced lips.

"I want my daughters back," Dad says. He looks up, finally, and stares at the statue of the Sacred Heart of Jesus. His lips move in silent prayer.

"Mr. Giovanni, that isn't going to be possible," the Monsignor starts to say.

"Why not? Send someone after him. Bring my girls home."

"Paulie," Father DiSante interrupts. "It's in God's hands now. You must put your faith in God and be strong for your sons."

Danny knows the strength of a bat, the power of wood against leather, shattering glass. He knows the strength of arms that cradle the pieces of a heart, stitch it back together thick with scars and memories. He knows the strength of walking down the long boards of the front porch, opening the door to a room full of priests with somber eyes, powerful men who know God by name, yet who cannot implore his strength to stop what never should have been.

"What the fuck does God know about it?" Danny blurts out. "She left with one of your goddamn priests. And you have the gall to say you can't do a thing about it?"

"Daniel," Dad says. "Not today." He shakes his head.

The corners of his mouth are sad and weak. "Don't talk to the Monsignor and the good Fathers like that. What has happened is not their fault."

"Raising your voice won't change a thing, Danny," Father DiSante insists. "What's done is done. It won't bring your mother back."

"What will then? You tell me! What will?" Danny hollers.

"Is Ma gonna come back for me and Danny?" Joey asks.

"Joseph," Father DiSante says. "Don't you want to be with your brother and your dad? Your place is here with them."

Joey cries softly. He tries to swallow it, but Danny hears his brother's small sobs. He wants to pick Joey up, put him on his father's lap, tell him to explain to his son how it is that his mama could do such a thing; how it is that his daddy prayed and prayed and didn't see that his almighty God let it all happen. How the all-powerful church can't do anything to change it now.

Anger bites into Danny's heart. Blood rushes to his fists. He wants to jump at the priests' throats, tear their words off their tongues, cram them back into the pit of their ugly mouths. He springs to his feet, twirls around, kicks the bottom step. Punches at the wall beside the crucifix hanging in the hallway at the end of the stairs.

"Daniel, calm down," Father DiSante says. "I know this must be hard for you, but you're going to have to learn to accept it."

Danny twists around and faces the priest. "You calm down! You learn to accept it!" he yells. The Monsignor and Father O'Brien come toward him to corner him, silence him. Father DiSante raises his hand and the two men step back, waiting. He grips the handle of the base-ball bat and offers the rounded, thicker end to Danny.

"Here, take this. Tomorrow you meet me at the ballfield and I'll pitch and pitch until your arms ache from swinging." His eyes are forgiving. Danny reaches for the bat and the promise of kindness. He grips the handle tightly and pulls it close to his chest.

"Tomorrow," he says. His arms shake as he squeezes the bat. "Can Joey come, too?"

"Yes," Father DiSante says.

He nods, and the Monsignor and Father O'Brien walk towards Danny's father.

Dad whispers into his hands, "Dear God, Marie, what have you done?" He slumps into his recliner and rests his head back. His face and eyes search the ceiling, for what, Danny does not know or care.

"Mr. Giovanni," the Monsignor says, "I hope you understand that we didn't mean to upset you and your sons any more than the situation already warrants."

Dad meets their eyes and purses his lips. "I am a man of God, Monsignor. I don't know how something like this could have happened. I tried to do what was best for my family, but it wasn't enough. I asked God to help me know what to do, but I..."

"This is truly a sad day for you and your family, Mr. Giovanni," Father O'Brien says. "The Diocese apologizes for Father Shaughnessy's actions."

"Help me get my daughters back. I don't care if Marie wants to be with him, just bring my girls back," Dad says. He sits up, alert now. Somehow God has breathed life back into his body. He's got fire in his voice. His eyes smolder.

"There isn't much the church can do to bring your children back," the Monsignor says. "Especially since they're already out of the diocese....Unless you want to press kidnapping charges. But that's a matter for your lawyer, Mr. Giovanni. Not the church."

"Ask the Archbishop. Tell the Cardinal. See what they can do. Surely someone will be able to help," Dad says. He pulls his rosary beads out of his pocket and shakes them at the priest's face. "I pray every day, Father. I'm a good man. I love my children."

"Yes, Mr. Giovanni, I'm sure you do," Father O'Brien says. "You must give that love to your sons now. They need you. Your faith will sustain you through this terrible loss. Father DiSante will be your spiritual counselor during this trying time. He can help you."

Danny squeezes his baseball bat. Bullshit. I'm sick of all their bullshit. Joey walks over to Dad's chair. He touches his arm, and Dad jumps, startled by his touch. "I busted the wall in the kitchen, Dad. I'm sorry. I'll mow lawns this summer and pay to get it fixed. And I knocked the milk bottle on the floor. I'll pick it up."

Danny thinks about the stained-glass window, the messy bits of colored glass littering the sidewalk in front of St. Joan's. Father DiSante knows he did it. He brought back his bat. But he didn't kick his ass about it. Maybe he'll tell the parishioners the wind blasted through it that terrible Friday in March, that night that the air howled and moaned like a wild dog, chasing its soul over the cold streets of Pisa.

Danny's mind chases now, over the highways, out past the edge of town, past the thruway, the countryside stretching out long and wide in front of his mind's eye. He follows the road as it curves and narrows, as it widens and swells with cars and trucks and people leaving for other places. Pisa is too small for sorrow. It cracks you open like a walnut and spills the fleshy pieces onto the sidewalk for everyone to step on. Tomorrow he'll call in sick, tell Mr. Johnston he's got a fever. Then he and Joey will hit some balls with Father DiSante. And afterwards, he'll stop by Mrs. M.'s house and offer to wash her windows or put up her screens or something. Anything to let her know that tonight won't ever slip out of his heart. He'll feel the warm tips of her fingers pressing comfort into the hard knot of his back for as long as he lives.

The Monsignor and Father O'Brien bundle into their coats, fit their hats snugly on their heads. "Mr. Giovanni, here is my card," the Monsignor says. He gives a small rectangle of thick paper to Dad and offers his hand to shake. Dad grabs the card and puts his fingers into the priest's soft palm.

"Goodnight, Monsignor. Father O'Brien," Dad says. "Thank you for coming such a long way to be with us tonight."

The visiting priests nod. Their eyes are full of sympathy and the kind of pity they dispense to old widowed women. Father O'Brien shakes Dad's hand, too, and then the priests leave. Their footsteps slap across the porch floor. The screen door flaps behind them, snapped by the wind and then released.

Father DiSante fidgets, anxious to be going. "Well, Paulie, I'll check in on you tomorrow."

"Thanks, Father," Dad says. He looks down at the rug again, as if he's searching for Peanut's face and Rosa's and Winnie's, too.

"And you boys," Father says, "I expect you to meet me at the Knights of Columbus ballfield by ten o'clock. Rain or shine."

"OK," Joey says.

"Yeah, Father," Danny adds.

The priest dons his hat, pulls his coat over his shoulders and heads for the door. His hand rests on the doorknob for a second, and he pauses, as if he's going to say something, but Danny knows there's nothing left to say. The silence rushes in to fill the holes left by words that don't mean anything anymore, anyway.

"Goodnight, Father," Danny says, releasing the priest from his obligation to heal the quiet.

"'Night," he says back. Then he's gone.

The room is full of ghosts: Peanut gawking at the June Taylor dancers on "The Jackie Gleason Show"; Rosa sharing a candy bar with Binkie; Winnie sucking her blanket; Mom calling one more time to "Come and get it" before supper gets cold. He can almost smell the smoke from her cigarettes, taste the sweet, tangy smell of her perfume. Heavy rocks of memories pin him to the couch. He tries to topple them, push them off, send them crashing to the floor. He nudges a few loose, but all that fall are pebbles, filling up his stomach.

"Dad, you want to make us some fish sticks or something?" he says to the quiet.

"You go in. Start the oven. I'll be in in a minute," Dad says.

Danny nods to Joey, and the boys head for the kitchen. He turns back to whistle for Zoomer and sees his father, head tilted back against the top of his recliner, fingering the worn beads of his black rosary. His lips move over the prayers like a kiss goodnight.

TWENTY-ONE

I keep telling myself not to worry. Mama will take care of everything, and now that she has Patrick to help, things will be better. She'll be happier, and it will be easier to love her 'cuz she won't have such a sad face. I want to believe it with my whole heart, but I'm not sure. I can't even tell if my heart's working anymore. It doesn't budge when I tell it that we're in Erie, Pennsylvania now, and we're never going back to Pisa. It's weird how I can say those words in my head, and my heart doesn't make a peep. Everything inside me is broken.

It's dark out now, and cold and windy still. It feels like spring will never get here. The wind is blowing and blowing. Mama's hair is flying all around her head like a bunch of dead leaves. It hides her face, and she pushes it back, away from her cheek, but the wind blows it in her eyes. She turns her back to the wind and heads for the trunk of the car. I pull my sweater up close around my neck and stick my chin inside. I shiver and lean against the side of Patrick's car and hang on to the cold door handle. Rosa and Winnie yawn, and the wind blows Binkie's ears and the corners of Winnie's blanket. They look like little leaves, waiting to be swept away. Mama's in back, rummaging through the trunk for something to put on her head, to keep her hair in place, and Patrick's lighting a cigarette. He cups his hand around the lit match, keeping the wind away from the flame. He puffs hard on the end of a Lucky Strike and flicks the dead match to the ground. He's grouchy. I shiver some more.

I can't remember if I put mittens in my grocery sack of clothes. I guess it doesn't matter. We had to rush so fast to get ready to leave, I'm sure I forgot lots of important stuff. Like Winnie's books. How could I let myself forget those? I'll have to sing to her to keep her busy, so she doesn't bother Mama and Patrick until we can get to Happy Town and buy some more. I think about asking Mama to check my A & P bag for mittens, but before I can get the question out, she slams the trunk shut and comes back with a scarf tied around her head. She walks over to Patrick and takes the cigarette out of his hand. She puffs it a couple of times and looks around like she's expecting to see somebody she knows. Patrick pulls out his wallet and looks at his money. A piece of paper flies out and he runs after it, steps on it and picks it up.

"Directions to Jack's house," he says to Mama. She nods. I wonder who Jack is until I figure out he's the guy Patrick knows who's gonna help him find a job when we get to Happy Town. I remember them talking about him a couple of times at Smiley's.

Patrick tucks the slip of paper back into his wallet, pulls a handkerchief out of his back pocket and wipes his face, but the little worry lines around his eyes stay put. He stares at the ground. He thinks hard about something, then he calls for Winnie to come walk with him. She and her blanket rush on over, pushed by the wind and the back of Mama's hand. Patrick bends down, picks her up and hugs her hard. She hugs him back and he kisses her face over and over again. "I love you, little one," he says.

Patrick looks at Winnie like he wants to swallow her

whole—like how Mama used to look at me when I was a little girl, before she had too many worries on her mind. And, for the first time, I get it. Somehow I finally realize that Winnie's more than just special. She's Patrick's little girl. Not Daddy's. And all at once everything inside me rushes to get out—pushes against my eyes, my mouth, my heart. I didn't kill the lost baby. I sold my soul to God for nothing. And all along He knew it. The lost baby was here the whole time. Winnie. It's Winnie.

Mama watches them and bites her lip. She cries a little. They're not sad tears this time, like how she cried in the car when Patrick drove out of Pisa. They're the kind you cry when you're scared that someone's gonna yell at you and happy that they haven't yet. I pull my sweater sleeves down over my hands and scrunch my fists up inside to warm them. Mama tosses her cigarette on the ground and snuffs it out with the toe of her shoe.

"Are you hungry, girls?" she says to me and Rosa. The wind blows her words into my face.

My stomach is empty, but I don't want to eat. Even though we've stopped, it feels like the car is still speeding inside me, and the smoke is swirling all around my head. I pop my fingers out of my sweater cave, grab her hand and hold on tight. I don't ever want to let go. If I do, she might forget about me, leave me here in the Erie Truck Stop Cafe parking lot, with the red-and-blue sign that blinks "Home Cookin'" at us, and the wind blowing its head off. I can tell this place is not friendly like Smiley's. Even from the parking lot, I can tell I'm not gonna like it.

"Let's go, girls," Mama says. The ends of her scarf whip around her head. I grab Rosa's fingers with my other hand and pull her along into the wind. Patrick's up ahead now, still holding Winnie real close and tight.

The Erie Truck Stop Cafe is noisy and crowded. There's no shiny malt machine like at Smiley's and no table-top jukeboxes, just a beat-up old thing in the corner by the bathroom. It's playing some song I never heard before. The lady on the record sings through her nose instead of her mouth. It's pretty, though, and I wish I could meet her. I bet she'd have a nice face, sort of like Betty, the waitress at Smiley's. Patrick walks through the restaurant, holding Winnie, and Mama and me and Rosa follow him. He slides into the booth and pulls Winnie in beside him. The rest of us catch up and join them.

"How's this?" he asks Mama. She smiles and slides in next to Winnie. Rosa and me sit across the table from them.

My face feels hot from all the wind. I sit real close to Rosa, hold her hand so I don't feel like leftovers, and I keep an eye on Mama. She and Patrick and Winnie remind me of a picture I saw once of Amelia and her mom and dad. Amelia was little, like Winnie, and in that picture she sat on a park bench with her mama on one side and her daddy on the other. They held on to her tight, holding her with one hand and holding on to each other with their other hands. It's like they were afraid somebody was gonna swoop on by, dash off with their baby, and leave a big hole in their hearts. I was jealous of how happy her mama and daddy looked, how much you could tell they loved her.

"You look funny," I told Amelia when she showed me that picture. It made her cry. I felt bad, but I didn't take it back.

"Winnie, you got a booger on your face," I say. Rosa giggles.

Winnie whimpers.

Mama checks and doesn't find anything. "Don't be mean, Peanut," she says. She snaps at me with her eyes. Patrick swipes a look at me, too. His eyes pin me to the seat, and my insides get all hot, like my windy face.

"Sorry," I say. I move closer to Rosa so there's only a tiny hair of space between us. She holds Binkie close with her one hand and holds my hand, tighter still, under the table. She won't let go. And I won't either. We're really leftovers now that Patrick has Mama and baby Winnie all to himself.

I wish we were at Smiley's right now, eating burgers and fries. I wonder if Betty will miss us. Maybe not this week. She'll just think one of us was sick or something, so we couldn't make it. But later, after we still don't show up, next week or next month, I wonder, will Betty wonder where we disappeared to? And the cat family daughters. Will they wonder where we are? Maybe they'll think our car got blown off the highway, and we tumbled over and over until we exploded in a dark cloud of smoke. Years later, they'll find dirty bones and pieces of hair and some teeth along the roadside. And maybe Mama's cigarette lighter. But maybe Betty and the cat family won't even notice that we don't show up at Smiley's anymore. I feel sad. Pretty soon Amelia won't remember me either. Even Zoomer will find somebody else to love. And I'll be all alone again.

This Erie Cafe place is smelly. Old tires and gasoline pumps stink up the front door. The tabletops have cigarette burns in them, and the waitresses don't smile. One of them comes up to our booth and gives five menus to Patrick, like the rest of us aren't even alive. She's got on a pink dress and a white apron with kitchen curtain lace running all around the edges. She chews gum and pops it loud between her front teeth.

"What'll it be tonight?" she asks.

She doesn't have any crayons for the girls or any mint candies, like Betty always does. Patrick flips through the menu and orders quickly. "Five burgers and a couple of orders of french fries," he says. "Two coffees and three milk shakes. Chocolate." He winks at me. "The milk shakes, not the coffee." I don't smile back.

"What's wrong, Peanut?" he says. "All that wind take your sense of humor away?"

"She's just tired, honey," Mama says to Patrick. "It's been a long day for all of us." She touches my hand and holds it for a few minutes. Her skin is warm, and I want to pull her away, run for the car, head home, but I can't even move my legs. They lay there tired from worrying.

Mama sits back in the booth and pulls her scarf off. She shakes her hair out and rubs her forehead. My mama with her sad, sad face. I look at her and my heart starts to wake up and all the feelings I have rush to my cheeks. In Happy Town things will be all better, he promised, I want to tell her. I want to believe it, too. But I can't. Not now.

Mama's mouth is turned under and her bottom lip sticks out. She's getting ready to cry. I want to cry too, but if my heart cracks open all the way, it will spill out everything. It will be a wild river and push Mama far, far away. Past the highway, past the towns we just drove by, past Pisa even, out beyond the edges of the sky into the deep, dark night. And I will be lost without her. I would call and call and my throat would be sore from yelling. And I would be cold, too. Colder than even now, with all the wind shouting at the windows, shaking the trees and everything else outside.

Mama, don't leave me, I want to scream. Even if God tells you that I traded my good twin soul so we wouldn't have to go to Happy Town. Even though I was wrong, and Winnie's the lost baby, and we're going anyway. Forgive me. I want to jump in her lap and hide my head near her heart. I want her to rock away the scary feelings I have inside, the ones that make me forget to breathe.

We sit and wait for supper to show up, and nobody

talks. Sometimes Mama looks at Patrick and he looks back at her, but mostly they both just stare at nothing. It's creepy, like they're looking at ghosts or something. Somebody in a booth across the way laughs real loud; somebody else calls, "Darling, I need more coffee," to one of the waitresses. And the music is there, still that lady on the jukebox singing like it's the only thing in life worth doing. I don't know how long we wait, but it feels like we'll never leave this place. Every once in a while the cafe door opens and the tiny bell jingles, and Mama gets jumpy as if she's expecting to see somebody she don't want to see. Maybe she thinks Daddy's on his way. Maybe Danny took Daddy's car, and he's looking for us. I hope they are. Please, God. Please.

When our food gets here, Patrick tells us to eat fast because there's still a lot of driving left to do before we find a place to stay for the night.

"Aren't we going home after we eat?" Rosa asks.

Mama settles her hands around her coffee cup, and she starts talking in that fakey way like how she talks to Mrs. Tanturri in the beauty shop, even though they can't stand each other. "No, honey. We're going to stay over-night in a motel and go to Happy Town tomorrow."

"What's a motel?" Rosa asks. She scrunches up her nose and chews a french fry with her mouth open.

"It's a place where we can sleep over, like Peanut sometimes stays over at Amelia's house."

"Is Amelia gonna be there?" Rosa asks.

"No Rosa, just us," Patrick says.

I think of Amelia's pretty room, with the walls painted light pink. "Blush," her mother calls it. Mama's cheeks are that color now, even though we're inside, away from the wind. I don't want to think about Amelia or hear her name. I won't be able to sit still, be quiet and calm like a good girl if I let Amelia crawl into my mind.

Mama's all upset now from Rosa asking questions. She ties her scarf back on and grabs for her purse. "I think we should go now," she says to Patrick. Rosa starts to cry. She doesn't know why she made Mama so mad, she just knows she did. Winnie cries too, but I think it's because she really is tired. I put my arm around Rosa and tell her it's OK, Mama's not mad at her. Patrick wipes Winnie's eyes and gives her a hug. Mama lights a cigarette and stands at the end of the booth.

"OK," Patrick says. "Let's go."

We pull our sweaters back on and head for the car. Mama hurries out of the cafe and runs ahead of us. When we catch up, she's wiping her eyes and blowing her nose and crying hard. Something's broken inside her, too. I can't stand it. I want to be as big as a house and strong as God and make her stop, tell her not to worry. It's the boys she's crying about. She says their names in between taking breaths and blowing her nose. Patrick holds her tight, and tells her it will be OK, we'll send for them. I don't believe him. He's lying again. Saying things to calm Mama down. But it's not true. He doesn't like the boys. He doesn't like me and Rosa either. He just puts up with us to make Mama happy. I want to run back into the restaurant, hide in the bathroom and never come out. I'll kick and fuss and yell for the cops if he tries to take us away with him. I'll scream so loud Mama will change her mind and come home with me. To Zoomer and the boys. And Daddy.

Winnie starts to fuss. She's cold. Rosa starts crying 'cuz Mama's crying. I wrap Winnie's blanket around her shoulders to keep her warm. I bend down and tell Rosa that if she stops crying, I'll tell her a story when we get in the car. Finally Mama calms down, and Patrick unlocks the car doors.

"Get inside now, girls," Patrick says. I lock my knees,

but he pushes my shoulders and I fall forward into the back seat. Winnie gets up front this time, with Mama and Patrick. Rosa crawls in back, next to me. It's no use. He wins. I can't run away. Not if Mama is going with him.

Patrick pulls out of the parking lot and the "Home Cookin'" sign in the cafe window blinks good-bye. I watch the people inside as we drive away. God is busy tonight, watching over the Erie Truck Stop Cafe; that singer on the jukebox, especially, needs God to hold her broken heart. I leave my bad twin soul on the corner, by the highway ramp, so the wind or a big truck can blow it away.

Patrick's speeding now. He's going faster than the wind. We fly through the dark, past more towns and more truck stop cafes. I tell Rosa a story, but she falls asleep halfway through. Winnie's sleeping, too, on Mama's lap. I listen to the quiet and watch the back lights of the cars in front of us. They shine like red lips in the dark. Mama's red lips, Mama's fancy hair on Friday nights. When we get to Happy Town, things will be different. No Danny. No Joey. No Daddy. No Amelia. No Zoomer. But I'll still have Mama. Maybe that will be enough, even though Winnie is Patrick's little girl.

Maybe we'll buy a record player, and get a new copy of *My Fair Lady*. I can put it on, and Mama and I can dance around the kitchen like old times. Maybe by spring, all Mama's worries will melt away, and maybe by summer, she won't be so sad anymore. She'll stop missing the boys, and everything will be OK. When we get to wherever it is we're going, I'll take the picture of the beautiful Blessed Mother out of my grocery bag and put it up in my room. I'll pray to her every day and maybe, after a while, Mama will sing with me, and we'll laugh again like we used to when I was little—before Mama and

Daddy fought all the time; before Patrick ever came to Pisa.

If none of that works, if Mama's still sad after all my praying and behaving, I'll sneak a phone call to Daddy. I'll wait for some afternoon when Patrick's not home and Mama's busy, and I'll call Daddy and tell him where we are. Then maybe he'll drop his rosary and come get us. Take us back to Pisa and leave Patrick with his priest friend in Happy Town. He's got to. He's got to.

I gotta try and not let it all get to me. Try to act happy. For Mama's sake. No matter what, I gotta try. I don't see any other way out of it, at least for now. I close my eyes, lean into the seat and think of only good things—the June Taylor dancers, Zoomer licking my face, and Mama's eyes smiling at me.

Mary Saracino is a freelance writer and
Shiatsu bodywork practitioner who lives in
Minneapolis. In 1991, she won a Loft Mentor Series Award for her fiction writing. Her
work has appeared in *Sinister Wisdom*, and
Writers Who Cook, an anthology of recipes,
prose and poetry (Herringbone Press).

Spinsters Ink was founded in 1978 to produce vital books for diverse women's communities. In 1986 we merged with Aunt Lute Books to become Spinsters/Aunt Lute. In 1990, the Aunt Lute Foundation became an independent non-profit publishing program. In 1992, Spinsters moved to Minneapolis.

Spinsters Ink is committed to publishing full-length novels and non-fiction works that deal with significant issues in women's lives from a feminist perspective: books that not only name crucial issues in women's lives, but more importantly encourage change and growth; books that help make the best in our lives more possible. We are particularly interested in creative works by lesbians.